About the author

Susan Parry began writing when her twin daughters were small, and she was working full time as a university professor at Imperial College. She now devotes her time to consultancy work, including forensic studies and archaeological investigations that form the basis for her writing. Her husband, Mark, is retired so they are now able to spend more time together in the family home in Swaledale, where the views from her farmhouse provide inspiration. Together they have walked many of the areas described in the books, accompanied by their Airedale terrier. Her grown up daughters, Elspeth and Alice both have careers in crime – on the right side of the law. Visit her website at www.SusanParry.co.uk.

By Susan Parry

DEATH CART

SUSAN PARRY

Viridian Publishing

First published in the United Kingdom in 2007 by
Viridian Publishing

This edition published in 2011 by Viridian Publishing

Viridian Publishing
PO Box 746
Woking
Surrey
GU24 0AZ

www.viridian-publishing.co.uk
e-mail: viridian.tc@virgin.net

ISBN 978-0-9544891-6-8

For Mavis & Tom

Acknowledgements

Although rare, chariot burials have been discovered in East Yorkshire and recently even in West Yorkshire. Information in this book has come from two main sources: the British Museum and Yorkshirehistory websites. Readers can listen to lectures by experts on the British Museum website, where there are photographs and details of the reconstruction of the Wetwang chariot. The British Museum has kindly given permission to reproduce the photograph of the skeleton from the Wetwang site on the front cover of this book. I am very grateful to Richard Hayton for providing me with valuable advice regarding the chances of discovering a chariot burial for the first time in North Yorkshire. Readers can find his excellent review of the subject at yorkshirehistory.com.

Chapter 1

'Vrishti?'

She was leaning on the doorbell as if it was all that prevented her from collapsing on the step. Even through the strands of long black hair that fell across her face, Millie could see she had been crying. Mascara was smudged below her red swollen eyes. She was shivering visibly in her thin party clothes although it was a warm night.

'How did you get home? Did someone bring you? Where did you leave your bag?' Phoebe asked anxiously as they helped Vrishti into the kitchen and sat her down at the table.

She remained hunched and shaking while Phoebe continued her barrage of questions but there was no response, and finally she gave up.

'Here, get this down you.' Millie gave them both a mug, sat down opposite them and sipped her tea.

'Where were you? We looked for you when we were leaving but we couldn't find you. I thought you'd already gone.'

She and Phoebe had shared a taxi from the Dean's house with some other second year students who lived in town. That was just before midnight and there'd been no sign of Vrishti then. Naturally they had assumed she'd left early since she didn't want to go in the first place.

'Well?'

Vrishti's hands gripped the mug as if for warmth. She didn't answer but lifted her shoulders slightly as if she was sobbing silently. Millie was wondering what she ought to do. What if she had been raped on the way home? Should she call a doctor? She had no bag, perhaps she had been mugged? Should she call the police? What if one of the men at the party had been pestering her and she had panicked. Although she knew Vrishti quite well, it was difficult to ask such intimate questions and she obviously didn't want to discuss it now. So they sat in silence and finished their tea.

'Do you want to talk about it?' asked Millie after a while.

'No, I'll be OK, really. I just want to go to bed please.'

She stood up, knocking over the chair as she lurched to the door. The two friends helped her up the stairs. She seemed disoriented and it amused them to think that the quietest one of them all was drunk. Once back in bed Millie lay awake worrying over what the poor girl had been up to and why she had come home in such a state. Finally she tiptoed over to Vrishti's room and peered in, to see her curled in a ball under her duvet, snoring gently.

The next morning, still in their night clothes, Phoebe was eating toast while Millie made a bacon sandwich. Vrishti said she didn't want anything for breakfast. Anyway it was nearly time to go to her brother's house for a large Sunday lunch.

'So what was the matter with you last night?' said Phoebe waving her toast at Vrishti.

'Nothing.' She looked uncomfortable.

'Too much to drink?' Phoebe persisted.

'I have to get dressed.'

Vrishti got up and left the room.

'Well I hope she lightens up a bit,' said Pheobe, raising her eyebrows at the door.

'I think she needs to recover first, and then she may. She's obviously upset.'

'What d'you think happened?'

'I don't know.'

Maybe she'd got entangled with another student and now regretted it, Millie thought, but she didn't like to discuss it with her friend. It didn't seem right. Vrishti was such a proper girl. She'd told them her parents didn't like her living away from home and her older brother had been told to keep an eye on her. Hence the enforced weekly lunch visit, on a Sunday.

'Well, I don't know about you but I'm going to soak in a long bath, then do my hair and nails. It will probably take most of the afternoon.'

'Fine,' said Millie. 'I think I'll go back to bed. I'm knackered after last night's fiasco.'

Vrishti poked her head round the door.

'I'm off to see Deepal,' she said, pulling a face. 'See if I can attempt to eat some of Priti's good Asian home cooking.'

Millie was pleased to see her smiling and joking again, even if her face looked strained and her eyes swollen.

'And thanks for looking after me last night.'

She was down the hall and out the front door before they could respond, or ask any further questions.

'Oh well, she'll tell us in good time,' said Phoebe disappearing up the stairs.

She reappeared in the doorway again. 'You know, it can't be anything bad, can it? She would have told us if it was really bad wouldn't she?'

Standing in her pyjamas with her ruffled blonde hair, her anxious face made her look like a small child, thought Millie.

'No, you go off and have your bath, it'll be all right.'

Millie followed her upstairs and went into her own bedroom. The window was open and the sound of children playing down below in the street came and went, while she dozed.

Late in the afternoon Millie was woken by a motorbike revving under her window. Dani must have been given a lift by the girl with the tattoos again. She got off the bed and stretched, peering through the grey net curtains to see the girls below. Her name was really Denise but she asked them to call her Dani, presumably thought it sounded cool. Millie disliked everything about her: the way she looked, the way she spoke and the way she treated everyone. Her hair was short and spiky, black and dried out from too much home colouring. She had a tattoo that resembled a piece of barbed wire round the top of her arm, five or six rings in her ear and her nose was pierced. Nose piercing could look nice, Millie was thinking, like the tiny jewel in Vrishti's nose, but not a large silver ring. She peered down to see what Dani was wearing as she stood on the pavement chatting to her friend. She always wore tight denim jeans and was usually dressed in black. Today it was a T-shirt with the tour dates of a heavy metal band on her back.

The front door slammed as the bike revved off down the road. Soon Dani was hammering on the bathroom door, and telling Phoebe to hurry up and get out, she wanted a pee. Millie sighed, pulled on her trainers and tied her hair back in a pony tail, ready to act as arbitrator in the impending domestic dispute.

- 4 -

'Can you get your little friend to stop curling her eyelashes and let me in?'

Dani almost spat the words at Millie.

'No,' said Millie, walking slowly down the stairs.

'What is it with everyone? I only want to use the bathroom. Is that unreasonable?'

She shouted after her but Millie just kept walking into the kitchen and turned on the tap, allowing it to run for a while until the water was cold enough to drink. The running water drowned the noise of the argument that was going on upstairs.

'What is it with that girl that she spends so much time in the bathroom? Has she got some obsessive compulsive disorder?'

Dani addressed no-one in particular as she prepared something to eat. Millie ignored her and continued to read an old magazine that lay on the table. Finally Dani sat down opposite her with a large plate of beans on toast.

'What did you think of the departmental bash then?' she said, with her mouth full.

'Professor McGrath's got a nice house,' Millie replied, without looking up.

'It's not bad, though it's not her place. It belongs to the university. She only gets to live there 'cos she's the Dean. The way she behaves you'd think she owned it. God she's such a stuck up cow!'

Millie turned another page slowly. Dani was wiping up the tomato sauce round her plate with the remains of her toast.

'Did you have some of that stroganoff? The meat was so chewy it was inedible. I thought she would get caterers but some of that stuff must have been homemade. I stuck to the quiches and cold food. Mind you, the drink was OK.'

Millie stared at the page, pretending to be engrossed in her horoscope for last month.

'Some of the staff were well drunk! Old Standing must have had a load. Did you see him flat out in the flower bed?'

'Phoebe and I left early.'

'Then you missed Gary Perkins having a go at Colin. They virtually had a fight.'

'Why?'

'Colin had his hands all over Joanna Armstrong.'

'So?'

'Like, his ex-wife?'

'They used to be married?'

'Duh – yes. Don't you know anything?'

'But they've got different names.'

'Hello, she's Dr Armstrong, like she was Armstrong when she got her PhD, see? You can't change your name once you become a doctor. I'll be Doctor Vincent my entire life.'

'Hmm. Well we didn't see any fighting, anyway.'

'Oh but *the Princess* was there.'

Dani said the words in a mock reverential way that was nasty. She always referred to Vrishti that way; Millie wasn't sure how it had started. She looked up, hoping to gain a clue about what had caused Vrishti to be so upset.

'Was she with anyone?'

But Dani jumped up and carried her plate over to the sink. She turned on the taps, ignoring her and started washing up.

'I was wondering how she got home,' Millie continued.

'Did she come home?' Dani didn't turn round.

'What d'you mean?' Millie pulled a face at the girl's back as she continued to rattle the dishes. She repeated the question but Dani grabbed the tea towel and finished drying her crockery.

After a few minutes Millie tried again.

'When did the party finish?'

'Just after midnight. The old McGross virtually told us all to clear off. Carmen and I went back to her mates and carried on drinking there.'

'Was Vrishti there at the end?'

There was a sound of a door opening upstairs.

'I'm next in the bathroom!' Dani shouted, racing out of the room without answering.

Millie and Phoebe had the television turned up loud to drown Dani's music from upstairs, so they didn't hear the car when Deepal brought Vrishti home later that evening. She tried to creep past the door unnoticed but Millie leapt up, offering her a coffee.

'Yes, but let me get changed and put this paratha in the fridge.'

'Good meal?' enquired Phoebe, who asked Vrishti the same question every weekend.

'Yes, Priti did herself proud, as usual.' She was generous with her praise for her sister-in-law's cooking. 'Mind you, I don't know how she puts up with my brother sometimes. He complains about everything. He told her it was overcooked, but he made us late, wanting to give me a lecture.'

'Why was that?' asked Millie.

'Oh, he was telling me I should work harder. Not go out so much. Can you believe it?'

'Why did he say that?' asked Phoebe.

'He said I look tired. I said it was because he makes me get up early on a Sunday to visit him!' She was laughing. 'He didn't think it was funny. He said he didn't go out at all when he was studying for his accountancy exams. He's worse than my Mum.'

'I think it's nice he worries about you,' said Phoebe.

'You wouldn't if you had to put up with it. It's really rather annoying. It's not like I go out much. Anyway, I shall stay in from now on.'

'Why's that?' Millie asked, looking across at Phoebe.

'Oh, I don't know. Perhaps it's best if I just stay in and work.' She laughed nervously. 'I must go and get changed. I'll catch you later.'

But she didn't reappear and Millie assumed she had gone to bed to recover from her late night.

It felt like a very bad Monday morning as Joanna Armstrong sat in her office preparing the lecture about her research. She had spent a disappointing weekend trying to make her new home more comfortable and felt she'd made a mistake moving to a dilapidated cottage in Wensleydale. Thinking a cup of coffee might make the day seem a little easier to cope with, she was about to go to the cafeteria when the door opened and Gary walked in.

He was always a mess and living on his own had made things worse. His hair was uncombed and the beard he had grown in Greece needed trimming. His corduroy trousers were worn at the knees, the old T-shirt was crumbled and dirty. Once, the unkempt look had made her want to care for him but now it repelled her.

'I'm surprised you have the gall to even come here after Saturday night,' she said, trying to sound remote.

'I came to say sorry,' he said with a sheepish grin. He was good at the boyish look and she was not taken in.

'It's Dr Hammond you should apologise to. You could have hurt him, pushing him down those stone steps.'

'Dr Hammond? Since when was it Dr Hammond? You were on more than first name terms as far as I could see.'

Joanna had been annoyed by Colin Hammond's advances and wished he would back off but she wasn't going to give Gary the pleasure of knowing that.

'I thought you were going to find a new lecturing post now you're back from your sabbatical.'

'I know, and I'm sorry. I'd had too much of the departmental booze allowance that night. I didn't mean to embarrass you.'

'You always do that. Now, I've got to get on.'

As if to prove it, she sat down with her back to him and continued typing. Gary hovered for a moment and then went out, leaving the door open.

She was just completing her notes when there was a sound from the corridor. A student was peering nervously round the door at her.

'I'm sorry Dr Armstrong, I didn't realise you were busy.'

The girl looked anxious and Joanna sighed; another student with problems she supposed. Being the tutor for the department, with responsibility for the welfare of women students, wasn't a job she enjoyed. There were far too many students with personal difficulties, particularly financial ones, and there wasn't a lot she could help them with. Also she wasn't supposed to tell them to come back another time. She checked the position of the tissue box almost unconsciously.

'Sit down. Now, what can I do for you, er …' She realised she didn't know this student.

'I'm Vrishti,' the girl said, 'you taught me last year. I came to see you because I was told you are the women's tutor.'

'That's right. Is there a problem?'

'It's very difficult. I don't really know what to say.' She sat looking miserable.

'Is it a financial problem?'

Judging by her clothes this student was not short of money but nine times out of ten it was the cause of anxiety.

'No, it's not. It's more personal.'

Usually Joanna would have no difficulty asking a student whether she was on drugs or perhaps pregnant. But there was something quite delicate about the girl and Joanna was worried she might be shocked to be asked such direct questions. So she sat and waited.

·'I wouldn't bother you,' the girl said politely, 'but it concerns someone in the department.'

'I see. In that case you were right to come and see me.' Joanna had no idea what the girl meant. 'Did you want to make a complaint?'

'Oh no, I mean I don't know.' The girl looked at her anxiously. 'Do you think I should?'

'Well, that really depends what it is about, Vrishti.'

Joanna was beginning to feel a little exasperated. She ha slides to finish and notes to copy before the lecture. But she really needed a cup of coffee.

'It's so difficult. I don't think I should say anything except I know it's not right. I don't want to get anyone into bad trouble.'

She suddenly burst into tears and Joanna reached for the tissues. It sounded to her as if this girl wanted to report some of her friends for drinking too much or drugs perhaps. The girl blew her nose and carefully wiped under her eyes where her mascara was running.

'Vrishti, listen. If something has happened you want to talk about, I'm here. When you are ready we can discuss it. Unfortunately I have to give my lecture now, but I am in all day and I'm very happy to see you again later.'

The girl took the hint and stood up. 'Yes, thank you.' She went to the door, turned to thank her again, and walked out, leaving Joanna feeling a complete failure.

'So, how's my favourite archaeologist today?'

Joanna looked up to see Colin Hammond at the open door.

'Very busy this morning, Colin. I've got to get on.'

'I thought I'd just drop in. Saw one of my tutor group leaving your office as I came along the corridor. Wondered if there was anything I could help with?'

'No thank you, Colin.'

'Are you sure? Wouldn't like to think that any of my fold were in need of personal help.'

Joanna was fed up with Colin and his juvenile attempts to engage her in conversation. He had caused enough problems on Saturday groping her in front of everyone. She was no longer going to remain polite with him.

'Please stop fishing and leave me to get ready for my lecture.'

'OK, OK. I'll see you downstairs but if Vrishti has been talking to you about personal problems I want to know!'

When Millie banged on Vrishti's door next morning there was no answer.

'Wake up Vrishti, it's the project lectures this morning. I'm leaving in half an hour!'

Millie was looking forward to a series of lectures from the staff in the Archaeology Department and she wasn't going to let her friend delay her. Opening the door she saw that Vrishti was not in bed.

Downstairs, Phoebe was still in her pyjamas.

'Revising again today?' asked Millie.

Her friend was retaking her Spanish exams.

'Yep.'

'Have you seen Vrishti?'

'She's gone already,' said Phoebe.

Surprised Vrishti hadn't waited for her, Millie shrugged and set off on the twenty minute walk alone. Their lecturers were going to talk about their research and, as she trudged through the outskirts of town, Millie wondered which of them might have vacancies for their projects that summer. She really wanted to experience a proper archaeological dig and practical excavation. It was what she had worked so hard for.

Vrishti was already seated when Millie arrived in the lecture theatre. The room was fuller than usual and there was an excited atmosphere. Several members of staff were standing at the front and soon they were joined by the Dean, Professor McGrath. She was dressed in a grey trouser suit and an old fashioned white blouse. Millie suspected she probably was younger than she appeared. There was just one face she didn't recognise.

'Who's that man with the beard and the scruffy clothes?' Millie asked Vrishti.

'That's Dr Perkins,' she replied. 'He's been working on pottery in Greece.'

'Is he the one you asked to work with in the summer?'

'Yes. He said I definitely could,' she said flatly.

'You don't sound very keen.'

'I'm thinking about it.'

Before Millie could ask why, Professor McGrath clapped her hands for silence and began introducing the speakers. The first two droned on about the intricate details of silverware and pottery leaving Millie quite uninspired, even though the projects were based in exotic locations and offered the chance to work overseas. Dr Perkins was on third and spent far too long on slides of sites in the Mediterranean. Dr Hammond gave the most entertaining talk of all. He showed them the archaeological site near Driffield, where they had discovered the latest in a series of cart or chariot burials.

'The burial sites date back to Roman times and are important examples of locations where the Brigantes were based. Does anyone know about the Brigantes?'

Millie had heard of them but didn't know where they were located. No-one volunteered to answer.

'Well, this map shows the area they covered during the Roman invasion. of 500BC. We think the site near Driffield was a base was used by the Brigantes for their raids on Roman camps in York. At the time the Brigantes were headed by a famous woman warrior, who led them into battle in one of these. You couldn't call this a cart could you?' He flashed up a picture of someone who looked like Boudicca in her chariot. Millie was impressed. The woman looked fierce, magnificent. She was leading her male warriors into battle with her red hair streaming behind her and her hands above her head in a shout of excitement.

'She looks well scary,' whispered Vrishti.

'Fantastic.'

'This is a very famous burial site at Wetwang.'

He put up a picture of a skeleton.

'This body is probably that of a priestess. She was buried with her chariot and they found a mirror with her which is why they think she was a mystic. If you want more details go onto the British Museum website.'

When he had finished his talk there was a buzz of discussion amongst the students.

'Quiet now,' shouted the Dean, 'we have one more talk from Dr Armstrong.'

Millie listened to the final lecture with polite interest. Dr Armstrong's area of research was in diseases in the Middle Ages and she talked about how she studied bones and teeth taken from a Medieval cemetery near York. The work she described was painstaking but Millie did not want to be stuck in a museum all day. At the end of the session the students gathered at the front of the lecture hall to indicate their choice of project. Everyone seemed keen to work with Dr Hammond and Millie stood with Vrishti in the long queue waiting to sign the appropriate list.

'I bet you're glad you're sorted already,' Millie shouted at Vrishti above the noise of the crowd.

'Well, I don't know. I'm not sure I've made the right decision.'

By the time Millie had fought her way to the front to sign up, there were about a dozen names on the list.

'I'll never get a chance to work with him,' she moaned.

'You could if you talk to the right person.' The gentle Welsh accent came from behind them. Millie looked round to see a thin lad hovering a few feet away. Although he seemed to be talking to her, he was looking at Vrishti.

'What d'you mean?' she asked.

'I'm Nige, Colin's postdoc. I work on the burial site near York. There's no way he's going to let any of you second years touch the chariot burial but there is another dig in Wensleydale that could, I say could, be quite exciting.'

He grinned at them in a creepy way, showing crooked yellow teeth.

'If you two want to come round to my office I can show you the website.'

Millie looked at Vrishti, who smiled and said, 'Good idea, let's go!'

'But you've got a project with Dr Perkins,' muttered Millie.

'I think this would be *much* better, all things considered,' She picked up her bag and followed Nige up the steps and out of the lecture hall with Millie in pursuit.

The Archaeology Department was on the top floor of the smart new building it shared with Earth Sciences and Geography. Nige's sweaty odour filled the tiny lift and Millie stepped out gratefully into the corridor. The office was cluttered, untidy and full of random objects - a bicycle wheel, traffic cone, plastic bucket and a cardboard cut-out of Indiana Jones. Nige sat them down at his desk, offering Vrishti his own comfortable chair. He'd begun tapping his keyboard when a good-looking student wandered in.

'Hey, this is Jake,' he said, without looking up. 'He's doing a PhD with Colin. I have to put up with him in my office.'

Jake smiled at them and clambered over the bucket to his desk by the window.

Nige tapped furiously.

'They wanted to work on the burial site but I told them there's no way Colin will allow that. So I'm showing them the Wensleydale site. I thought they might be able to help out.'

Jake looked over, shaking his head, 'We don't even know whether there is a chariot there, do we? It's not where you'd expect one and Colin isn't sure about it.'

'Well.' Nige tapped the screen with a dirty fingernail, 'I can show you what we've done so far and you can come and see the site yourself if you like.'

'That would be great,' said Millie, looking across at Vrishti.

She could see herself now, working on the site and making a really exciting discovery. If she played her cards right she could continue working on it after the summer and make it her final year project.

Nige spent a long time describing Iron Age funeral rituals and showed them several sites around York where chariots had been found in graves.

'Now East Yorkshire is really quite interesting because in the Iron Age the dead were buried in large graves and the bodies were crouching, which is a bit weird. You don't get many artefacts buried with them, just a pot and sometimes a brooch.' He paused for effect and looked at Vrishti. 'But there are some big graves where the body is buried with a chariot and then they have weapons and food buried with them.'

Millie was disappointed to hear that out of seven only two were graves of women. He found a plan of the burial site at Wetwang giving the location of each bit of the chariot as it lay over the body. They could see where the metal tyres and other bits of the vehicle had survived.

'Now here's a plan of the site at Wensleydale. It's near Bainbridge, which I'm sure you know was a Roman fort,' Nige explained, leaning back in his chair.

Millie didn't, but she wasn't willing to show her ignorance in front of Jake, who had come over and stood watching them.

'We've been studying the site ever since it showed up as an anomaly in a geophysical survey carried out a few years ago.'

When they'd had lectures on surveying Millie had struggled over the technical side of it. They'd done a practical session measuring the resistance of the ground. It was supposed to show up where there were stones and they had looked for a buried wall. It sort of worked but the student who was helping them said the equipment was old and played up sometimes.

'Nige is a techy,' explained Jake. 'He knows all about magnetometry and GPR, he did it for his PhD.'

'Yeah, well, ground penetrating radar is rather impressive.' Nige rubbed his hand over his lank hair and smirked. 'Most interesting part really but you've got to investigate once you've spotted something, so now we're delving into the site a bit. Not got far mind you.'

Jake smiled across at Millie. 'We're taking some equipment over there tomorrow if you want to have a look. It doesn't mean Dr Hammond will let you help though, you'll have to wait and see what he says.'

'Right, good, I mean yes please!' said Millie.

'And me.' Vrishti looked anxiously at Nige.

'Great. We're taking the Land Rover back to the flat tonight for an early start so you'll have to meet us there. D'you know the chip shop on the way into town, with a big fish hanging outside?' he asked.

'Yes,' they replied.

'We live above there,' Jake added. 'And when Nige says early he means nine o'clock. That's early for him.'

'There's a door at the side of the shop. Ring the top bell,' Nige instructed. 'We'll see you there, then.'

Millie and Vrishti giggled together about Nige as they made their way down to the cafeteria. Once they were sitting drinking coffee, Millie asked Vrishti why she had changed her mind about working with Dr Perkins.

'I don't know. There's no special reason. I just thought it would be better if I stayed round here I suppose. Dr Perkins said I would have to go over to the site in Greece for the summer and I don't think it would be a good idea.'

'Would he be there too?' Millie asked, thinking maybe he was the problem.

'Oh yes, I wouldn't have to go on my own,' Vrishti replied, evidently missing the significance of Millie's question.

'Does your brother have a view?' Millie tried again. This time she seemed to hit a nerve.

'Oh no, he doesn't know about any of this.' She seemed flustered. 'He would want me working in a stuffy museum with Dr Armstrong.'

'Why? You mean because she's a woman?'

'Because I'd be safely tucked away in a museum, I would think.'

Now she was beginning to open up.

'Vrishti, tell me if I'm prying but what was the matter on Saturday night?'

'I'm sorry Millie but I really can't discuss it. It's too difficult for me and it's not something you can do anything about. I must sort it out in my own way. I'm sorry.'

Her cheeks were flushed and she avoided Millie's gaze. She took her mug to the trolley, returned to pick up her bag and gave a weak smile, 'I'll see you later.'

It had all gone wrong again. Millie watched Vrishti leaving, wishing Mum was still alive to tell her what to do. She would know whether to leave well alone or try to help. She had been really good at things like that.

Chapter 2

It was raining heavily and Millie's back felt damp. Her new all-weather jacket seemed to be letting the water in and her jeans were wet. Only her feet felt dry in her new expensive walking boots.

'Look, there it is!'

Vrishti pointed excitedly at the white Land Rover parked further down the road. Millie could make out the university logo on the door, and the words "University of North Yorkshire" painted down the side.

'Must be the right place then,' remarked Millie, stopping outside the chip shop, where a pigeon was pecking at the contents of a soggy bag on the pavement.

Just past the shop was the front door that Nige had described and a set of three doorbells. Vrishti pressed the top one timidly and stepped back. Millie couldn't hear it ringing, so when no-one responded she pushed it again herself, firmly, and for a good long time.

'OK, OK, OK!' Feet pounded down the stairs and the door was flung open by Jake.

'Give us a minute!' He grinned. 'It's a long way down you know.'

He turned round and started up the stairs again. Millie shut the door behind her and followed Vrishti up the two flights to the boys' flat.

As she'd expected it was in the same state as Nige's office. The front door opened directly onto a tiny sitting room packed with the sort of furniture that comes in student accommodation. She was used to the chairs not matching, in garish flowery patterns, curtains and carpet that clash, the ornamental gas fireplace with cheap knick-knacks on the mantelpiece. Millie and her friends had managed to change their student house by replacing the odd curtains, putting throws on the chairs and bringing pictures from home. The boys didn't appear to have made any effort to make the flat more comfortable.

'Make yourself at home, we're nearly ready,' said Jake, disappearing through a door into what looked like a bedroom.

They sat down and grinned at each other. Dirty glasses adorned the window-sill and other surfaces around the room. There was the debris of a pizza delivery on the table. In the corner of the room was a bicycle in pieces and a pile of laundry. Millie couldn't work out if it was clean or dirty.

Nige came in through an archway eating a piece of toast. He was dressed in the same clothes he had worn on the previous day and his hair looked even greasier.

'Hi, we're nearly ready,' he said with a mouth full of food. 'D'you want a coffee?'

'No!' Millie answered too quickly and was grateful to Vrishti who added, politely, 'We just had some, thank you.'

'Right.' He went through into the bedroom.

'Nice flat,' muttered Millie and Vrishti collapsed in giggles.

'Shh! They'll hear you.'

Someone was coming back into the room.

'Have you got waterproofs?'

Jake was carrying a large jacket and a pair of wellingtons.

'Only what we've got on,' Millie replied.

'It's really muddy on site. You might find you get wet if it stays like this all day.'

'Oh well, we'll survive.'

That's Vrishti, back to her optimistic self this morning, thought Millie. Personally, she was not sure she would survive so well if she was going to get even wetter *and* covered in mud.

The back of the Land Rover was full of ropes, spades, buckets, trowels, flags and plastic boxes. Nige moved some of the equipment forward so Millie and Vrishti could sit on the seats facing each other by the back door. Nige was driving and Jake took the passenger seat in the front. The windows were steamed up and there was little of interest to see when they set off so Millie found herself dozing, waking only when Nige braked suddenly at traffic lights or a junction.

Vrishti had cleared part of her window to see out and Millie thought she recognised the town. She wanted to ask Jake but the Land Rover was so noisy she didn't think he would hear her.

'I'm sure this is Richmond,' she told Vrishti.

'It is, we've just passed a Richmond Theatre.' Vrishti pointed back down the road.

Now they were driving along the route she knew so well to upper Swaledale, where her grandmother had lived, but their goal today was Wensleydale and soon they were driving past the turning to Reeth, following the sign to Leyburn. She could see over the dry stone walls into fields where sheep stood miserably in the rain, and rivers ran fast and brown. Soon the sign indicated they were entering Leyburn and Millie excitedly pointed it out to Vrishti as they flashed past and along the Wensleydale road towards Bainbridge.

When Millie saw the site she was surprised at how small it was. She had figured it would cover a large area, perhaps several acres but there were just a few trenches, forming a series of symmetrical lakes across the tiny field.

'One of the problems is they fill up with water very quickly here,' pointed out Nige, rain dripping from his nose and hair.

Millie held the umbrella over Vrishti as they stood staring across the site.

'Let me show you what we've got so far,' shouted Nige, waving his arms excitedly. 'Over here we've dug three test pits and there are definitely signs of Brigante occupation.'

'How do you know that?' asked Millie.

'We found some coral beads that looks like the right period. They've been sent off for examination.'

He strode off and they followed, stepping carefully between the trenches together, keeping the umbrella over them both. Millie could feel the water trickling down her legs and although it was a warm day she had begun to feel chilly. Nige chattered on, clearly enjoying his chance to impress her friend. She watched as he gave his lecture on Brigante raids directly to Vrishti. He asked her what they had covered in class on the period and then explained very carefully about chariot burials. Millie couldn't put into words why she found his behaviour so irritating; after all he was the last person she fancied. On the other hand, Jake, who remained firmly in the dry back in the Land Rover, was much more her type.

Finally, after what seemed like another hour of lecturing from Nige, Jake appeared beside them.

'This is crazy, Nige. You're soaked. It's nearly lunch time – why don't we head for the pub?'

'Well, I suppose we won't get anything done today. Cause too much damage anyway.'

Millie was relieved, at last the chance to dry out *and* get to know Jake better. But Vrishti had other ideas.

'I think we should get back to uni. Don't you, Millie?'

'Well … actually, I …' She didn't want to argue with her friend but so far it had been a pretty tedious day. At least a drink with Jake might cheer it up a bit. 'Let's at least get something to eat first.'

'If you like.' Nige was rubbing the water off the end of his nose with the back of his hand in a particularly unpleasant manner.

The pub in Bainbridge was quiet and they sat awkwardly with their drinks, even after their sandwiches arrived. The weather had dampened the atmosphere and as soon as Vrishti had swallowed her last mouthful she suggested they moved on.

'Hang on!' Jake looked surprised. 'We've only been here a few minutes, surely we deserve another drink?'

'And I've got a seminar at four, I meant to say,' Nige admitted.

Jake scowled. 'Well in that case mate, just drop me at the farm.'

Millie wondered what he meant. She looked at Vrishti who was turning with a smile to follow Nige.

'Why do you need to go, Vrishti?' Millie called.

'I have to see Dr Armstrong this afternoon.'

'Why this afternoon?'

'Er, it's about my project. Yes, my project. I have to get permission to change it.' She was blushing.

'Can't it wait until tomorrow?' Millie had never seen Vrishti so obstinate.

'No, no. I must see her today!'

'Right, we'll get going then,' said Nige.

Millie climbed in the Land Rover without speaking to Vrishti. She didn't want to show her disappointment. Jake was talking quietly to Nige although she couldn't hear for the rain beating on the roof of the vehicle. Finally he turned round to her.

'If you want to, you could come back to the farm to get dry. It's quite near here. We can go back to town later. Mum or Dad can give us a lift.'

Now it was Millie's turn to blush.

'Are you sure? I mean, won't they mind?'

'No, they're OK and it's not far.'

He turned back to Nige. 'Just go down the main road for a bit. I'll tell you where to turn off.'

It wasn't far and soon they were bumping down a narrow track to a large farmhouse, surrounded by outbuildings and barns.

'You can sit next to me now,' called Nige when Jake got out. Vrishti grimaced as she climbed down and went round to the front. Millie nearly slipped on the mud as she got out and Jake grabbed her arm.

'Careful.'

'Jakey! It's Jakey!'

A small boy came running out and then stood back in the porch while the Land Rover reversed and sped out of the yard. Jake ushered her to the door and took the boy's hands.

'Hiya Toby, how's you?'

'I've been made monitor and I have to look after the hamsters in the holidays.'

'Well, that's … brilliant.'

He grinned at Millie and indicated for her to go into the house. A woman came into the hall wiping her hands on a tea towel.

'Hello. I didn't expect you back so soon!'

'Just passing. Mum, this is Millie.'

'Come in, both of you. You're soaked. What have you been up to?'

They followed her into the warmth of the kitchen.

'Take off your jacket and stand by the Rayburn, I'll get a towel.'

Millie felt in need of more than a towel and was grateful but slightly embarrassed when Jake's mother returned, not only with towels but an assortment of clothing.

'There are some trousers and a sweater, why don't you go to the bathroom and dry yourself off properly. If you bring the wet things down I can dry them here.'

Millie was directed upstairs to the family bathroom. There was no way she was going to bring her underwear downstairs to dry, so she pulled on the fresh clothes over her damp knickers and bra. The jeans were too big and rather short and the sweater was baggy. She did not think the image in the mirror would attract Jake, unfortunately. She towelled her hair but it was too long and thick to dry properly without a hairdryer. Now she looked even worse. Finally she ventured downstairs again and was rewarded with the offer of a mug of tea and cake. Jake was not there.

'So, are you doing a PhD as well, Millie?'

'No!' Millie realised she didn't know what to call Jake's mother, she didn't even know his surname. 'I'm just in my second year. Jake and Nige were showing us the site.'

Jake's mother laughed.

'So you've met Nige, have you? Isn't he awful? I feel like giving him a good wash and a haircut. And when I see that place they share in town – well, really what a tip! I'm sure you must have a much tidier flat – or are you in halls?'

'No, I share a house with some other girls, but yes, it is tidier, I guess.'

Toby, who had been sitting at the kitchen table, slid off his seat and came over with a sheet of paper.

'I've drawn you, out in the rain.'

He offered her the picture. She had stick arms and legs but her face was neatly drawn with her hair coloured in, bright red.

'That's nice.' She took the paper and pointed at a ball with four legs. 'That's a lovely sheep.'

'No, it's not a sheep,' he said with a frown, 'it's our dog, Dash.'

'Well, it's beautiful.'

'You can have it if you like,' he said, turning back to the table, 'There's plenty more where that came from.'

Jake's mother smiled at her and shook her head.

'He's just like Jake was at his age, only worse I think.'

'What d'you mean, like me?'

Jake was standing at the door rubbing his head with a towel. He had changed into a shirt and trousers that made him look tall and slim.

'Mum says I'm worse than you were when you were my age,' piped up Toby.

Jake sat down at the table with him and idly tidied up the boy's crayons.

'Where's Dad?' asked Jake.

'He's gone over to Martin's to see about taking some more pasture towards Bainbridge.'

His mother poured him tea.

'When will he be back?'

'Not till tea time. Why?'

'Thought he might give us a lift back.'

'He will if you give him time to have his dinner. He won't miss that. But you'll need something to eat anyway.'

'If that's OK with you, Mum?'

'Of course, you daft thing. What d'you want to do until then?'

'Is the pool table still in the barn?'

Toby jumped up and ran to stand beside his brother.

'Can I play?'

'If you want. Come on, let's go.'

Millie followed the boys out of the kitchen and into a large room at the end of a long passage. There was no ceiling, just a high roof and rafters. It was dark until Jake opened a shutter on the window in the end wall. Across the fields, in the distance, Millie could see a large hill with a flat top.

'That's Penhill,' said Jake. 'It dominates the view round here. Did you notice it when we were at the site?'

'No I didn't, but then I didn't see much at all in the rain.'

'It'll be better tomorrow. It's a brilliant place and when it's dry there's a lot to do. Nige was a bit of a pain this morning but I think he was trying to impress your friend.'

'Vrishti? I don't think he'll get far there, she's a bit preoccupied at the moment.'

'No!' Jake rushed over to Toby who was wielding a cue at the table, despite the fact he could hardly see over it. 'Wait until I can help you little bro.'

Millie had only played pool a few times before and wasn't really sure of the rules. They had to lift Toby up and try to prevent him from damaging the table, which meant the game was rather haphazard. Soon Jake's mother came to tell Toby it was time for a snack. The rain had stopped and the sun was shining. Millie went over to the window.

'Do you want to have a look at the farm?' Jake asked, putting his cue down.

Millie was glad of any excuse to stop making a fool of herself on the pool table. In the yard the fences and gates were steaming in the sunshine and it felt warmer outside than in. Jake showed her round the barns where there were hens scratching. He explained that some of the sheep were on the fells but thirty or forty were grazing in the fields close to the house. As they wandered back, a Land Rover appeared in the yard. A middle-aged man jumped out of the driver's seat and opened the rear door to release a border collie that raced up to Jake. Millie wondered who the man was until he shouted, 'Hello son, who's this then? Bringing lady friends back home eh?'

She felt her face turning bright red.

'Ignore him,' muttered Jake, rubbing the dog's back, 'he does it to embarrass me, not you. Dad, this is Millie from uni. We've been up to the site today. Got rained off.'

'I see, you been playing truant have you?' He grinned.

'No, just drying off really. Dad, can you give us a lift back tonight?'

His father frowned. 'Don't see why not, so long as I get me tea.'

'Oh yes you'll get your tea. C'mon Dash!' Jake strode towards the house with the dog close at his heels and they followed him inside.

Millie was impressed by how well Jake got on with his parents. She was still having trouble with Dad's girlfriend, even though she'd been around for several years. It meant she preferred to find reasons not to visit them and envied friends who looked forward to going home. The conversation flowed at dinner with the topics changing rapidly as they discussed Millie's course, Jake's studies, and various items of news from the dale. Millie learnt that Jake's mum, Bridget, had a small business making cakes for special occasions. Jake asked how it was going and she gave them a list of weddings and christenings that were keeping her busy.

As soon as the meal was over Jake's father, Robert, suggested they got ready to go back. He wanted to get home at a reasonable time and was anxious to be off. Bridget had dried Millie's clothes and she changed back into them in the bathroom, using the opportunity to give her hair a brush and tie it back into a pony tail again.

The family car was more comfortable than a Land Rover and Millie was glad to relax on her own in the back. The stone walls drifted past and the music on the radio was soothing, with a background of low mutterings as father and son discussed the hay-making. The villages and towns passed by quickly and soon Robert was dropping Millie off outside her house. Jake jumped out and thanked her for coming with him.

'I should thank *you*,' she said, 'I really enjoyed today.'

'I do hope we can do it again, I mean, go out somewhere.'

'Get a move on you two. I want to get home tonight!' shouted Robert from the car.

'I'd better go. I'll call you!'

Millie laughed. He didn't have her number so he couldn't, but she'd see him tomorrow when they went back to the site. He was so nice. Too nice? It can't last, it won't last. It'll be like the others. There'll be something wrong with him, there always was. Wait till she tells Phoebe.

Vrishti was standing outside her office when Joanna arrived back from invigilating the first year resit exams. She could see the student was anxious and tried to be as patient as possible, considering that she had a huge amount of marking to get through before the next day.

'Come in and sit down. It's Vrishti isn't it?' The girl nodded without speaking.

Joanna perched on her desk and looked down at the girl, who was sitting on the edge of her chair.

'So what can I do for you? Is it about our chat the other day?'

'Yes, I mean no, Dr Armstrong. I'm here because you're the project co-ordinator.'

Joanna sighed with relief. She could cope with projects but personal stuff - that was tricky.

'I wanted to ask if I could change my summer project to work in Wensleydale, with Nige and Jake.'

'You mean Dr Hammond's site? Who were you supposed to be working with?' Joanna asked.

'Dr Perkins.'

Vrishti blushed and Joanna had the usual uncomfortable feeling that occurred when her ex-husband's name was spoken by an attractive young girl. She took a deep breath.

'Vrishti, do you want to tell me why you don't want to work with him any more?'

The girl looked uncomfortable, 'I don't really want to say, it's awkward.'

'Awkward?' Joanna could feel her heart pounding.

'I don't like to speak about it, you know.'

Joanna didn't know what to think. She didn't want to press her; she didn't want to hear what she had to say.

'Well, if Dr Hammond is happy to have you, there's no problem with changing from my point of view.'

Joanna smiled down at the girl, who now looked relieved and grateful.

'Thank you so much, you don't know what this means to me.'

'And Vrishti, if you want to talk about any problems you are having, my door is always open you know.'

Joanna watched her leave the room, wondering what she should do regarding the situation and whether she should mention it to anyone at all. It could seem odd if anything embarrassing came out about Gary later, when she hadn't reported it. She sat staring out of the window, wishing life was less complicated and Gary had stayed out in Greece permanently. There was nothing for it, she would have to tell the Dean.

Millie was up early, excited by the prospect of seeing Jake again. Vrishti had not appeared by the time the Land Rover was due to pick them up and Millie ran up to her bedroom, only to find it empty. She woke Phoebe to ask her if she had seen Vrishti when she got home the previous evening but Phoebe had assumed she was already asleep.

They were still discussing what to do when Jake arrived to take Millie to Wensleydale. There were two other students waiting in a battered old blue Land Rover and there was no time to tell Jake about Vrishti, except to say she would not be coming with them. Climbing reluctantly into the back she settled herself down beside an excitable summer student called Edie, who talked at her for the entire journey.

When they arrived, the other students went straight off to work at the edge of the site and Jake came over to her.

'Hi there. Do you want to do some work today?'

'Yes please.'

She followed him over to a test pit, which was about a metre square. It was away from the main work area and she suspected that it was less important, since she had so little experience.

'Have you done the second year practical course?' he asked.

Millie noticed that his hair had a touch of red in it, and that it was even more obvious in his stubble beard.

'Yep, I've done that. D'you want me to clear this area?'

'Yes but very gently. We've got all sorts of things to work with here, toothbrushes, toothpicks, lolly sticks, but let me know if you uncover anything. We've found some buckles and beads here and we think there could be more. I've got the tools in the Land Rover.'

He wandered over to the vehicle and came back with an armful of trowels, brushes and plastic bags.

'Here's a marker pen. Keep notes of anything you find and let me know. I'll come over and help once I've sorted the others out.'

He made another trip and returned with a bundle of paper.

'These are the record forms,' he said, pointing to the top of the first sheet.

Millie studied the series of boxes entitled "colour", "composition", "compaction", "coarse components". It went on and on, until she reached "artefacts" at the bottom of the page.

'Have you filled these in before?'

'Yes, of course,' she lied.

They had gone through them in class but she'd not done it for real.

'Well, start at this end and work through, sieve as you go and record everything! If you find anything let me know straight away and don't do anything until I've seen it.' He started to walk away. 'Call me if you need a hand. There's a bucket for washing things over by the gate.'

'OK.' Millie was feeling distinctly nervous.

It was a beautiful clear day and she could feel the heat of the sun on her back as she crouched down on the blue plastic sheeting round the pit. Her excitement at the prospect of working with Jake had completely obliterated her worry about Vrishti, for now she had to try to remember everything that she had been taught about cleaning. She waited until Jake returned and checked with him on how to do this and that. He had a soft voice with a pleasant Yorkshire accent and she listened to his explanations, thinking up new questions so she could continue to engage him in conversation. Soon she got into a rhythm with her brushing and sieving, and the morning passed quickly until it was interrupted by a loud yell.

'Jake! Jake! I've got something!' The silly girl who had chattered non-stop on the way was waving. Jake ran over to her and Millie stood up, wishing it was her that was attracting his attention. A crowd gathered round Edie, who was holding out something covered in soil about ten centimetres long. Jake took it from her and rubbed at it very gently.

'I think it's a blade,' he announced to the group, looking very pleased. 'Well done Edie, that's brilliant.'

The girl beamed and one by one they congratulated her on the find. Millie left them to it until the excitement died down and then went back to look at it more closely. It was small and insignificant, like a child's ruler covered in soil but Millie could see it could be a small dagger.

'Pretty exciting, eh?' Jake said, putting it carefully back in its plastic bag.

Millie sighed. 'I don't suppose I'll find anything like that.'

'No, but other things are just as important. A tiny bead, a buckle, a comb, they're all clues to who lived here.'

Soon everyone was back at work and the find was almost forgotten.

At lunch time Millie sat at the edge of the site with Jake, eating the packed lunch she had brought, and chatting about nothing in particular. He asked where Vrishti was but she just shrugged. It sounded rather silly to say she was "missing", so she just said she hadn't turned up that morning.

'Does she often disappear like that?' Jake asked.

'No, never. Not Vrishti.'

'Nige didn't mention anything yesterday.'

'Where is he today?'

'Down near Driffield, at the chariot burial site. He was up amazingly early today. He was getting a lift.'

'*He* might know what Vrishti was going to do today.'

'She did seem keen to get back early yesterday.'

'That's because she wanted to see Dr Armstrong about changing projects.'

They looked up at the sound of a diesel engine.

'Hey up, it's Colin. Jump to it!'

Dr Hammond climbed out of the white university Land Rover and marched across the field, zigzagging to avoid the test pits.

'Hello there, Jake! And who is this young lady?'

Jake introduced Millie and explained about her wish to take part in the excavation as a summer project. He asked her a few questions about what she had been doing and what year she was in. Millie was flattered by his attention and reddened when he asked her what she wanted to do when she completed the course.

'I'd like to carry on studying, really.'

'Good, good. Well keep up the good work. I hope you enjoy working here over the summer. Now then Jake, anything of interest to show me?'

They strode off together to the test pit where Edie had found the blade and Millie waited while they studied the artefact. Eventually Dr Hammond walked back to the Land Rover with the plastic bag and was gone.

'He didn't stay long!' Millie commented when Jake returned.

'No, he had to get back to a staff meeting. Anyway he was suitably excited by the blade. He thinks it might be Iron Age.'

*

Joanna gathered up her papers and set off for the Council Room. It was the last staff meeting of the academic year and the agenda was longer than usual, meaning it would go on for most of the afternoon. Gary was sitting next to the departmental assistant and Joanna chose a seat as far away from him as possible. There was no sign of Colin and Joanna hoped he would not appear. Colleagues drifted in and chatted in groups until the door was flung open by the Dean. Clapping her hands for quiet, she asked everyone to sit down at once and motioned to Gary to open the window behind him. It did little to cool the air and the room became stuffier as time went on. Joanna watched Colin creep in half way through the afternoon. His hair was a mess and there were sweat marks under his armpits. Joanna stifled a yawn and stretched her legs under the table. She watched the cars building up on the main road and thought about the journey home. She imagined the queues in the supermarket and wondered how much longer the meeting would go on. They were working slowly down the agenda and were now about three-quarters of the way through. Angela McGrath was fond of her own voice and she dominated the meeting with her views, giving the staff little opportunity to comment.

'Now, Joanna. What about the summer projects?'

The Dean had reached the penultimate item, which related to Joanna's role as project co-ordinator.

'They're all organised, Angela.'

'That's good to hear. Any problems?'

'Not really.' Here was her opportunity to mention the Vrishti business without being specific. 'Although one student has had a few issues but I think they are sorted out now.'

'What do you mean "issues"?' The questioner was Colin Hammond.

'I can't really discuss them here. But don't worry, they've been sorted out.'

She kept the irritation from her voice and managed to avoid looking across at Gary.

'Well, perhaps we should leave it there then.'

The Dean moved to any other business and Joanna settled back, glancing at her ex-husband, who appeared to be engrossed in sending a text message on his mobile phone.

When the meeting finally came to an end, Joanna fiddled with her papers until Gary had left the room. There were only a few people remaining, including Angela who was speaking to Colin. As Joanna headed down the corridor she heard her name and saw her ex-husband waiting by her office door.

'JoJo, I wanted to have a word. I didn't have a chance to speak to you properly before and there's something I wanted to put straight.'

'Well, I don't have time now Gary.' She couldn't face another row with him at this time in the day.

'I thought we might meet away from here, at my place … or yours?'

'I don't think that's a good idea, do you?'

'Why not? We're both adults. Surely we can have a sensible grown-up conversation?'

'Perhaps … later in the week maybe. I'll let you know.'

She turned into her office and shut the door firmly behind her.

By the time she left, the cleaners were already vacuuming the corridor but tonight she spared herself the pleasantries and headed for the car park. Colin was waiting for her in the entrance hall.

'Well I thought I must have missed you.' He breathed alcohol at her as they stood face to face. 'Except I saw your car outside. I wondered if you would care to join us for a drink?'

'And exactly who is us, Colin?'

'Well, actually at the moment it's just me but some of the students said they'd be along later.'

'I'm sorry Colin but I've got shopping to do. Perhaps another time?'

She knew immediately it had been a mistake to add that.

'When? When would you like to make it? Tomorrow? Maybe Friday?' He had moved nearer and the smell of alcohol was stronger than ever.

'Well, I didn't mean it literally, Colin. It was more of a phrase, something people say.' She took a deep breath. 'What people say when they really mean "no".'

'Mean "no" what?'

'Mean "no thank you but I really don't want to have a drink with you, ever". Sorry.'

He was staring at her, his face close to hers. 'What d'you mean?' He looked puzzled.

'I mean I don't really want to go out for a drink, thank you.'

'You miserable bitch.'

He stared at her for several seconds. She moved back and he made to step towards her and then stopped.

'You'll change your mind, and I'll be waiting. Oh yes, I'll be waiting.'

Joanna walked quickly, almost ran out of the door into the car park. She didn't look back until she was in the car and driving out past the building. She could see him in the entrance hall staring out at her. There was something in his manner that was decidedly unpleasant.

Chapter 3

The day had passed quickly for Millie. Her back ached, her neck was sore with sunburn and her hands were scratched and dry. She was sure she looked an absolute sight, her hair had been scraped back so many times it felt lank and sweaty. Her makeup had disappeared hours ago and without a mirror she was even unsure whether her mascara was smudged. When it was time to leave the site she tried to climb into the back of the vehicle unnoticed.

'Millie, d'you fancy a drink when we get back to uni?'

Jake was calling through the window. Millie nodded, and then spent the journey trying to make herself presentable by spitting on a tissue she found in her pocket and rubbing her face and hands. Edie was so full of herself over finding the blade, Millie had no time to think about much else on the return journey.

The university bar was housed in the Students Union. It had been recently refurbished and attracted both students and staff early in the evening. Millie noticed that Dr Hammond was sitting drinking alone. Jake took her over to a table in the corner and introduced her to his fellow postgraduate students. She asked for a lager and sat happily listening to their chatter. Jake was telling them about the find at the site and one of the students, called Ben, was particularly interested.

'That's amazing,' he said. 'I'd like to have a look at that. It sounds similar to one I saw when I was working in Northumberland. Where is it?'

'Don't know,' said Jake. 'Usually stuff like that is logged and goes in the artefact room for storage, unless it's displayed in the Council Room. Colin brought it back … if you want to ask him he's over there.'

'Right!'

Ben jumped up and went over to the bar. They watched him in conversation with Dr Hammond, who was talking loudly and waving his arms enthusiastically. When he returned, Ben told them Colin had the blade in his office.

'He's had a bit too much to drink and he's becoming a bore, so I got out of it quick,' he added.

Millie was distracted by the sight of Dr Perkins ordering a drink, talking to Dr Hammond, who was standing at the bar next to him. She couldn't make out what was being said but soon they were squaring up to each other and voices were being raised.

'Oops, trouble at mill! This should be interesting,' said Ben, turning round.

When the two men started pushing each other he strode over and spoke to them.

'Gary is Ben's supervisor,' explained Jake.

'Isn't Dr Hammond your's, Jake?' Millie teased.

'Yes but I'm smaller than Ben. And I want to get my PhD next year.'

The barman came out and took Dr Perkins to one side, hanging on to him until Dr Hammond had left and then letting him follow.

'I don't know, these academics,' Ben said, returning with a pint in his hand. 'Still, the management was properly appreciative!'

The roads were already busy with evening traffic and the supermarket in town was packed with shoppers.

Joanna idly scrutinised the baskets of the people in front of her while she queued patiently. She noticed that many of the customers were like her, dressed for business and buying items for one, ready-made dinners. Occasionally she made the decision to eat real food but it was always disastrous. She would buy fresh ingredients and then something would crop up. Several late evenings, the odd working lunch and she would have to clear the rotting food from her refrigerator. Finally it was her turn to unload her shopping onto the conveyor belt, stacking the items neatly. This was the result of years of training. Her mother had been the headmistress of a large private school for girls and so Joanna and her sisters had virtually run the family home as teenagers. She knew how to cook but she didn't see the point. Generally she snacked on cheese and microwaveable meals, on the basis that it gave her more time to work in the evenings.

'Thank you!'

The girl at the till handed the man in front his receipt and started on Joanna's goods. When she handed the girl her credit card she recognised her as one of her first year students. She was about to say hello but realised the girl was blushing, so she simply thanked her and took the receipt.

She left the supermarket car park with a sense of relief, joining the A1 until she left the busy road, heading for Richmond. Once she was travelling through the familiar countryside she relaxed. Before long she was through Leyburn and on to Redmire, planning her evening as she drove. She needed some fresh air so she would jog round the circuit before heating her supper, and so it would be eight or so before she would eat. She swerved to avoid a white

Land Rover parked on the bend in the narrow lane and cursed the farmer who must have left it there.

It filled Joanna with pleasure and pride each time she arrived at her cottage. It represented her independence, her ability to support herself and her decision to live in the countryside. The property needed work and she would have to spend the summer painting and decorating but it was worth every minute to live in such a beautiful spot. The door groaned when she opened it and she picked up flakes of paint that had fallen off the dried wood. Dumping the groceries, she ran upstairs to change and, stopping to check she had the keys, she jogged out of the cottage and slammed the door.

As she set off up the hill she heard an engine behind her. It was catching up as she ran and soon it overtook her and continued round the corner. It was only when it reappeared a few moments later she recognised the driver and stopped to stare as the vehicle accelerated and veered towards her. Instinctively she threw herself at the side of the lane but there was nowhere to go as she felt metal pushing into her side and the hard impact of the stone wall at her head.

The moment Millie let herself into the house, Phoebe burst into tears and began to tell her about the row she'd had with Dani.

'That bitch is at it again! She called me everything under the sun when I confronted her about it. She did it before when I was out and I told her I knew. I said to her …'

Millie listened for several minutes but was none the wiser about what "the bitch" was supposed to have done.

'What did Dani *do*?' she asked patiently.

'Well, I said, I saw her coming out of Vrishti's room this afternoon. I told her I'd seen her. I came in and was going up the stairs when I saw her shadow flit out of her bedroom. At first she denied it but I knew it was her and I told her so.'

'What did she say?'

'Nothing. She told me to 'ef off.'

'That's not very nice.'

'No, and I said so. Don't tell me to 'ef off, I said.'

Millie let Phoebe continue, while she put the kettle on.

'So did you find out what she was doing?'

'She said, she said she was looking for cotton wool balls. I ask you – cotton wool balls!'

'She might have been.'

'She wasn't.'

'How d'you know?'

'Because I can't imagine, for one minute, that she uses cotton wool balls!'

Millie couldn't help smiling.

'What?' Phoebe looked indignant. 'It's not funny. She called me names when I accused her to her face that she was stealing from Vrishti. And then she was horrible about her.'

'Was she?'

'Yes, she said "Why would I want to take anything from a pathetic little princess who freaks out the minute anyone lays a finger on her." I don't know what she meant but I hope she hasn't been bullying her.'

'Did you ask her what it meant?'

'Yes, she just laughed.'

'Did you tell Vrishti about Dani being in her room?'

'No, she hasn't come back'

'Oh shit. I hope she's all right.' Millie tried calling her mobile but it was on voicemail. She left a message.

'Vrishti, it's Millie. Where the hell are you?'

Next morning Phoebe insisted they ring the police.

'She's never stayed out all night. We've just got to report it,' she pleaded. 'Please, Millie. What else can we do?'

Millie had been awake most of the night thinking about it. The sensible approach would be to contact Vrishti's brother but she didn't know how to, and anyway she was nervous of how he might react. So far the only explanation for her disappearance was that she was staying with him. A call to Deepal would confirm it but if she wasn't there he would worry and there was probably a perfectly rational explanation.

'We wouldn't panic like this if Dani didn't appear for a few days, or even you or me.' Millie knew this sounded feeble.

'I know, but Vrishti is not us and certainly isn't Dani. She doesn't do this. I think we should tell the department at least!'

'Technically it's not even term time now …' Phoebe was about to interrupt her. 'But I agree we ought to tell someone.'

'OK, we'll go and see Dr Armstrong. She's the departmental tutor, or women's tutor, or something like that.'

The Departmental Assistant was eating a jam doughnut when they arrived in the office. Giggling, she licked her fingers as Millie asked whether Dr Armstrong was in.

'Isn't she in her office?' asked the girl, with a polite smile while flicking sugar off her silk top.

'No, and the door's locked,' said Phoebe. 'It's really urgent.'

'Well, they don't tell me their movements, especially in the holidays. Maybe she's taken the day off.'

'Then who do we see? We wanted to talk to her 'cos she's the women's tutor.'

The girl looked confused. 'I don't know. There isn't a deputy. You'll have to wait until she's back in, I'm afraid.'

'We can't.' Phoebe looked flushed. 'We have to speak to someone, it's really important. There should be a deputy – we're not leaving till we see someone.' She grinned at Millie triumphantly.

The administrator shrugged, got up and walked through to an inner office. Millie could hear her talking softly to a second person. The two of them returned and Millie recognised the Departmental Secretary, Mrs Weiss.

'Now then girls, Chantelle tells me you have a problem.'

Her tone was patronising, her smile artificial. Now it was Millie's turn to be cross.

'We want to see Professor McGrath, it's urgent.'

The woman looked surprised but her smile remained intact. 'I'll see what I can do but I can't promise anything. What is it about?'

'It's a personal matter.'

'About Vrishti,' added Phoebe.

The woman strode back into her office and carefully shut the door behind her. Millie and Phoebe stood motionless while Chantelle started work on her keyboard. A few minutes later the inner door opened and the secretary, no longer smiling, announced the Dean would see them now.

'You know where to find her? It's the third door on the right.'

She went back into her office and closed the door.

Phoebe looked triumphant but Millie was nervous of what the Dean might think of them. She let Phoebe do the talking.

Professor McGrath was sitting behind a highly polished antique desk when they entered. She rose and indicated to them they should sit down opposite her. Millie could hardly see round the pile of paperwork in front of her.

'So what can I do for you?' she asked, peering over her gold-rimmed half-glasses.

She didn't smile but she seemed willing to spare them some time.

Phoebe looked at Millie, who nodded at her and remained silent.

'It's about our friend Vrishti.' Her voice was almost a whisper. 'We haven't seen her for a while.'

There was silence. Finally Professor McGrath asked, 'Is that unusual? I imagine you students come and go pretty much as you please. Maybe she's gone home?'

'But I'm sure she would have told us,' tried Phoebe. 'It's so unlike her.'

'So what would you like me to do?' The Dean's voice was calm, almost motherly. She fiddled with her necklace.

'We thought we should inform the police.' Phoebe reddened.

'Don't you think it might be a bit early for that? Why not come back in a few days, if she hasn't reappeared. I'm sure you must be anxious but we don't want to waste their time, do we?'

She stood up as if to dismiss them.

'She wouldn't go away without telling us,' said Phoebe sulkily.

'I tell you what.' The Dean smiled. 'I'll contact her parents, just to let them know we're concerned, how about that?'

Millie was relieved. 'Thank you. Thank you very much. That would be really helpful.'

She raised her eyebrows at Phoebe and her friend followed her out of the office. As soon as they were outside Phoebe burst into tears.

'Don't be silly Phoebes.' Millie put her arm round her friend. 'Everything will be fine. Vrishti's parents will contact Deepal straight away and he'll know what to do, if she hasn't turned up at the house by then. Come on, I'll buy you a coffee.'

Term was over and most undergraduates had gone home for the summer, so the cafeteria was nearly empty. A few students, including Phoebe, were re-sitting exams they'd failed and some, like Millie, were working on research projects. Otherwise the only students around were postgraduates, including Jake and Nige, perched on stools at a high table by the window.

'That's Jake.' Millie nudged Phoebe and pointed over to their table.

'Which one?'

'The one with the sort of beard – the nerdy one is Nige.'

'You go over, I'll get the drinks,' offered Phoebe.

Jake immediately asked whether they'd seen Vrishti yet. Millie explained how they had been to see the Dean because Dr Armstrong was not around.

'That's because she's disappeared,' Nige broke in.

'How d'you know?' asked Millie.

'Because Colin told me. She's not been in and no-one can contact her. Actually he's quite shaken up about it.' He grinned.

Phoebe arrived with a tray.

'We wondered if you knew what Vrishti was doing when she got back to uni on Tuesday,' said Millie.

'She was going to see her tutor so I dropped her in the department before I took the Land Rover back.'

'And you didn't see her after that?' asked Phoebe.

'Nope, I went off to town straight away, to the supermarket.'

'I thought you said you hadn't got any food in?' Jake looked puzzled.

'Not food. I needed a new printer cartridge.'

'You could've got some food while you were there,' Jake muttered.

'Too busy, couldn't stop.' Nige grinned at the girls.

Millie looked at Phoebe. 'So you don't know what her plans were when you left her then?'

'Who, Vrishti? Why should I? What's her problem?'

'Well, actually *she's* disappeared.' Phoebe was nearly in tears. Climbing off her stool, she picked up her bag and tugged at Millie's sleeve.

'We've got to get back. She may be there or trying to get hold of us.'

Millie smiled across at Jake and he jumped up. 'Will you be coming to the dig tomorrow?'

Millie looked at Phoebe, 'Yes, I don't see why not. I'm sure it will all be sorted by then.'

As she turned to go he signalled he would call her.

*

Deepal was waiting outside the house. He jumped out of his BMW as they turned the corner and was standing by the front door when they arrived, blocking their way.

'Where is she?'

They led him into the kitchen but he refused to be seated, pacing up and down the narrow space between the table and the sink. His hand moved between the knot of his tie and the handkerchief in his top pocket. He dabbed his forehead as he turned sharply to Millie.

'I have been trying to reach her for days. Where is she? I want to speak to her.'

'I'm sorry, I really don't know. I thought she might have been staying with you.'

He sat down, looking suddenly deflated, crumpled. He leaned his elbows on the table and then lifted them up again quickly, rubbing his jacket sleeves. He spoke quietly in an exasperated tone.

'You could have tried to find out. Isn't that what your mother would want if you went missing?'

Millie felt a lump in her throat and tried to stop tears forming.

'I'm sorry. I really am.'

She was saved by Deepal's mobile ringing and she went over to fiddle with the mugs in the sink. He spoke quietly and quickly so at first Millie didn't realise he wasn't speaking in English. Suddenly he finished the call with 'OK I'll see you soon.'

'Would you like a cup of tea?' asked Phoebe.

'No. I must go. My wife has to go to the doctor's.'

'Oh dear …' Phoebe began.

'No, no, no. Nothing.' He seemed distracted.

'Vrishti,' he said, 'I assume there is a boy involved? What do you think? I mean a boyfriend …

- 51 -

did she have a boyfriend?' Beads of sweat were appearing on his forehead.

'No, no she didn't have a boyfriend.'

Millie thought Phoebe sounded too defensive. It was true but they didn't know what had happened at the party. Perhaps there had been someone.

'Well no-one you could call a *boyfriend.*' Millie added.

'There was someone then?' Deepal's eyes were wide with alarm.

Phoebe looked at Millie for support. 'No, not that we know of. I've never seen anyone.'

'If I find him, I'll, I'll … well he just better not show himself.'

He pulled out his handkerchief again and wiped his forehead. His mobile rang and he looked at it quickly.

'It's Priti again. I must go now.'

He glared at them in turn. 'You must tell me anything you know. I will tell the police at once and I expect they will wish to speak with you.'

He gave them his mobile number and Millie wrote it down on an old envelope out of the recycling box. Then she followed him to the door, watching until the BMW disappeared round the corner. It was going to be official then, Vrishti was now a missing person. Part of her was frightened for what may have happened but mostly she was sure there was a perfectly logical explanation. She tried to recall if there was a field trip or a visit that she had mentioned and they had forgotten about. The police would ask them things like that.

Back in the kitchen Phoebe was playing with small scraps of paper, absently fitting them together into a rectangle.

'Millie, I've been thinking. If Deepal is registering Vrishti as a missing person we'd better go and tell the Dean.'

Millie nodded. 'What are you doing?'

Phoebe continued to re-arrange the pieces as if she was doing a jigsaw.

'I found them in the envelope you used, I think it's a letter.'

'Whose is it?'

'Well, the envelope is addressed to Vrishti.'

Peering over Phoebe's shoulder, Millie saw the scrawled handwriting. It didn't take long to fit the pieces together to form a letter, written on half a sheet of A4 paper: *I am sorry about what happened at the party and I hope you will accept my apologies. I am sure you will agree we all had a bit too much to drink and I can assure you it will not happen again. We need to discuss a matter of extreme importance and I would like you to come to the archive storeroom at 5 pm tomorrow to discuss it. Failure to do so may result in serious consequences.*

'Who's it from?'

'It doesn't say … unless there's another page, but it looks as though it's all there.' Phoebe started stuffing the pieces back into the envelope. 'We should give it to the police. It could be a very important clue.'

'But it could be from anyone!' The mention of police had scared Millie. It made Vrishti's disappearance seem too significant, too important.

'It's obviously from a member of staff.'

'No, it's not, Phoebe. It could be another student. It could be …' Millie tried to think of a student who would suggest meeting Vrishti in the departmental store.

'Dani, it could be Dani!' Phoebe shouted.

'Or Nige … or anyone.'

'No, but wait. It could be Dani, after all the note wasn't posted, was it?'

'But ...'

'And she was in Vrishti's room on Wednesday.'

Millie read the letter again. 'It doesn't sound like Dani. It's too formal, isn't it? It's quite polite. We really can't tell from this.'

'We can tell from the handwriting. I'm going to give it to the police.'

Millie's mobile rang and she was relieved to see it was a call from Jake.

'Hi.'

'Hi Millie. I just wondered how things were going.'

'Fine.'

'Really? You don't sound it.'

'Oh it's just stuff. You know.'

'Any news about Vrishti?'

'No.'

'Look I just wondered if you wanted to do something tomorrow? We could go into Leeds or …'

Millie wanted to go to the family farm again but didn't want to ask. 'What about Bainbridge?' It was near the farm and a good excuse. 'You know, the Roman Fort.'

'Could be tricky getting there,' said Jake, 'but if we visit the excavation we could use the departmental vehicle.'

'Even better. I'd like to get a proper look at the whole thing. You can explain it to me.'

'Right, leave it to me.' He rang off.

'So shall we take it to the police?' pleaded Phoebe.

'OK but we should wait until we hear from Deepal.'

*

Nige was hunched over his desk, peering at his computer screen when Dani came in carrying two paper cups. He grimaced and leaned back in his chair, rubbing his eyes. It was six thirty and most people had left the department.

'What do you want?' Dani didn't normally spare him the time of day.

'Well that's a nice way to talk when I bring you a coffee.'

She placed the cup carefully on the only clear space in front of him and sat down by Jake's desk.

'What do you want?' Nige repeated, gazing at the screen.

'Just a chat. I wondered how things went down in Driffield today.'

'Fine. In fact quite good, actually.'

'Great. Did you use the new Land Rover?'

'Yes, it goes like a bomb.'

'D'you know who used it yesterday?'

'No I don't, but whoever it was has scraped the nearside wing already.'

'Really?' She sipped her coffee slowly and peered over the cup at him. 'You took it to Wensleydale on Tuesday, didn't you?'

'Yes. Look, what is with the Spanish inquisition?'

'It's just I heard you took Vrishti and I wondered what she did after you brought her back.'

'What's it to you?'

'Nothing.'

She stood up and walked out, nearly bumping into Jake.

'Hey Nige, what's she doing? You kept quiet about her.'

'She's weird. Asking me loads of questions about Driffield and Land Rovers and the girl that's gone missing.'

'Didn't think she cared about Vrishti. From what Millie says none of them get on with Dani.'

'And she brought me this coffee.'

'Well, perhaps it's your body she's after really then!'

Nige reddened. 'I don't think so,' he said, his accent getting stronger with his increasing irritation.

Jake picked up his rucksack and set off home leaving his flatmate working in the office. But Nige wasn't the last to leave the building. Jake could hear Dani's raised voice as he passed her office door.

'Leave Vrishti alone. Stop following her, stop trying to contact her. Because if you don't I'll make sure everyone knows and that'll stop your career in its tracks. I can look after myself but the poor child doesn't know what's hit her. I'm warning you, stop now or it'll be you finished!'

Jake could hear the phone being slammed down as he continued down the corridor.

Chapter 4

Staff nurse stood at the end of the bed surveying the new patient. Dr Joanna Marianne Armstrong, age thirty four, road traffic accident, was lying on her back oblivious to the student nurse, who was washing her arms and drying them very gently, patting them carefully with the threadbare hospital towel.

'Still not conscious?' Staff asked.

The girl shook her head slowly, without looking up. 'No.'

Staff studied Joanna's notes. She knew the woman had been in a traffic accident but it was her first shift on the ward for a week and she had missed the details. It must have been pretty serious to have crushed both legs and her pelvis. There was massive blood loss, which had been stabilised but the concern was what had happened to her head. The scan had shown a subdural haematoma. The outlook was uncertain and the family would have to be given the bad news when they arrived.

Joanna could hear muffled voices and sensed something touching her arm, first one side and then the other. It was dark, pitch black. She felt sick and her head hurt so much, much worse than a migraine. If she concentrated very hard she could hear someone talking but she couldn't tell what they were saying. She was tired and didn't want to try any more, she just wanted to sleep.

'Poor love,' said the girl, neatly setting Joanna's arm down by her side.

She looked at the patient with her head on one side and then, picking up the wash bowl and towel, she left the room. Staff remained at the foot of the bed reading her notes until she was disturbed by the receptionist saying they had spoken to the university and now they had a contact, an ex-husband, who could inform the patient's relatives.

When the ex-husband turned up an hour later, no-one was sure whether he should be allowed to see Joanna or not. The man, wearing a torn shirt and denim shorts introduced himself as Gary Perkins, *Dr* Gary Perkins. He kept running his hands through his thick curly hair, which made him appear even more unkempt. He seemed very concerned for Joanna and Staff didn't see why she couldn't discuss the patient's condition with him. He wouldn't take a seat but stood looking lost, rubbing his forehead furiously.

'Can I see her?' he asked.

'Of course, but she won't be able to speak to you, or even hear you, I'm afraid.'

'No, I just want to see her.' His voice wavered.

Staff led the way to where Joanna lay motionless. She pushed a chair to the edge of the bed and made him sit down. She explained what the monitors did and what the tubes were for. He didn't appear to take any of it in but sat staring at Joanna's face, his lips pressed hard together with emotion. She found a nurse to keep an eye on them and went back to the office, to discover whether an ex-husband was considered family in this situation.

The academic staff had taken to popping into the departmental office to ask for news of Joanna. Chantelle was tired of repeating the same brief message Dr Perkins had given her and had jokingly offered to post a bulletin on the door. Dr Hammond had been in several times badgering for more details and didn't believe her when she told him she knew no more than he did. She'd helped Dr Perkins arrange flights for Mr and Mrs Armstrong from Scotland because he was going to meet them at the airport late that evening and drive straight to the hospital. She had become quite sad at the thought that the only relatives Dr Armstrong had were her parents and she'd shed a tear, which was quite embarrassing because the Dean came in but she was really kind and chatted to her about it. Professor McGrath suggested a collection for some flowers and, despite being the Dean, she offered to take them to the hospital herself. So Chantelle popped quickly to the newsagent's on campus to get a card.

When they found the departmental office empty, Phoebe dragged a reluctant Millie along the corridor to see Professor McGrath. Although the door was shut when they knocked, a friendly voice told them to enter. The windows were wide open and the breeze gave the room a cool airy atmosphere. The older woman was sitting at a computer on a side table and as they entered she pushed back her chair and stood up. Her hair was a pale blonde in the sunlight but Millie noticed the roots were beginning to show through white.

'Hello again, girls.' She smiled at them both.

'Good morning, Dean,' Millie replied formally but Phoebe plunged in immediately.

'We thought we should come and tell you that Vrishti's brother has gone to the police to report her missing.'

The Dean continued to smile. 'Good. Yes. That's probably the best thing to do. I was going to suggest it myself … if she hadn't turned up.'

She walked across to her desk and perched on the edge. They sat in silence.

'What did her parents say?' asked Millie.

'They were obviously concerned about their daughter. I told them we'd do everything we can to find her.'

She smiled at them in a way that reassured Millie. The Dean was a very competent woman and they had done the right thing to tell her.

'Well, thank you both for keeping me informed and do let me know the moment you hear any news.'

There was nothing more to say, so they walked back to the house in silence.

Detective Inspector Ernie Brown drove slowly down the wide suburban roads of the modern estate on the outskirts of town. The route was unfamiliar and it took him some time to locate Nuthatch Drive from amongst a number of streets associated with birds. Deepal Bhatt must have a bit of money to live in this neck of the woods, thought Brown as he parked outside number eleven. Picking his file off the passenger seat he made his way to the front door, noting the BMW in the drive and the open double garage containing a people carrier.

'Hello love. Is your husband home?'

The door had been opened by a slim attractive woman carrying a chubby baby.

'Deepal! There's someone for you!' she called up the stairs and almost immediately a young man in tracksuit and trainers came running down to meet them.

'I'm sorry to bother you sir, but you reported a missing person.'

'Yes, yes, please come in, come in. This is an excellent service, please come in and sit down.'

Deepal turned and spoke quietly to his wife. She disappeared down the hall, while they went into the lounge. It was decorated elaborately and the furnishings were draped with throws and cushions, laid out carefully in symmetrical patterns. Deepal motioned for him to take a seat on the large sofa in the bay window.

'It's my young sister, Inspector,' Deepal began, thrusting a photograph into his hand. It showed a young attractive girl wearing a sari, surrounded by exotic plants and flowers.

Ernie took a pen from his jacket. 'If you don't mind I'll ask you some questions while I complete this form.'

He hated this sort of work. Anxious people worried sick about missing relatives and bugger all they could do about it. He would register the case and then they would file the paperwork until anxiety became desperation.

The wife came in with tea on a gilt tray. He had some difficulty holding the delicate china cup and saucer in his large hands, and he fumbled with the sugar lumps. She offered him cake but he declined. He managed to take all the details despite constant interruptions as Mr Bhatt found more photographs of his sister.

The couple followed him out onto the drive when he left and he could see them in his mirror, side by side, his arm round her shoulders, standing motionless. Back at the station he would make a mug of coffee and finish off the documentation before he went off shift. It was obvious to him that the girl had just gone off with a friend, probably a local lad that the brother didn't approve of. It would all come out in the wash, although the missing girl would be in big trouble when she did come home. He knew about these families that controlled their daughters and married them off to men back in India. It still happened even these days, you could see it in the papers. He thought about the photographs, the happy holiday shots. They seemed a decent enough family to Ernie but they all did, to begin with.

'Someone on the phone asking about our traffic accident lass,' said the ward receptionist, holding out the receiver. Staff took it with a sigh.

'May I ask who is calling?'

'I'm a colleague, a close friend – well, a very close friend actually.'

'May I take your name?'

'Yes, it's Colin Hammond. I need to know how she is. Is she conscious? How bad is it?'

This time Staff knew the rules. 'I'm afraid I can only give information to relatives. I'm sorry.'

'But I can visit, yes?'

'No, no visitors at the moment I'm afraid.'

The man at the other end slammed the phone down.

'Am I in the right ward for Dr Armstrong?'

A smartly dressed woman was standing in the doorway holding a large bouquet. Staff guessed she was in her forties but she could be older, she obviously looked after herself. For a second she couldn't place a Dr Armstrong but then realised that the woman was referring to their new patient.

'Yes, that's right, traffic accident. She was admitted yesterday.' The woman was too young to be her mother surely? 'Are you a relative?'

'No, I'm a work colleague, well her boss actually. I'm Head of Department, Dean.' She offered her hand. 'Angela McGrath.'

Staff explained as politely as she could that only relatives were allowed in and she couldn't really discuss the patient with her but she was so persuasive and the flowers were so lovely she found herself leading the way down the corridor to where the poor girl lay. Of course she didn't leave her alone with the patient but remained discreetly in the doorway while the woman stood by the bed.

'Poor Joanna. She looks so vulnerable lying there. I do hope she recovers consciousness soon.' Although the woman had her back to her, Staff could see her wiping her eyes surreptitiously. 'Do you know how it happened?'

'Struck by a car. Unfortunately she was squashed against a wall and that's what did the damage.'

'How horrible.'

'Yes and the driver just left her lying there.'

They stood in silence staring at Joanna until Staff noticed the reading on the monitor above the bed. She ushered the visitor out and bleeped the doctor. Something was happening and it didn't look good.

Joanna's parents looked shocked and drained. They sat with their ex-son-in-law in the relatives' room, waiting to speak to the consultant.

'Do you want anything to drink, Marjorie?' Gary put his hand on her arm.

'No thank you, dear.'

'Arthur?'

'No.' The older man sighed and rubbed his hands together.

When a doctor came in they all stood and he motioned for them to take a seat.

'I'm Joanna's consultant neurologist. I've had some tests done and we're sure now there is significant swelling in her brain. It may subside but the next few hours are critical.'

'Doctor, can she recover from this, if the brain … if it goes down?' asked Joanna's father.

'It's difficult to say but normally there will be some brain damage. Even the best prognosis is a significant personality change.'

'So what are you doing for her?' This time Gary was asking the question.

'There are drugs we can use to help and we can operate *in extremis*. We are providing some treatment and we are monitoring the effect. However, I must emphasise Joanna is critically ill and the next few hours will tell us whether she is going to pull through with any hope of any kind of quality of life.'

'Thank you, doctor,' said Marjorie, dabbing her eyes.

The consultant didn't seem to know what to say and after a second or two he left them alone again.

They stayed in the relatives' room all day. Gary fetched coffees from the machine down the hallway and at lunch time he bought sandwiches that no-one ate. Other visitors came and went and they stayed rarely speaking, flicking the pages of old magazines, pacing the centre of the floor and sitting slumped in the hard plastic chairs. The room was hot and unwelcoming but they remained there regardless. Eventually the news came that they half expected and yet could not acknowledge. Joanna had died as a result of a head injury caused by a hit-and-run road accident. The police had been informed.

Chapter 5

Saturday morning was clear and breezy. Millie was still trying to decide between jeans and shorts when she spotted a white Land Rover drawing up outside. She pulled her jeans back on as Jake rang the bell and before long they were flying down the A1. Millie leaned back, enjoying the breeze through the window. When she opened her eyes they were parked in a small village. She hoped she hadn't snored, had her mouth open, or worse, drooled.

'We're here.' Jake smiled across at her. 'Bainbridge. There's not a lot to see to be honest. We can take the footpath up there and you can look across to the mound.'

They wandered through the meadow past the hill where the fort had been built by the Romans.

'OK, so what can you tell me about it?' Millie teased.

'Not a lot, though I did look it up on the internet last night. Let me see. It was built around one hundred AD on a glacial mound and was occupied throughout the Roman period. It's rectangular and you can see there was a gate on each side. Actually it's been excavated quite a lot in the past so it's been disturbed. There would have been buildings to house the soldiers and officers. And that's about it.'

'So that's it – a mound?'

'Yeah, but it was really important. Roads go off from here in several directions. We could go up there and I can show you the one that goes all the way to Ingleton.'

Millie was still grinning but he suddenly looked serious and taking hold of her arms he gently turned her round to face him and kissed her, on the lips. She was surprised, but pleased, her interest in Roman soldiers obliterated by how comfortable Jake's arms felt round her. She wondered how significant this was as they walked slowly back to the Land Rover.

The lane was signposted to Semer Water and, once they had passed through Countersett, Millie could see the lake below them.

'Can we get down there?' she asked.

'Yes, sure,' replied Jake, as he swung them up a sharp right turn in the opposite direction, 'on the way back.'

They climbed steeply round a crag and then down to a fork in the road. As they parked, Millie could see a wide track of rough stones extending in both directions.

'Is this it? Is this the Roman road?'

'Yes.'

Jake leaned across towards her but she opened the door and jumped out, shouting, 'Let's go for a walk!' to cover her confusion.

He carefully locked all the doors before they set off up the rough track. It was a beautiful day and Millie strode happily along holding Jake's hand.

'How far exactly are you intending to go?' he asked. 'Ingleton?'

'What happens if you walk the other way?' asked Millie.

'It goes back to Bainbridge.'

They ambled along for about half an hour, talking about their families and university ambitions. Jake admitted he hadn't really thought about what he would do when he finished his research.

'I suppose I hope to stay on and continue what I'm doing now,' he admitted.

Soon, inevitably, Millie was reminded of her friends disappearance. She told Jake about Deepal's visit and their talk with Professor McGrath. He listened in silence, until she had finished.

'He sounds a bit heavy, the brother, doesn't he?'

'A bit, but I think he was just worried. Actually I've got a really bad feeling about it now but I don't know what we can do.'

'The police will know what to do.' He put his arm round her shoulders and they walked back along the track in silence.

'We could keep going all the way down to Bainbridge,' suggested Millie.

'Yes, but then the Land Rover would be here and we would be there, idiot.'

'And I want to see Semer Water.'

'OK.' He looked at his watch. 'Then we'll scrounge something to eat off Mum.'

There were several cars parked beside the lake. Children were paddling, their father was skimming stones and a black dog was running into the water for sticks. Jake described the Iron Age village that had been built out in the lake on stilts.

'We used to bring the dogs here in the summer,' he said. 'It's possible to walk here from home, over the tops. We'd do it as kids, anything for a paddle when you're little.'

'We should have brought Dash with us, he would have liked that.'

'We would have had to bring Toby as well, and that would be a pain. Can you put up with him if we go back home?'

'Of course, but you'd better let your Mum know. Will she mind?'

'I already rang her.'

They drove in a comfortable silence back down the narrow lanes to Bainbridge. Millie wasn't sure exactly where the excavation was from there but asked whether they could go to the site on the way.

'No, because it's not on the way and we don't need to. It's Saturday, you know, a day off.'

'Oh.' Millie couldn't keep the disappointment from her voice. 'I thought I'd get a chance to find out more about it before I started my project properly.'

'You have started properly. But if you want, we'll go this afternoon. Just seems a shame to be working on such a nice day.'

Soon they were turning off the road and up the long track to the farm. Bridget was out in the small garden.

'Toby's out with his Dad. He'll be disappointed he missed you. Perhaps you'll stay for tea, he'll be back at five,' she said as she followed them indoors and immediately began preparing food.

'Maybe.' Jake was flicking through the paper while his mother moved around the kitchen.

Dash treated Millie like an old friend and soon he had brought a ball for her to throw. He didn't stop bringing it back to her and when she grew tired of the game he kept pushing his toy into her hands.

'Dash, into your basket and stop bothering the poor girl. Now, I know what I wanted to ask you, Jake. Someone told me the woman who was run over in Redmire worked at your place.'

Jake looked up and across at Millie. She felt a weird feeling in her stomach 'What's her name?'

'Armstrong. Dr Armstrong they said.'

'She's my lecturer,' said Millie.

'Well I heard she's right poorly. Mrs Anthony who does some of the holiday cottages over that way, she heard from Mrs Thomas who works in the hospital. Apparently it was a hit-and-run.'

'How awful. She was giving us a talk on Monday.'

'I heard that she's critical.'

'Where did it happen, Mum?'

'In the lane by her cottage. Luckily the farmer who has sheep up the road was coming by soon after it happened and he called an ambulance. Proper shaken up he was.'

She dried her hands on her apron and brought a plate of sandwiches to the table.

After lunch Millie and Jake set off in the Land Rover with Dash, promising to return for supper when Toby and Robert would be home. As they turned up the track, Jake stopped the vehicle.

'That's odd, the gate's open.'

Millie was disappointed. 'Surely there's no-one working here today?'

'Not that I know of.' He jumped out and closed the gate behind them.

'There isn't anyone here,' said Millie, wandering over to the test pits.

'I hope no-one's been in.' Jake looked worried.

'Why would they?'

'Sometimes thieves raid sites, but there's nothing significant here. Possibly walkers or kids. Still it looks OK.'

He called the dog over and made it lie down.

'So,' said Millie, 'are you going to explain exactly what's going on here. The full lecture please.'

'To be honest I don't actually think there is much of anything interesting here. Although there's evidence of settlements, like Addleborough over there, and Bainbridge fort, the chances of there being anything here is pretty remote.'

'So why are we here?'

'Some kid with a metal detector found a Roman coin in the field and so work was started as a student exercise. We've found a few bits of pottery, Iron Age of course, and then we found a couple of coral beads over in that pit.'

'So what have I got to look out for when I'm sieving?'

'Pottery, any bits of metal, like buckles.'

'Or like the blade we found this week.'

'Well, yes, but that was quite a rare event. You're more likely to find beads. They're really tiny and so they can easily be missed, but they'll prove someone important was around here. Dr Hammond seems a bit obsessed that he will find a chariot burial here but to be honest it would be very unlikely.'

'Why?'

'Because, my dear, every other single one has been over in the East of the county and there is no reason to expect to find one here,' he said, kissing her on the nose.

'And are they really chariots?'

'More like carts. They've got two wheels and they're dismantled, with the body buried in a crouching position in them. Wetwang is the most famous. The body was of a woman and they found a mirror and beads buried with her. That's why Colin, Dr Hammond,' Jake corrected himself, 'is so positive about this site because of the beads.' He suddenly looked up, 'Hey, come here you rat.'

Dash was scratching at the soil in the corner of the field, looking up when called but then continuing to dig. It took a number of expletives from Jake before the dog trotted slowly back. He was bundled into the Land Rover while Jake showed Millie where the blade had been found and explained how it would be studied and catalogued before being displayed, either at the university or, if it proved to be significant, in the British Museum. Millie was thrilled by the idea of her find on display in London. It made her even more excited about her project and determined to discover something really important during her studies.

'I took a birthday cake over to Mrs Anthony in West Witton this afternoon,' began Bridget as they sat down to supper that evening. 'She was talking about that lecturer, the one that was run over.' She paused to pass the potatoes to her husband. 'It seems she's not survived the accident. She died last night.'

'They'll be keen to trace the driver in that case,' said Robert, passing the dish to Millie.

She didn't feel hungry. It still gave her a strange claustrophobia when there was talk of someone dying, especially when they were young and it was unexpected. She remembered the feeling when Mum died, so suddenly without warning, when they thought she was clear. Millie pushed the food around her plate and wished she didn't feel so close to tears.

'Anyway, there's bound to be an inquest,' Robert was saying. 'Toby, will you stop mashing your food up like that!'

The focus turned to the boy and the conversation moved on, while Millie tried hard to think of anything but Dr Armstrong lying in hospital.

'Millie, you haven't eaten much.'

Bridget was collecting up the plates and bringing out pie. Millie didn't eat any more but sat politely while Jake's family tucked in, chatting about their day and their plans for Sunday.

'So what are you two up to tomorrow?' asked Robert.

'Nothing, Dad.'

'Well, I can always use a hand with the hay.'

Millie was disappointed when Jake replied they did not plan to do that but Bridget laughed and said it was far too much like hard work and they were supposed to be using their brains not their muscles.

On the way back to town they sat in silence until Millie plucked up the courage to tell Jake what she had on her mind. She wanted to show that she was thinking about Dr Armstrong, even though she didn't know her well. It seemed important and she wanted to do something. She didn't know who to send a sympathy card to because it didn't seem right to send it to an ex-husband did it? Jake laughed because he couldn't understand why she was concerned and Millie thought it was probably because it was the anniversary of her mother's death soon and it made her silly and emotional. But she said nothing.

'Next you'll be putting a bunch of flowers at the spot where she was knocked down.' Jake really didn't understand.

'Actually that's a really good idea.'

'You're not serious!'

Millie didn't answer. She didn't want it to be the source of an argument between them, not so soon. So she sat without speaking until they drew up outside her house. Jake leant over to kiss her but to her relief they were distracted by the front door flying open and Phoebe bursting out.

'Thank goodness you're back!' she shouted, pulling at the passenger door. 'The police came round today to ask about Vrishti. It was awful.'

'I'll call you tomorrow,' said Millie, climbing down onto the pavement.

'Oh Millie, I wish you'd been here. It was terrible. They asked me so many questions and I didn't know what to say. They asked about boyfriends and her family. They kept asking about her brother and they wanted a list of her friends, and they wanted to know where she went.'

'Did they search her room?' asked Millie, ushering Phoebe indoors.

'Yes. I don't think they took anything away though. Oh, they asked for her toothbrush – don't you think that's weird?'

'Have they any idea why she's missing?'

'They didn't tell me anything. They weren't very pleasant to be honest, just had a list of questions and kept going through them. They got a bit funny with me when I said she didn't really have many friends. Well she didn't, did she?'

'So what happens now?' Millie felt suddenly very tired. She had been enjoying herself with Jake, when she should have been helping Phoebe talk to the police. She'd been upset by Dr Armstrong's death but this was much worse.

'I don't know what the police will do. They are treating her as missing now, so I suppose they will start some sort of search. They didn't say.'

'What about photographs – did they want any photos of Vrishti?'

'They didn't ask but I guess the family have plenty of those.'

'Are they coming back, Phoebe? Do they want to talk to me? Should I go to the police station?'

'I think they've got everything they wanted. It's just so horrible not knowing where she is.'

'It hasn't really sunk in yet. Today I just forgot all about it most of the time and it was only when I heard about Dr Armstrong that I began to feel …'

'What about her, who is she?'

'Oh, she's my lecturer. She was, now she's dead.'

'Dead?'

Phoebe's hand went up to her mouth and she began to cry, big tears and howls of anguish. Millie wanted to join in but knew she should comfort her friend and try to keep them both steady. She made tea and they sat together in the stuffy kitchen not really talking but keeping each other company until they were so exhausted that they went off to bed. It wasn't really dark so Millie left the curtains drawn back and the window wide open, listening to the sounds from the street. She felt helpless and it made her angry. Determined to do something constructive the next day, she planned to look after Phoebe despite the fact she had wanted to visit Redmire, where Dr Armstrong had been knocked down. Perhaps they could justify looking in Vrishti's room to see if anything might indicate where she had gone.

Dani sat motionless in the dim light waiting for the sound of movement outside in the corridor. Her body was alert and she held herself stiffly ready to move quickly if she needed to. She knew it was dangerous to meet here, where no-one would observe them, but she had to make it known she meant business. It wasn't only for her benefit, although the cash would come in handy, but she was going to make it clear that it had to stop, that it could not carry on, this elimination of anyone who stood in the way.

There were a few minutes to go before six o' clock, so Dani allowed herself to move between the open stacks looking at the labels on the drawers. They were mostly worthless items used for the practical classes, pieces of pottery, different metals and ceramics for identification studies. The more valuable pieces were in the stacks at the end and they were closed off. To open them she would have to switch on the motor and press the buttons that operated the stack of heavy shelves. That would be noisy and she wanted to hear when the footsteps came down the corridor. She returned to the table, sat down facing the door and waited.

A few minutes later there was movement outside, a shadow cut across the light under the door and the handle turned. It opened slowly and a dark figure was silhouetted in the door way.

'What do you want to meet in here for, Dani? Couldn't we have done this in my office?'

'I thought you would prefer somewhere more discrete.'

She stood up, leaning on the table for support.

'Why do you say that, my dear? Are you suggesting some sort of indiscretion, down here in the storeroom? Is that what you have planned?'

'Not with you, so just keep your distance.'

The door had swung gently closed and there was very little light in room again.

'Dani, tell me why you've asked me here. On the phone you suggested you had something to discuss.' The voice was smooth.

'I told you, I saw you with Vrishti at the party last weekend. I know you've been harassing her and now she's disappeared. I don't know what you've been up to but it's sure as hell frightened her off. I could go to the authorities.'

'What are you after, Dani? Just get to the point.' The voice was harsher now.

'Well, I was also wondering why you were driving the new Land Rover on Wednesday evening.'

She was feeling more confident now, breathing deeper.

'What do you want?'

A fist banged down hard on the table in front of her and Dani stepped back.

'Well. It must be worth a hundred or two.' She was aware that her voice was wavering.

There was a hesitation. 'A hundred pounds? Why on earth should I give you a hundred pounds?'

'Because if you don't,' Dani's voice was quiet, 'it will be all round the department.' She walked quickly to the door without looking back; her legs were like jelly. Once she was outside she ran to her office and locked herself in, with hands shaking visibly.

Millie spent the next morning with Phoebe deciding whether they should look in Vrishti's bedroom. First they thought they would and Millie led the way, pushing open the door and marching into the centre of the room. But once they were there they stood motionless, surveying the familiar possessions that reminded them of the fragile, gentle girl. Her clothes, her soft toys and even the room, smelt of her. Somehow, in tacit agreement, they both withdrew and returned to the kitchen.

'It might be best not to disturb anything,' Millie said, finally. 'The police might need to make a proper search if ...'

She stopped without uttering the words that seemed so final and kicked the table leg in frustration. She found it so difficult to sit doing nothing and was relieved when finally her mobile rang and she saw it was Jake.

'I was thinking about what you said and I want to take you to Redmire.'

'Are you sure, Jake?'

'Yes, it's a good idea. I'll take you in the Land Rover. No-one will know.'

'I'm not sure. Phoebe might like to come with us, for a change of scene.' Millie was worried about leaving her friend alone again.

But she shook her head, 'No I want to stay here, in case there's some news. You go out, I can always text you.'

Millie felt guilty when she finally pulled the door behind her and climbed in beside Jake.

'I don't think I can stand hanging around all day waiting for something to happen,' she said. 'It's so frustrating not being able to do anything. If she was a relative I could ring round the hospitals but being just a friend it's hopeless, really.'

They drove in silence until they reached the Dales, stopping only to buy petrol. Millie jumped out at the garage and purchased a bunch of flowers. There was very little choice and the carnations, wrapped in bright pink paper, looked half dead already. She was disappointed she had not planned the trip more carefully.

Jake drove slowly when they turned into Redmire and peered down each junction until he was apparently satisfied he had the correct turning. They drove for about half a mile down the narrow lane, bordered with a high stone wall, finally reaching a tiny cottage on the left just as the road began to climb. On the right hand verge a bit further on, Millie spotted a large bouquet lying against the stone wall and asked Jake to stop. They walked across in silence, and stood staring for a while at the bunch of roses and lilies wrapped in cellophane. Millie bent down to read the card, realising she hadn't thought to put a message on her flowers. She couldn't, or perhaps didn't want to read the personal message but she could see it was signed "all my love Gary".

'It's not in the right place.' Jake had wandered off and was now back. 'You can see where the car hit the wall up there.'

Millie followed him back up the lane, where he pointed to a deep gouge in the stone, extending about a metre along the wall. Bits of moss and vegetation had been torn from the stone and fragments of pink and white flowers lay on the ground with the mangled stems and leaves.

'It might not have been, you know, the actual vehicle. It might have been a tractor that did it earlier.' Millie protested, not wanting to believe this was where the woman, who so reminded her of her mother in many ways, had been left injured.

'Well, it's all very new – you can still see the paint'. He was running his hand along the stone and pointing his upturned finger at her, it was covered in white powder.

'That's just the stone isn't it?'

'I don't think so. I think it's paint.' He wiped his fingers on his jeans. 'If you look closely you can even see metal on the last section of wall.'

'Really?' Millie wouldn't look.

'If you don't believe me I could get it tested in the forensic archaeology lab. It wouldn't take long. They do it for oil paintings.'

Millie listened to Jake's explanation. How the technicians could take a tiny piece of material from an old master and measure the elements in it, like a fingerprint.

'All I need is a tiny sample.' He pulled out a penknife and took a piece of paper from his jacket, first looking at it and then folding it into four. He scratched at the groove in the wall, catching the powder in the folded paper and tucked it carefully in his back pocket.

'There, I'll give it to Jeff tomorrow and he'll tell us whether it's paint or stone but I bet you a pint it's paint.'

It won't make any difference to Dr Armstrong, thought Millie. She was dead and her family were hurting, just like she hurt when Mum ... There were hot tears on her face, then Jake holding her tight, and she allowed herself to let go for just a little while. They wandered slowly up the lane, Jake still holding her close, and when the road petered out into a track they continued to follow it into a hay field and over a stile into a meadow full of sheep. Finally they sat with their backs resting against a dry stone wall and Millie shut her eyes to avoid the glare of the sun. Finally she was sufficiently calm to face whatever awaited them at her student house and she suggested to Jake that they head back.

Millie need not have worried. Phoebe had left a note to say the police had been in touch but there was no news and so she had gone to a friend's for the evening. Jake stayed with her until late and left promising to pick her up next day to go to the excavation site. Millie was in the kitchen drinking hot chocolate when Dani wandered in, slamming the front door behind her. She looked tired and Millie wondered whether it was because she had very little makeup on. She looked almost frail without the dark eyes and lips. When Millie offered her a drink she accepted a coffee without any clever remarks and drank it in silence. It was only when Millie got up to go to bed that Dani spoke.

'By the way, is there any news of Vrishti?'

'No, nothing, not yet. The police came round yesterday. Phoebe saw them.'

'What did they want?'

Millie thought the girl looked worried. 'Just to find out who her friends are, where she goes, that sort of thing.'

She decided not to mention they had looked in her bedroom. Dani had been snooping in there, hadn't she?

'Have they checked hospitals and ... other places?'

Millie knew what Dani meant. She assumed the police did all that.

'I suppose so.'

'I do hope nothing's happened to her.'

Millie sat down again. 'What makes you say that? Do you know something?'

Dani looked sideways, avoiding her gaze.

'No, nothing. It's just wrong isn't it? I mean, if I went off for a week or even more, no-one would care would they?' She was looking up at Millie now, her face almost angry. 'If I disappeared no-one would think anything of it.'

'Of course we would.' Millie knew she didn't sound convincing.

'You know what I mean. It wouldn't be ... what do they call it? Out of character.'

'I know. Vrishti isn't the sort of person to leave without telling anyone. To be honest I'm beginning to wonder if we really knew her. Perhaps she has gone off with someone, you know, eloped to avoid her family.'

'I think you and Phoebe would have known if there was a significant other, Millie.'

She was sure Dani knew more than she was letting on.

'If you know something about this, you must tell the police.'

'Oh I will,' she said, 'if I find out anything about it.'

Millie had had enough. She dragged herself up the stairs and threw herself on the bed. Phoebe arrived back later and there were raised voices downstairs. Just as Millie decided to go down and stop them, there were heavy footsteps and the door to the next room slammed. Dani had gone to bed. Soon she heard Phoebe in the bathroom and then finally the house was still.

Millie remained awake for a long time thinking of plausible scenarios that explained Vrishti's sudden disappearance; ones that were not so unpleasant that she could not entertain them. Perhaps the girl had been secretly in love with a distant relative. She once mentioned a cousin in India who she'd had a crush on when she was younger. But what if she was being married off to some old man she didn't like but the family favoured? She concluded that the only sensible suggestion was one Phoebe had made, that she was lying ill and unrecognised in hospital somewhere.

Millie took a deep breath of fresh Wensleydale air. She had felt surprisingly positive when she woke next morning and had a good feeling about the day. She looked in on Phoebe and told her she was sure that they would get good news today. The sun was already hot when she left the house and by the time they reached the excavation it was very strong. The breeze down the valley kept them comfortable but Millie had to stop frequently to sit in the shade of the stone wall and drink from her water bottle.

Jake was busy with the other students but she was happy working on her own pit. She'd finished the top layer of soil, everything was labelled and recorded, and she was making a start on the section below. The soil was baked hard and Millie had to break it up with her trowel before filling the sieve. She worked steadily, enjoying the mindless activity of sieving, recording and sieving again. She was so engrossed in her thoughts she almost ignored the small grey lump as it went into the bag. She picked it out again and studied it, assuming at first that it was a stone. But the shape was quite symmetrical, so she wandered self-consciously over to the bucket by the gate. Jake had his back to her, so she held the lump under the water and rubbed it gently. Now it was still grey but there was a kind of grain in it, like wood.

'What've you got there?' Jake was standing over her.

'I don't know. Here,' she said, passing it to him, 'it's probably nothing.'

He studied it, turning it over in his hands, and then smiled.

'This,' he said, pausing dramatically, 'is a piece of pottery. Anglo Saxon by the look of it. It may not look exciting but it's probably about two thousand years old.'

Millie was so pleased she couldn't stop herself from laughing out loud.

'Come over here and I'll show you how to document it properly.'

He called to the others and went round showing them her find. Millie watched the stir it caused with considerable pride. Once the excitement had died down, she returned to her pit with renewed enthusiasm and studied every full sieve in great detail, disappointed when each grey lump crumbled into a handful of soil. The morning flew past and Millie had to be persuaded to stop for a lunch break. Jake seemed amused by her enthusiasm and teased her, pretending to find artefacts in the grass, offering his hand and grabbing her when she came over to look. They were rolling around in a mock fight, with the other students shouting ribald remarks, when the entertainment was halted by the sight of an old tractor moving up the track. Jake jumped up, smoothing down his hair.

'That's Dad, I wonder what he wants.'

Robert jumped down from the cab, followed by Dash. The dog leapt at Jake and then rushed off to investigate the students and their lunches. Robert handed a plastic box to his son.

'Sorry lad, your mother insisted I brought this when she heard I was up this way. It's some cake she's been baking; there's a piece for yon young lady as well.'

'Thanks. What's the tractor for?'

'Helping old Will with his mowing for a bit. He's not feeling too good these days.'

Millie was half listening, watching Dash rushing around the field. She didn't want him going near her test pit. Now he was in the far corner by the old tree where the grass was high, where he had been digging before.

'Oh no, he's at it again!' Jake started across the field. 'Dash! No! Dash!'

The dog looked up but kept digging. Millie caught up with him as he grabbed Dash's collar and dragged him away. She turned to follow but something blue on the ground caught her eye. With a jolt she thought she might have made another find and bending down she cleared the soil around it. It was only a bit of cloth, silky to the touch. She tugged and the earth fell away revealing something pink, like an animal. She brushed it with her finger and then realised it was a hand. She dropped the sleeve and shrieked as she recognised the silver ring that she had bought Vrishti for her birthday.

Chapter 6

Ernie felt a buzz at the police station he hadn't experienced since 'eighty-three, the year when there had been two apparently unrelated murders that had turned out to be the work of a serial killer. As a young constable, Ernest Brown had been involved in the house to house enquiries and the early morning arrest of the man who had killed the young women in quick succession. Not since then had he felt the excitement of policing in the same way. It had made him determined to become a detective. It began as hard work and it had remained so for him.

Mitch Turner, his young sergeant, had rung to let him know that the missing girl had been found and he immediately asked his young sergeant to accompany him to Wensleydale. The lad reminded Ernie of himself as a young copper, willing to learn, always happy to fetch tea and keen to listen to his superiors. He enjoyed showing off his driving skills to the youngster and even after thirty years he felt a thrill of anticipation as they flew along the country lanes.

By the time they reached the crime scene, the local uniforms had set up a barrier at the entrance to the site. On the field a crowd of scruffy youngsters were gathered by their battered vehicle. Among them, an older woman in a suit identified herself as Professor McGrath. Ernie listened politely while she explained what they were doing there and how the students had discovered the body. As soon as he could he went over to join the local force. It was their patch but she was his missing girl and so he wanted to ensure he would be leading the enquiries. The pathologist had been contacted and while they waited for him Ernie arranged for the details of the students be taken. Then he told them all to leave: the scruffy students, the smart professor and the farmer with his tractor. He had seen the girl who found the body but she was a bit hysterical and so he'd talk to her later. Nothing much to see there, he thought.

The dapper man climbing out of his Volvo turned out to be the pathologist, Doc Carter. Ernie watched him unpack his equipment and make his way to the lad who was managing the scene. By now uniform were manning the barrier and were recording comings and goings.

'Good morning, sir.'

Ernie escorted the pathologist to where the body was cordoned off and he signalled to Mitch to follow him. In his experience scientists like this guy provided the most valuable information. He watched him from a distance. He knew better than to ask questions and he didn't want to be embarrassed in front of the lad. The sun was hot on his back and it would be a long time before the evening would provide some cooler weather. Well, the girl wasn't going anywhere now.

'It seems a strange place to bury the body, sir, if she was killed in town.'

'If she *was* killed there,' said Ernie. 'She could have died here. She's one of them archaeology students. She could have been killed out here.'

'Might be clearer when we know how she was killed and whether she was raped.'

'Well, we can be sure she didn't bury herself. Someone wanted to hide her.'

Ernie wiped his forehead with a yellowing handkerchief.

'Didn't expect a dog to be looking, otherwise it's not a bad spot, sir. An archaeological site's ideal if you want to dig a hole without raising suspicion. Nobody would think twice if they saw you, would they?'

'I suppose not – if you're an archaeologist.'

'D'you think that's right, sir?' He looked pleased.

'Yes, Mitch, I reckon you've got something there.'

Professor McGrath had told them all to go back to the university and carry on as normal. She asked them not to gossip about what had happened and not to talk to the press. Turning to Jake, who was holding Millie tight, she suggested they come to her office and speak with her on their return. Robert expressed concern about Jake driving the Land Rover but he insisted he was all right. He also spoke in a fatherly way to Millie and told her she was welcome to come to them if she wanted to. She couldn't help crying as they had to leave with Vrishti still in the soil. She knew it would be a while before she would want to return to the site.

She asked to go straight to Phoebe but Jake insisted the Dean wanted to see them as soon as they got back. She was waiting for them with tea and sympathy. Millie needed the older woman's words to help but they didn't. She sat in silence while Jake explained exactly what had happened. The Dean offered to ring Millie's father and she agreed. He wouldn't be any use, what could he do? Tears came easily again and this time it was Angela McGrath who had her arm round her, comforting her. Somehow it helped, almost like having Mum around again, and Millie felt a calm filling her body. Afterwards she blushed to think how she had hung onto Professor McGrath while the tears poured down her face and made a dark stain on the older woman's ample bosom. Eventually the Dean suggested Jake took Millie home, but not before she had insisted they let her know of any further news, and secondly they come and see her again the next day.

Phoebe came running downstairs the moment they arrived back. They hugged and clung together.

'The police came back,' she told them. 'They want to talk to you and they said they'd be taking stuff away.'

'When are they coming back?' asked Jake.

'Not till tomorrow but we mustn't touch anything.'

'Are you OK Phoebes?' Millie thought her friend looked too bright almost too lively.

'I took something. I feel better now.'

Jake looked at Millie but they said nothing. He insisted on making them something to eat but they all sat and played with their pasta. Most of it was scraped into the bin. Millie would have liked to have got away from the house, with the room upstairs full of Vrishti, but how could they go and leave Phoebe?

The three of them sat in front of the television and drank a bottle of wine Millie had in her room. Phoebe brought down half a bottle of vodka and when they had finished it she went to bed. Millie and Jake dozed together on the sofa throughout the night with the flicker of the TV screen lighting the room.

Ernie's office was hot and stuffy. The small window only opened a fraction and there was no breeze at all. The fan on the window-sill was broken and he'd ordered a replacement weeks ago. He sighed, drawing his hand across his forehead and wiped the sweat on his trouser leg. Mitch came in carrying a large package.

'Is that the pathologist's report, son?'

'It's from his office, sir.'

Ernie ripped open the envelope and pulled out a handful of evidence bags. Each one contained a separate item. A ring, a necklace, a piece of metal.

'What's that, Guv?'

'It says "ornamental blade" on the label.'

He turned it over and felt it through the plastic bag. It looked like a blunt and rusty blade but it had quite an ornate handle, brassy looking. He picked up another bag and peered at the tiny stone in the corner.

'What's a "nose stud"?'

'Like an earring, sir. It goes at the side of the nose. Like Nina has.'

Ernie hadn't noticed anything in the young policewoman's nose but he didn't like girls on the force and avoided them if he could.

'Is that an Asian thing then?'

'Yes, but my sister has had her nose pierced. Lots of girls do.'

Ernie picked up the blade again.

'Maybe this is Asian too.'

'We could ask Nina,' offered Mitch. 'She could be a great help, particularly with the family.'

'You're quite right,' agreed Ernie, 'we need to go and see the family.' It was time they paid that brother a visit. 'But we don't need any help from the girls, thank you very much.'

It was nearly nine o'clock by the time they reached the edge of town and the suburban street was deserted. Uniform had been and gone, delivering the message that the missing girl was dead. Now it was their turn to talk to the brother. He looked drawn when he opened the door and waved his arm feebly in the direction of the living room, where the wife sat in the same impassive manner as before. This time there was no baby in her arms.

'It's all right Priti, it's the detectives again.' He turned to Ernie, 'Would you like some tea?'

'No thank you, sir. I've just a few questions and then we'll be away.'

Ernie went through the set of routine questions. He would have to visit the parents but they lived over a hundred miles away and probably didn't speak English. It would be a real pain dealing with them and he'd find someone else to do it. It was the brother, living close by, keeping an eye on little sister that interested him.

Deepal answered his questions calmly, even helpfully, until Ernie began to probe.

'So, I expect you kept an eye on your sister, eh?'

'Yes, of course, it's my duty to look after her. I did my best but ...'

'Quite so, but you couldn't be with her all the time could you? Girls will be girls, won't they? Make up, parties, boys.'

'What do you mean? What are you saying?'

'Girls these days, they like to be independent, do their own thing.'

'Not Vrishti. She's a good girl. She didn't have a boyfriend.'

'Are you sure?'

'Yes. I asked her. Just last week I told her to tell me.'

'So you had a bit of a discussion about it, did you?'

He made notes in an ostentatious manner.

'Yes. I'm sorry to say we did have words on the subject.'

They said goodnight and left Deepal standing on his doorstep staring after them as they drove slowly back to the station. Ernie felt pleased with the way the evening had gone.

'Mitch my lad, did you see those daggers in the cabinet? Quite a few of them. Nice and shiny but they looked like the weapon I reckon. I wouldn't be surprised if we haven't got ourselves a suspect.'

'And the motive, sir, would be …?'

'You know these Asian families Mitch. Arranged marriages, honour killings, you've just got to see the way the wife just sits there. We should get him in and question him first thing tomorrow.'

Back at the station, in the canteen, Mitch told Nina about their visit and what his boss had in his mind. He was diplomatic about Ernie's views on Asians but Nina could sense where it was going.

'Mitch, if you think it would help I'd be happy to be involved. It might be useful.'

She didn't want to push it but she'd seen Ernie putting his size tens in it before. He'd embarrassed her on several occasions, partly just because she was a woman but mainly because of her background. She liked Mitch and she knew he quite fancied her, so she used her best smile and gave him her pleading look.

'I'll suggest it to Ernie,' he offered with a wink.

Nige was in his office when he learned what had happened in Wensleydale. He waited but when Jake didn't come back to the department he went to the flat and remained there. In the morning he looked for Dani, thinking she might have some information but her office was empty. He decided to spend the day on site and walked down to the parking bay to pick up the Land Rover. A piece of paper was fluttering, pinned under the windscreen wipers. It was typed on departmental headed notepaper and was addressed *"To whom it may concern."* Nige read on. *It has come to my attention that this vehicle has been damaged without the incident being reported through proper channels. Will the person responsible for the damage please contact me immediately to complete an insurance claim.* It was signed by the Dean.

Nige walked round the vehicle checking the paintwork. He examined the offending damage, an unpleasant scratch exposed the metal where someone had caught a gatepost or something pretty solid. He referred to the log book in the cab but only his signature appeared on the last two pages. No-one else had driven it, or at least they hadn't signed it out. There was no way he was going to drive it now. He stuck the note back under the wiper blade, locked the doors and walked slowly to the department.

He spotted Dani in her office. 'Have you been out in the new Land Rover?' he demanded.

She swung round and glared at him. 'No. Why?'

When he explained about the note from the Dean, she laughed. 'Not guilty. I've not driven it yet. Are you sure *you* don't know anything about it?'

'No, but someone must.'

She grinned. 'It'll be insured. Worse things have happened.'

'Too right … compared to that bad business with Vrishti.'

Dani stiffened visibly. She apparently hadn't heard the news and so Nige told her everything he knew about what had happened. To his surprise she became very upset and he had to fetch her water. She asked him loads of questions. Who was there? Who found her? How long had she been there? Did they know how she'd died? When Nige finally left her, she was picking up the phone and pressing the keys angrily.

Millie had never felt so completely helpless. Vrishti was dead and there was nothing that could be done to help. The police had asked her about finding the body but there was nothing much to say. She did recall Dash digging in the same corner on Sunday, so she told them about that but she couldn't help them with how the body had come to be there. It made it worse, thinking of Vrishti lying there all the time when she and Jake had been so happy. Anyway, she had signed the statement and the police tramped up and down the stairs carrying away a computer and piles of paper. They said they might be back and they sealed Vrishti's room when they left. Phoebe gave the sergeant the envelope containing the letter to Vrishti inviting her to meet in the archive room. The officer thanked her and shoved it in a box of papers he was carrying. Millie sent Jake home and sat with Phoebe, passing the morning with mugs of coffee and the crossword from the weekend paper.

When her mobile rang, Millie saw it was her father and sighed. 'Hi, Dad.'

She listened as he acted the concerned father. He asked her if she wanted to come home. Did she want to have time to recover from the trauma? Should she see someone? Counselling perhaps? She waited until he had finished.

'Dad, I'm fine. I'd rather stay here, really.'

He put Fiona on, like she really wanted to have to talk to the girlfriend. Millie listened in silence.

'Thank you, I'm fine. I'll call soon, bye.'

She pressed the button to cut her off and grimaced at Phoebe.

'I'm sure they're just worried for you,' said her friend.

'Yes, you're right but the last thing I need right now is someone fussing over me. I just wish we could do something to find out what happened to Vrishti.'

Mitch was showing Ernie the letter that Phoebe had given him. It lay in pieces on his desk. His boss was uninterested and waved him away.

'Not relevant, lad. Stick it in the file and let's get down to the brother's place before he does a runner back to Pakistan or wherever he comes from.'

Mitch sighed and picked up the authorisation to search. The boss had been like a cat on hot bricks getting through the formalities but he had a bad feeling about this. He'd been talking to Nina to find out more about arranged marriages and honour killings. She had convinced him it was extremely unlikely that a Hindu family would be forcing their daughter into a marriage she didn't want, and an honour killing was unheard of in a family like Vrishti's. He tried to tell Ernie about his concerns as they sped back to the suburbs.

'Listen Mitch, did you not hear about the young lass murdered last year because she wanted to marry someone unsuitable.'

'Yes I did. She was a Muslim.'

'She was a graduate, had a good job. She was killed by her brother.'

'Yes but that doesn't mean this case is the same. For a start the family are Hindu.'

'How d'you know that?'

'It's obvious just looking at their home, the pictures, the clothes, everything.'

'They still have arranged marriages don't they?'

'Yes but it doesn't mean they marry against their will … ask Nina she'll tell you.'

'Oh I see. You've been doing some homework have you? You sly dog! Better watch out her old man don't catch you!'

The younger man looked out of the window and sighed. There was no point trying to talk to him and they sat in silence until they reached the house. Mitch took a deep breath before climbing out of the car, ready to face the ensuing fiasco.

'Hello, Mr Bhatt,' Ernie announced cheerily as the door swung open before they had the chance to knock.

'We've come to have a chat and a look around your property. I'm sure you won't mind, eh?'

The young man looked puzzled and stepped back as Ernie pushed past him into the hallway.

'I'll go upstairs, you do down here.' He took the steps two at a time.

Mitch remained with Deepal and explained the terms of the authorisation to search. He asked lots of questions but Mitch simply told him he was helping them with their enquiries. They could hear Ernie above them, opening drawers and slamming cupboard doors. Mitch was relieved that the wife was out with the baby. He sat the suspect down and self consciously searched the living room and kitchen. It was not even clear what they were looking for but he asked him to unlock the cabinet containing the daggers. Mitch picked up the beautifully crafted blades and Deepal's face lit up when he asked about their origin.

'They're mainly copies of old pieces. I collect them from India,' he said. 'This one is a khukri.' He picked up a curved blade and stroked it. 'The shape is a symbol of the third eye of Lord Shiva.' He gently placed it in Mitch's hand. 'That one is a copy of an eighteenth century khandjar.'

Mitch noticed the brass hilt and ornamental designs on it.

'And this one?' He pointed to the dagger in a leather sheath.

'That's a copy of a Sikh weapon.'

'I'm afraid I'll have to take them back to the station, sir.'

The young man seemed astonished. He opened his mouth and then shut it again, wiped his upper lip with his hand and sat down suddenly on the leather sofa behind him.

'Can you tell me what is going on please? What has this to do with my sister?'

'I can tell you exactly what it has to do with it, Mr Bhatt.' Ernie was standing in the doorway. 'We are taking you in for questioning regarding your sister's death.'

'Am I under arrest?' He stood up and strode towards Ernie.

'Oh we'll see about that, Mr Bhatt, once we get you down to the station.'

Chapter 7

Just when they thought they'd seen the last of the police, two men appeared at the door and showed them their identification. The older man was wearing a rumpled blue shirt open at the neck with baggy black trousers. Millie noticed the large sweat stain under his armpit as he wiped his pockmarked face with a dirty handkerchief. His colleague looked much cooler in chinos and a polo shirt.

'Sergeant, you go up and have a look at the young lady's room.'

They showed the inspector into their sitting room.

'Have you met the brother?' Ernie was referring to his notes. 'Deepal, he's called.'

'Yes, he came here last week looking for her.'

Phoebe offered the information readily while Millie was more cautious. She didn't like his tone.

'What was his mood like? Was he pleasant?'

'Well, he was rather agitated because Vrishti hadn't been in touch,' Phoebe replied.

'It was after she'd gone missing,' added Millie. 'He was really worried about her.'

'But what sort of brother was he, do you think? Did she get on well with him? Did he bully her?' Ernie sat with his pen poised.

'He looked after her,' Millie said.

'Ah, you mean he kept an eye on her?'

'No, I didn't mean that ...' Millie tried to see what he was writing.

Ernie interrupted, 'We are very concerned about your friend's brother. He's helping us with some questions down at the station at the moment. If you have any information you might like to add, please let me know.'

He stood up, shut his notebook and called Mitch. The girls exchanged glances.

'You're not arresting him, surely?' asked Millie.

'Too early to say yet.'

He stood up as Mitch came downstairs. 'Just let me know if you have anything to add,' he shouted as he left with his sergeant.

As soon as they were gone Phoebe suggested they contact Deepal's wife.

'What can *we* do?' asked Millie.

'There must be something. Imagine your husband being arrested for murdering his own sister. She must be in a terrible state.'

'Phoebe, he hasn't been arrested. He might be home by now.'

But Millie couldn't persuade her friend to leave it alone. Their only contact was the mobile number that he had given them. Phoebe rang it and Millie heard one side of a difficult conversation. When she had finished talking, Phoebe was jotting down an address.

'She was in such a state, Millie. I said we'd go over to see her.'

'I heard you. What are we going to do there?'

'I don't know but we've got to do something. Vrishti would have wanted us to.'

They had to take a bus into town and then another to get to the smart suburb where Priti and Deepal lived. When they walked up the road they could identify the house by Deepal's BMW parked in the drive. A man was loitering across the road and when Priti opened the door he ran forward with a camera and began taking photographs.

'Please come in quickly,' she said, shielding her face from the reporter and ushering them inside.

Millie could see two Asian women seated in the living room with the curtains drawn and she felt they were intruding but Priti welcomed them in and led them through to meet the other women. One was her sister, the other was a detective. Millie was immediately struck by the contrast between the three women. In some respects they were quite similar in age and physical appearance. All three had straight dark hair; Priti's was a beautiful dark glossy stream, hanging free in the way Vrishti usually wore her hair. She was dressed in jeans that clung to her slim figure, her height accentuated by her high heeled boots. A bright turquoise top showed off her slim waist. Priti's sister did not share her fashion flair; she wore a pair of drab trousers and flowery blouse. Her hair was scraped back into a bun.

'Nina has been asking me questions about Vrishti but I only see her once a week, whereas you two girls were with her all the time.' She turned to the detective with a smile, 'They will be able to help you better than I can.'

But Nina said nothing. The police officer had her hair in a pony tail, giving her a harsh appearance. Her black suit looked hot and uncomfortable.

'We've already spoken to the police, several times,' said Millie.

'I'm sure it's all a huge mistake,' added Phoebe.

'Of course,' agreed Priti. 'Deepal will come back home soon. We haven't said anything to my in-laws, it would be too dreadful for them. They have hardly been able to accept what has happened to their daughter.'

She sat down rather suddenly and wiped her face with a handkerchief.

There was an awkward silence. Millie was trying to remember the name of their baby so she could ask how it was but she couldn't so she kept quiet.

'Well, I think I've finished here, Mrs Bhatt,' said Nina, getting up to leave. 'We'll keep you informed with any developments.'

She smiled at the young mother and tried to convey sympathy. The poor woman must be distraught under the calm exterior, she thought. She wished she could say more, give her some hope, but it was not in her power to do that. Only Ernie had the wherewithal to bestow such comfort.

'So you are Vrishti's housemates,' started Priti, when the detective had left. 'It is so nice to meet you. She spoke so much about you and what good friends you are.' They smiled. 'But I think there is a third housemate that she did not get on with well?'

'Oh Dani!' said Phoebe. 'None of us like her, I'm afraid.'

'I think she is a bit rough, rather loud perhaps?'

'Yes, that's right,' agreed Millie.

There was a cry from upstairs.

'That's Sunil. He must have woken from his nap. I'll fetch him.'

Priti disappeared upstairs for several minutes and returned with her tiny son. The girls made a fuss of him and she asked them in turn to hold him. Millie felt extremely uncomfortable at first but gained confidence when he smiled at her. Phoebe was much more at ease with the boy and he settled down in her arms.

'Millie, you were there … you were there, when they, when they found Vrishti.'

'Yes.'

'I don't understand, you see. I don't understand why they took our ornaments.'

'Ornaments?' Phoebe asked.

'They took our khukris, some of them belonged to my father. Do you know why they would do that? They haven't told me anything much about, you know, how she died. But they were very interested in daggers. I don't understand why they took them all away.'

'Did they explain to you what was happening to Deepal?' asked Millie.

'Not really. I was too upset. That's why they called my sister.' Looking across at the other woman, she lowered her voice. 'She is very shy and rather nervous of the police.'

'The police officer seemed very nice,' suggested Phoebe.

'Nina? Yes, she seems genuinely sympathetic but that might just be the way they are told to behave. She's like a family liaison person, what with Vrishti being ... killed ... and Deepal being taken in for questions.'

'Is your sister staying here with you?' Phoebe asked rocking Sunil gently.

Priti laughed. 'Oh no! She has five children to care for and so she must get back before school finishes.'

The other woman nodded and looked at her watch.

'I could stay if you liked,' offered Phoebe, looking down at the baby. 'I could help you with Sunil, you know, if Deepal needed you to go to see him.'

Priti looked across at her sister, who shrugged her shoulders. 'That would be very kind. I feel I'm nearer Vrishti when her friends are here. Perhaps just until

Deepal comes back from the police station. He won't be long.'

Millie raised her eyebrows at Phoebe who studiously ignored her gaze. It was agreed that Millie would accompany her sister back to town while Phoebe would stay to help Priti.

The sister remained silent except to thank Millie profusely when she showed her the correct platform for her return train journey. Millie wandered back into town to find herself a large hot chocolate with cream on the top. She needed to do some serious thinking. Half an hour later she was walking, almost jogging, back to the university to find Jake. After several false starts she tracked him down in the library, where he was surrounded by books on material science.

'What are you doing?' she asked in a whisper.

He was flicking pages rapidly. 'Looking for the composition of paint,' he replied without looking up, 'I know it's titanium oxide but I just want to check the trace elements.'

'What?'

She sat down opposite him and watched while he moved from book to book. She picked up a large tome and opened it at the index. 'Titanium dioxide. Is that it?'

'Yep.'

She found the page and moved her finger down the text. Titanium dioxide. There was a lot of detail on particle size, heat resistance and abrasion characteristics. She turned over the pages until she reached a table of data which included the elements in white pigment.

'There are some figures here – lead, copper, zinc.' She turned the book round so that he could see.

'That's it! Look. Jeff gave me an analysis of the powder from the wall in Redmire. It's mainly titanium but there's a whole range of other elements at really low concentrations. Jeff reckons it's the pigment from the white paint but I wanted to check.'

'Does that mean it's the paint from a car?'

'Yep. Jeff said it would explain zinc being there, because cars are coated with zinc before they're painted.'

'So the car that hit Dr Armstrong was white?'

'I guess so. The scraping was white, no sign of any colour.'

'Well, you proved you were right. I stand corrected. But we knew she was hit by a car so it doesn't really add anything does it?'

'It shows that it was a white car.'

Millie laughed, 'Well, yes, but what will you do – tell the police you know the colour of the car?'

'Of course not. I just wanted to prove the point. You owe me a pint now.'

As they walked to the bar, Millie described her visit to see Priti and how Phoebe had offered to stay with her until Deepal was released. Jake had been trying to find out how long it would be before they could access the site in Wensleydale again.

'I don't think I ever want to go there again,' Millie declared.

'No. Don't you see? We could take flowers like we did for Dr Armstrong. Her family will want to visit, won't they? You mustn't think of it as a dark place forever.'

'Well, I will at the moment.'

Millie was upset by Jake's apparent lack of feeling and assumed he was simply anxious to continue his studies.

The bar was busy but Jake spotted Nige sitting in the corner and went over while Millie bought him his pint. When she joined them they were deep in discussion about white paint and the new Land Rover.

'Well the Land Rover is white,' insisted Jake.

'And it has been in a scrape on the passenger side,' Nige added.

'I think you're both completely mad. It would be too much of a coincidence for the departmental Land Rover to be involved in an accident with a member of the staff miles away from uni.'

'Not necessarily,' replied Nige seriously. 'Not if it wasn't.'

'Wasn't what?' Millie spluttered into her drink. 'Not an accident?'

Jake leaned forward, 'You mean someone drove the Land Rover to Redmire with the intention of running her down?'

'No! What I meant was it wouldn't necessarily be a coincidence for a departmental vehicle to be near her house, would it? Someone might have been visiting her.'

Millie put her glass down. 'I suppose that's true. But, even if it was an accident, it means someone from the department was driving it.'

'True. But the question is who?' Jake looked at Nige for an answer. 'Who had the vehicle for that day?'

'No-one signed the log. My name is the only one down all week. Well, since it was delivered actually.'

'Hi there! Room for a small one?'

Dani was dragging a stool over to their table, spilling her beer and almost toppling over as she sat down next to Millie. They all fell silent as she became the centre of their attention. Millie noticed her lack of makeup except for a smudge of mascara round her eyes. Her hair was flat and she was in the same clothes that she had been wearing when Millie saw her the previous week. Her sweaty proximity told Millie she had not showered recently.

'Hi Dani, where have you been? You still got the key to the archive store?' Jake's voice was spiky.

'Well that's a nice welcome,' she slurred. 'I've been around. Actually I was down in Leeds for a gig with some mates. I don't suppose anyone missed me.'

'Where's the key, Dani?' Jake repeated.

'What d'you want it for?'

She took a gulp from her pint glass and slammed it back on the table.

'Actually I'm looking for something Edie found at Wensleydale last week.'

'What, the blade?' asked Millie.

'Yes. Colin said he didn't have it, so it must be down there.'

'I thought he said it was in his office.' Nige looked puzzled. 'D'you remember, in here last week?'

'Well it should have been logged in if he was doing it properly, but since when did he do anything properly?'

'Too right, the bloke's a total …' the rest of the sentence was drowned as Dani finished her pint. 'Must be off, see you guys.'

'How long has she been here?' asked Jake, as they watched her stagger out of the bar.

'She was in when I arrived and she's been drinking the whole time,' observed Nige.

Millie sat quietly listening to the two friends discussing what would happen about the excavation in Wensleydale. Apparently Colin Hammond had asked the department to get the field opened up again as soon as possible. She could see they were worried about the effect of the police tramping over the site but it seemed heartless to put the archaeology first. She was also worrying about Dani and wanted to get back home in case she was there. So she excused herself and, assuring Jake she would call him, she made her way back to Jubilee Street.

Music was being played at full volume as she came down the road. The house was vibrating with the sound and when she went upstairs she found Dani in her room, sitting on the floor, her back against the bed, eyes shut.

'Dani!' There was no response. 'Dani!'

Millie was shaking her, beginning to panic, when the black smudged eyes opened, staring at her without recognition.

'What d'you want? Leave me alone.'

Millie didn't know how she did it but she persuaded the girl to get up and shower. She made her coffee and brought it up to the bedroom. The poor girl seemed grateful and wouldn't let her leave, insisting she sat down on the bed so that she could tell her something.

'Don't tell anyone this, will you? Promise me. Go on, promise!'

Millie was exasperated.

'OK, I promise.'

'It's about your friend.'

'Who? Phoebe?'

Dani was always complaining about her.

'No, no, the other one … the Princess.' She smiled.

'Vrishti?'

'Yes, her. It's about her. I know who was after her. But don't you worry,' Dani waved a finger at her. 'I'm going to talk to them and sort it all out.'

'You mean you know who killed her?' Millie was appalled.

'I didn't say that did I?' She stared with a vacant look again. 'Did I?'

'No you didn't.'

Millie was frustrated. Dani was talking utter nonsense. Goodness knows what she had taken in addition to the beer. She told her to have a rest and left her to sleep it off. It was early evening when Millie heard the door slam. Dani had gone out, presumably to get drunk again.

Not long afterwards Phoebe arrived back.

'Not staying long. I said I'd go back. I just wanted to get more contact lenses and other bits. They've arrested Deepal.'

'How's Priti?'

'Devastated but keeping it together for Sunil. He is so sweet!'

Sometimes she could be so naïve, thought Millie.

'Are you sure about this, Phoebes? Isn't it a bit dodgy getting too involved?'

'You don't actually mean you think Deepal is guilty do you? Listen, I've been talking to Priti and she's told me how anxious Deepal has been about Vrishti. When she went missing he was almost off his head with worry. He wasn't sleeping. He was ringing the police every few hours. Surely he would have kept quiet if he was responsible. And why would he go to Wensleydale of all places? I asked Priti and she didn't even know where it was!'

'I guess so.' Millie was worried for her impetuous friend.

'The other thing is that the policewoman, Nina, is apparently really nice. Priti's sure that she believes Deepal even though her boss thinks he did it.

'Well that's something I suppose.'

She helped Phoebe pack a few things, gave her a hug and made her promise to keep in touch.

'We should stop meeting like this Dani, people will start to talk.'

Dani had planned this carefully, which was good because she felt like rubbish now. It was hot, her head hurt and she was thirsty. She had insisted on meeting while there were still people in the building and her mobile was near to hand. She'd made a point of being in the archive store well before the appointed time and had ensured she was within easy reach of the door. When it opened she stood her ground and the dark figure had to move past her, leaving her escape route clear.

'Have you brought the money?' Dani wanted to get it over with quickly.

'Yes I have it here, but first I want a guarantee this is the end of the matter.' The voice was calm, matter of fact.

So far everything was very civilised but it made Dani mad to think what this piece of shit had got away with.

'What matter would that be, then I wonder? Would it be sexual harassment or something more serious?'

Now she had a bit more information she could press harder, make even more money.

'I don't know what you mean.' The dark form was wandering around the store, pacing between the shelves.

'I mean,' Dani was irritated by the constant movement, she was losing it, she always did and she was cross with herself. 'I mean I saw you in the Land Rover on Wednesday.' The shadow stopped moving. 'I just wonder exactly what you were up to. Were you doing some late night excavation perhaps?' Her legs were shaking and she was becoming breathless.

'Don't be silly, I wasn't driving a Land Rover on Wednesday. It must have been someone else.'

The figure disappeared behind the shelves and she heard a heavy drawer being dragged open.

'Come out here. I can't see you.'

'What a wonderful specimen, just look at this Greek amphora! What would that be, 300 BC?'

Dani peered into the gloom as the figure reappeared from behind the stacks with a large piece of pottery held high. She backed away as it moved towards her, sensing the wall at her back. She struggled to escape as the amphora came smashing down on her head.

Chapter 8

Jake had become obsessed with the missing keys. He'd tried the departmental office and asked all the other postgraduates but no-one had seen them. Even if Dani still had one, there should be a second set in the department somewhere. So he had arrived outside Colin Hammond's door early, determined to catch him when he arrived for work. But someone else was already there.

'Hello Jake, are you looking for Colin as well?'

Gary Perkins was leaning against the wall with his arms folded. He looked as though he hadn't slept for days: his beard was straggly, his hair unkempt and his T-shirt was spattered with food.

'Yes. I'm trying to find the key to the archive store. No-one seems to know where it is.'

'Really?' Gary was looking into the distance above Jake's head.

'It's important. I need get something out of there.'

'Right.' Gary nodded and stared into space.

Jake gave up. 'I'll come back later.'

He set off down the corridor just as Dr Hammond came in sight, smiling amiably.

'Colin!' Gary was calling behind him and Jake observed the other man's features change. Recalling the fracas in the bar, he scooted round the corner and off to his office.

'Hello Gary,' Colin called keeping his voice level.

The man was obviously distressed and he didn't want an argument now, not now that Joanna ...

'Colin, old chap. I wanted to talk to you.' He paused. 'It's about Joanna.'

Colin looked up and down the corridor. Unlocking his office he ushered Gary inside and cleared a pile of papers off his chair.

'There you go. Now how can I help?'

'Colin, I know I've been a bit of a plonker in the past but I've been thinking about Joanna. Well, about Joanna's funeral to be precise.' His voice wavered as he tried to pull himself together. 'I'm helping Joanna's parents plan her funeral now they've released her body.'

'Oh, right. I thought they might have an inquest or something.'

'There will be an inquest but we can bury her now the post mortem is over.'

He felt exhausted. He really didn't want to be talking to this man but he knew it was what Joanna would have wanted.

'Look, old man ...' Colin began.

'No, let me finish what I've got to say. I know she would have wanted you to have some say in all this, in view of your ... relationship. So I would like you to say a poem or something, whatever you want.'

There, he had done it. The man looked genuinely surprised.

'I didn't expect that, Gary. I really didn't expect I would be invited to attend.'

'Of course, mate. I know you were close.'

'Look, I think it would be best if I stayed away. It wouldn't be right somehow.'

'No, I insist. I'm going to put it in the order of service. Shall I just put "a few words from a friend"?'

It was hurting him to do this but it was for Joanna.

'Whatever.' The man looked uncomfortable.

'Call it a colleague, then?'

'OK, if you really want me to.'

'Good. That's sorted then. Now I can get it printed.'

He rose to go and then came back to the desk.

'It's on Friday in the chapel here. And, thanks mate, no hard feelings, eh?'

He offered his hand and Colin took it in his clammy palm.

Gary wandered down the corridor to his office and locked himself in. It was still a surprise to him that everything looked the same. Nothing had fallen down or disappeared, it was exactly as he had left it just a few days ago. He looked out of the window towards the town. If he stood up he could just see the flat where he and Joanna had first lived when they moved here. They'd even shared this office until his sabbatical – no, let's be honest – until the divorce. He sank down into the seat at his desk and turned his computer on. The e-mails flew in and there was one from the Dean giving details of the funeral.

'Oh, JoJo! Why did I make such a mess of everything? You know I loved you all the time, even after you left.'

He opened the top drawer and took out a half bottle of whisky. He took a swig, wiped his eyes, coughed and started working on the pile of mail on his desk.

Jake was complaining to Nige about his abortive effort to talk to his supervisor.

'Don't worry mate. I'm sure the blade is safe.'

'And how would you know that then, Nige. Are you suddenly psychic? Or do you know where it is?'

'No, course not. I just think you're getting in a state about nothing. It's not important in the scheme of things is it? Everyone else is absorbed with thinking about Vrishti and there's Joanna's funeral on Friday … and you're obsessing about missing keys!'

'Right, so I just forget about it, then, till someone else needs something from the store?'

'Yep.' Nige resumed typing without looking up.

Jake read his e-mails, including the message about Dr Armstrong's funeral service. Then he tried Millie's mobile but it went to voicemail.

'It's no good I've got to get out of here,' he announced to no-one in particular.

He jumped up and strode off to the cafeteria, where he sat until Millie called him an hour later.

'Are you OK? You sound weird, Jake.'

'I'm fine. I just wanted to speak to you.'

'What is it?'

'Nothing special. I just miss you.'

They chatted for a while and soon Millie was rushing into town. She had asked Jake to meet her at a "proper" florist's and there they spent a long time choosing Vrishti's flowers. As yet there was no date for the funeral but Millie wanted to do something. She didn't know if they would be allowed back in the field where her body had been found but Jake had suggested she might like to take flowers. At first the police had been a bit cagey but then the inspector offered to meet them down there when they were escorting Vrishti's parents to the scene and so she was now surrounded by blooms, uncertain what to choose. She didn't want anything formal, something bright, yellow perhaps? In the end they agreed on sunflowers on the basis that the birds could also enjoy them. The florist added some reds and oranges to set them off.

'For anyone special?' she asked, as she wrapped them in fluorescent orange paper and offered her a card to write a message on.

'Yes, someone very special.'

Millie took the flowers and pocketed the card, planning to write it when they got to Wensleydale.

Ernie was already on site when they arrived. This time he was accompanied by the woman officer, Nina, who was taking care of Vrishti's parents. They stood quietly in the corner of the field where Millie had discovered their daughter's makeshift grave. When he saw them, Ernie strode over and instructed them to stay where they were until Mr and Mrs Bhatt were ready to leave.

Nina was guiding the elderly couple across the field towards them, warning them to avoid the test pits, taking Mrs Bhatt's arm as she led them over and introduced Millie.

'I thought you might like to meet Mr and Mrs Bhatt. They wanted to meet Vrishti's friends.'

Millie didn't know what to say. Feeling very immature she offered, 'We all really miss her.'

Mrs Bhatt pulled a handkerchief from the sleeve of her tunic to wipe her eyes and blow her nose. She looked tired and bewildered. Her husband stepped forward and smiled.

'Tell me Millie, what is the work that is going on here? Nina tells me it is something to do with the university.'

'Yes, it's our archaeological site. We think it might be an Iron Age burial site,' she said proudly.

'So these holes are where you have been digging?' He seemed genuinely interested.

'We think it might be a chariot burial site. Someone important like a princess could be buried here,' she explained.

'You know, Millie,' Vrishti's father moved closer to her, 'last Monday, when you found my daughter lying here, it was July the sixteenth, a very important day for me.'

'Yes of course.'

'No, you don't understand. My family come from eastern India, Orissa. Last week people across India would have been celebrating Rath Yatra. Don't you think that remarkable? We were going to have a party to celebrate the Chariot Festival. In Puri, my family home, there is a festival for the Lord Jagannath, with three great chariots.'

'She doesn't want to hear about that!' Mrs Bhatt looked anxiously at her. 'It's a long story.'

'Do please go on,' insisted Millie.

'I will be brief, my dear. Lord Jagannath, his brother and sister, travel to their country palace from the famous temple in Puri in three huge chariots, forty five feet high they say. They are each drawn by four horses, different colours for each chariot.' He stopped abruptly. 'Anyway, it is good our daughter was close to a chariot of her own and she died on the earth. We will go to London at the end of the month and celebrate Rath Yatra in Trafalgar Square with our fellow Hindi. We took Vrishti a few years ago and we were all happy then.' He took his wife's hand.

'Vrishti told me about visiting your family home, Mr Bhatt. She said it was beautiful.'

'Oh yes, it is. You know the temple is famous throughout India. Puri Jagannath - the home of Lord Jagannath. And, you know, that is the origin of your word Juggernaut!'

As they moved away, Mr Bhatt turned back and, taking Millie's hand, spoke slowly but firmly.

'She is too young. We cannot believe it has happened, and we will never overcome the sadness we feel. She is our only daughter and she was our joy. But now we have to think of our son, he is alive and needs our prayers.'

He turned and Nina followed with his wife, helping them back to the car.

'Right, we'll be off then,' said Ernie in a brisk tone. 'Yon lass is staying, she's to wait for the pathologist. He wants another look round before the site's all yours again.'

'What? You mean we can start work again, soon?' Jake asked.

'Yes, first thing Monday, as far as I'm concerned.'

He went over to where the Bhatts were waiting by the car.

'I think I'll go and put these flowers over by the tree.'

Millie took a deep breath as she walked towards the corner of the field.

'Hold on!' Nina was calling her. 'I'm sorry but do you mind waiting until the pathologist has been? He's due in a few minutes and he won't take long.'

So the three of them stood in the middle of the field in silence with Millie clutching her bouquet.

'So, you probably knew Vrishti better than most?'

It was more a question than a statement.

'I don't know, I suppose so.'

Millie wasn't sure she knew her very well.

'We'll need all the facts we can get, so I expect we'll want to chat to you again some time.' The woman smiled sympathetically. 'It must be terrible for you.'

It was the first time Millie had admitted to herself, never mind anyone else, that actually it was awful.

'There are various bits of information we are interested in,' she continued. 'One puzzle is the ornamental blade that ....' She stopped, as if she shouldn't be telling them. 'Well, there's this blade, and there is a view that it comes from India. To me it seems very different to the daggers which were taken from the suspect's house.'

'What sort of blade?' asked Jake.

'It looks rather old to me but I don't know. I thought, since you're archaeologists, you might know about such things?'

'I could always have a look if you like,' Jake offered.

'Well, it's actually a bit difficult because it's evidence.' She paused. 'And my boss is convinced it belongs to the suspect.'

When Millie heard the word "suspect" again she thought of Deepal and how distraught he had been when Vrishti disappeared. She pictured Priti, sitting alone at home with her tiny baby. Except, of course, she wasn't alone, she had Phoebe for company. She was about to ask what would be happening to Deepal when she saw a car making its way up the track.

'That's Dr Carter, the pathologist.'

Nina almost ran across the field and was beside the driver's door as he opened it.

'I'd like to have a look at that dagger,' said Jake.

'Well she won't let you have evidence, that's for sure,' Millie said quietly as Nina came back across the field accompanied by a stocky man with a ruddy complexion and flowing white hair.

'These are the deceased's friends,' Nina said cheerily, 'and this is Dr Carter. He'll only be a few minutes.'

She led him over to the corner of the field and left him there.

'He wants to collect pollen samples, bits of vegetation from around the scene,' she explained.

'What will he do with those?' Millie was puzzled.

'He will get someone to match them with material he's found on the body.' She looked uncomfortable.

'It's OK,' said Millie, 'please go on.

'Well, they look for pollen to match it with the scene of the crime.'

'How?' asked Jake.

'He can retrieve pollen samples which have been breathed in by the deceased at the time of death. If he can find a match, then he knows she died here where she was found.'

They turned to watch him picking up pieces of grass, and bits off the tree, placing them into bags and writing on each one carefully. When he was finally finished he took all the bags back to his car and Nina told them it was time for her to go.

'About that dagger,' Jake said as she set off. 'If you'd like me to have a look at it, I'd be happy to.'

She turned and waved, calling back, 'Thanks, I might just do that!'

Millie left Jake and walked unsteadily across to the corner of the field. She placed the flowers carefully beside the tree and sank down beside them. She wanted to talk to Vrishti, tell her how she missed her and how awful it was to think of her, but this wasn't her grave and she wasn't there to hear her.

'Oh Vrishti, what happened to you? Who could possibly have wanted to hurt you?'

She tasted the tears running past her mouth and heard herself wailing like an animal. It was embarrassing but she couldn't help it. When she finally stood up and stepped back she felt Jake's hands on her shoulders.

'There's no rush, take as long as you need,' was all he said.

She didn't turn round but leant back against him and sobbed until her emotions subsided. She was still shaking but was silent now. She turned and they walked slowly back across the field.

'I don't suppose you'll want to come back to work on the site now.' He sounded miserable.

'Oh yes I will.' Millie smiled. 'I feel closer to Vrishti here than at home. I want to come back if we're allowed. We might even come across a clue that the police have overlooked.'

'Yeah, right! How d'you work that out?'

'Well, we know the site better. We know Dash was sniffing around over in the corner when we came on Saturday, which means she was there then.'

'Do the police know that?'

'I don't know, they haven't asked us anything about the site really, have they?'

Jake looked puzzled, 'So exactly when did Vrishti go missing? She was here with us on Tuesday, wasn't she?'

'Yes, and she went back to uni with Nige. We never saw her after that.'

'You're not suggesting that Nige …'

'No, of course not. Well, I don't think so. It's difficult to imagine anyone …'

'So she was killed between Tuesday and Saturday, I suppose,' said Jake.

'She disappeared on Tuesday and she would have come home if she was able to, so she was either dead or being held by someone from Tuesday onwards. She could have been brought here any time from then until Saturday.'

They had reached the Land Rover and Millie turned to take a last look at the field.

'It's so sad that Dr Armstrong had her accident last week as well,' she said, reminded of how she had placed flowers by the wall in the lane not many miles away. 'You know, Dr Armstrong could have been the last person to see Vrishti alive. She was going to see her when she got back on Tuesday. In fact, it could be that Vrishti was the last person to see Dr Armstrong before her accident.'

'You don't think the two things are related in some way?'

'You're not still on about the hit-and-run vehicle being from the department!'

'Well, the paint matches and it convinced Nige. What if it's not a coincidence and there's a connection between the two … events.'

'I can't think of any reason why there should be. Vrishti hardly knew Dr Armstrong, and we don't even know if she did get to see her on Tuesday.' Millie paused. 'And anyway, who would we tell?'

'I dunno. I don't suppose the police would listen and Gary's in such a mess he wouldn't be any help. I saw him this morning when I was waiting for Colin to try and get the store key. Now he's the person we should be talking to!'

'Dr Hammond?'

'Yes. Nige said no-one had signed the log book for the new Land Rover but he was definitely using it when he came over here on Wednesday morning.'

'Was he?'

'Yes, don't you remember? It was soon after Edie found the blade. He trawled up and stayed for all of fifteen minutes before dashing back. Said he had a staff meeting.'

Millie recollected the lecturer leaving in a cloud of dust but couldn't remember what he was driving. It could have been a Land Rover. She was beginning to feel weary after the emotional strain of the afternoon and when Jake suggested calling in to see his family she said she would prefer to go straight home.

She expected the house to be empty when Jake dropped her off but inside the radio was playing and she assumed Dani was back. To her surprise it was Phoebe who was in the kitchen busy ironing.

'Hi, I came back while Vrishti's parents are staying with Priti. The police brought them over this afternoon and I felt a bit in the way.'

'I met them over at the site today,' said Millie. 'They seem nice.'

'They're absolutely devastated, it's so awful with Deepal being charged with … well … you know.'

Phoebe put the iron down on its rack and looked at Millie gravely.

'You don't think he did it, then?' asked Millie.

'No way, Priti has convinced me he couldn't harm Vrishti. He was devoted to her.'

'But isn't that the point? He might have been jealous and overprotective?'

'Millie, she told me he hardly slept once she disappeared. He spent all his waking hours trying to think where she might be, who he could contact.'

'Well, if he's been charged the police won't be looking for anyone else, that's for sure. And they won't listen to us.' Millie changed the subject. 'So how did you get on at Priti's? Did you help with the baby?'

'Sunil, you mean Sunil.' Phoebe went into raptures, describing his daily routine in detail.

Millie told Phoebe about her visit to the archaeological site and they both fell silent as they remembered their friend and realised how empty the place felt without her. It was never like that when Dani was out of the way, in fact they relished her absences.

'Seen Dani since you've been back?' Millie asked Phoebe.

'No, is she out today?'

'I haven't seen her since she got ratted yesterday.'

'Good riddance,' declared Phoebe, picking up the iron and sweeping it vigorously across a pair of jeans.

'She'll be OK. That girl is always turning up when you least expect her and least want to see her!'

Back in the department Jake found Nige at his computer typing furiously.

'Hi.'

Nige didn't look up. 'Where you been?'

'Over in Wensleydale. I went with Millie. She wanted to take flowers, to put where Vrishti was found.'

Nige looked up with a sympathetic grin. 'That's nice.'

'Yeah.'

Jake went over to his desk and turned on his computer. He looked at his e-mails while Nige carried on typing.

'You busy?' Jake asked, hoping his friend might join him in the bar.

'Mad busy, mate. I asked Dani to do the risk assessment for the student projects down in Driffield and they were supposed to be ready for the meeting today. She's buggered off and I can't find her anywhere. Disappeared off and dropped me in it. Now I've got to give them to Colin before the end of today "or else" he says.'

'She's probably sleeping off a mega hangover,' suggested Jake, 'after yesterday's performance.'

'Right.' Nige was hunched back over the keyboard.

'I'm going to find Colin to get this key off him. Shall I tell him you're on the case?'

'Yeah, nice one.'

Jake shut the door quietly behind him and set off down to the ground floor, where the staff had their offices. It was already five o' clock but Jake knew if he wasn't there, the chances were Dr Hammond would be in the bar.

'Can I see you for a minute, Colin?' Jake was standing at the door and his presence seemed to almost intimidate the man, who was sitting at his desk about to make a call. He put the phone down again and turned his chair round to face Jake.

'Yes?' He was abrupt.

'The key to the store, can I have it?'

His supervisor looked confused. 'What key?'

'The one to the store.' Jake repeated slowly. 'The archive store.'

'Ah.'

'Chantelle says you're the last person to borrow it.'

'Am I?'

Jake moved into the office. 'I want to have a look at the dagger Edie found at the Wensleydale site last week. You took it away and you said you put it in the store.'

'Did I?'

'Yes you did.'

The older man fidgeted in his chair. 'I did have it but I can't find it at the moment.'

'You said it was probably in the store, so I would like the key.'

'I thought it might be in there, but I'm not sure now.'

'Do you have the key, Dr Hammond?'

He fumbled around in his pockets and finally went through his desk drawers. He stood up and went to the coat rack, where a light jacket was hanging. He felt in each pocket and produced a key ring containing two keys. He held his open palm out to Jake.

'Are these them?'

Jake took the keys and studied the tag. It simply said "store".

'I think so.'

'Can you make sure you give them back to Chantelle then?'

'Yes Dr Hammond.'

Jake sighed and left the room. The guy seemed to have become a complete disaster area. At least with the key to the store he could check if the dagger had been put there for safe keeping. He ran down to the basement, keen to search the room and then catch Nige before he left. He deserved that drink and his friend would probably feel the same. It was dark and he had to switch on the lights to make his way down the corridor, past the boiler room and the cleaners' cupboard, to the storeroom. The first key didn't fit but the other one turned and he gently pushed the door open.

He hadn't remembered the room smelling so musty before and he stood outside as he fumbled for the light switch. Once the room was illuminated he stepped in and looked around. Jake tried to rationalise what he perceived but it was difficult to create a sensible scenario for a foot sticking out from between the stacks at such a strange angle. He ran to where the leg protruded and pressed the button that controlled the movement of the stacks. As the shelves parted the body rolled into the space between and his brain registered it was Dani, whose life had been literally squeezed out of her between the shelves of ancient artefacts.

Chapter 9

His mobile had no signal in the basement and Jake had to climb the stairs to the entrance hall on legs that were shaking with shock. He called the police, then sat and waited, knowing the door was locked and he had the key. He wanted to ring Millie to make sure she was safe. Two of her housemates had been murdered and he was anxious for her. Perhaps it was shock, maybe he was being too calm, but he felt it was best to wait and see what the police told him to do. Several members of academic staff were off home for the evening, but he watched them in a trance as they left, without saying a word. Soon a blue light flashed outside and two uniformed officers appeared, looking round as if they expected to find a commotion.

'It's in the basement,' he said to them as he stood up and without further words he led them to the stairs.

When they reached the door he unlocked it but he wouldn't go inside. He let them find Dani lying there lifeless. He couldn't face the sight again. There were questions, they shouted at him sometimes and eventually he led them upstairs to the Dean's office. She took over and he was able to sit on the sidelines without having to speak. More police were called, entrances were sealed off and any members of staff and students who were still in the building were corralled into the lecture hall.

Jake was relieved to see a familiar face.

'Hello, Jake. What's going on?' Nige asked.

'It's … it's … it's Dani.'

'What d'you mean?' Nige looked confused.

'I found her ... in the store ... she was ... she was ...'

'Oh no, not ...' He seemed to understand, to know what Jake meant. He came over and put his arm round his friend. 'She's not dead, is she? She can't be, not Dani?'

Jake couldn't answer, the tears wouldn't stop and he wanted to get away, hide away, but he couldn't. He felt everyone was watching him, Colin, Gary, the Dean, Chantelle.

In turn the police worked systematically through the rows of people seated in the hall. Jake watched as a policewoman approached them one by one and went through the same performance. She would lead them over to the man in plain clothes who was perched awkwardly at the end of the front row. His papers were balanced on the small wooden ledge that was provided for the students to lean their notes on during lectures. She would indicate for the next interviewee to sit down next to him and she would sit on their right. The man would ask questions, writing furiously. Sometimes the person being questioned would chatter away, gesticulating, turning to the policewoman now and then for reassurance. But most of them simply nodded or shook their heads, jumping up as soon as the questioning was over to rush away home, the whole experience for them was presumably a mere inconvenience.

Jake sat until nearly everyone was processed and at last it was Nige's turn. It didn't take long and as he left the hall he indicated he would wait for Jake outside.

'Would you like to come and speak to the sergeant now please?' the woman asked.

She reminded Jake of his mother as he followed her down to the front of the hall. The guy was pleasant enough and asked him to explain exactly what had happened. Jake felt fine until he got to the bit when he unlocked the door and then he thought he might be sick.

'Take your time, lad. We've got plenty of time. It's important that you tell us everything you remember. Anything however small might be very important.'

He took a deep breath.

'I unlocked the door and I noticed it was very stuffy, well quite musty actually. I put the light on before I went in and it was then I saw her foot, sticking out, like someone was lying down between the stacks.'

'And what was the position of the stacks at that point.'

'They were together, close together. As soon as I went in I could see someone had been squashed between the shelves, so I pressed the control to move them apart. Then I realised it was Dani, despite the colour and everything I could see it was her.'

He paused as the picture formed itself in his mind and he resisted the urge to throw up.

'Go on.'

'I was pretty sure she was dead but I touched her face. It wasn't cold really, it was warm down there. I did try to find a pulse but I wasn't really thinking straight by then and I freaked out a bit.'

'Don't worry, she had been dead for some time. There was nothing that you could have done.'

'There was no signal so I had to go upstairs to call you. I locked the door before I left and then waited in the entrance.'

'You did the right thing. Thank you for giving us a statement now. We'll want to chat to you again down at the station. You can sign the statement then, when it's typed up. Do you have any questions at this time?'

Jake shook his head. They took his contact details and he made for the door, leaving the police busy poring over their paperwork. Outside Nige was waiting with Phoebe, and Millie was running towards him.

'Back in a minute,' he called as he made for the toilets.

He returned a few minutes later, rather sheepishly. His stomach was calmer now and he gratefully fell into Millie's arms.

'Nige told us what happened so we came straight down,' said Millie.

'You need a beer, mate,' suggested Nige and led the way to the bar, where they sat in the corner furthest from the door, silently sipping their drinks.

Last time they were there Dani had staggered over and broken up the group. Millie was desperately trying to recollect what she had been on about. She asked Jake and Nige but they couldn't remember anything in particular and then Millie began to recall their conversation back at the house. Dani had been very drunk and Millie had gone to see if she was all right, and she'd said she knew what had happened to Vrishti. What had Dani said? She knew something and she was going to deal with it.

'I don't know what it all means,' announced Millie, 'but I'm sure Dani knew who murdered Vrishti.'

Her friends were dumb-struck by her declaration.

Finally Phoebe spoke, 'You mean what happened to Dani was to do with Vrishti's death?'

'I believe so.'

'In that case,' said Phoebe, 'we'd better go down and talk to the police.'

'Don't you think they might already be looking at the connection between them? After all they did share the same house.' Nige was looking unusually alert and intelligent beside Jake who was beginning to slump down in his seat.

'Are you all right Jake?' Phoebe asked anxiously. 'Millie, I think Jake needs to go home.'

'Yes, we need something to eat. Do you want to come back to our's?'

Millie's invitation was mainly directed at Jake but Nige accepted swiftly and helped Jake to his feet. They passed through two police checks on the way out and in the main entrance a manned desk had been set up to record the comings and goings. Reporters were hanging about outside but no-one was concerned with the group of friends as they made their way slowly out of the building and along the road to Jubilee Street. Nige offered to buy pizza on the way home but no-one was hungry. They let themselves into the empty house and slumped in the sitting room. Finally Phoebe broke the silence.

'I suppose the police will want to come here soon,'

'Just like before,' agreed Millie. 'They'll search her room and take stuff away.

'They'll want to question you too,' said Nige. 'They haven't spoken to you yet, have they?'

'No.' Millie said absently.

She was thinking about how Nige had taken control in the hour after Jake had found Dani's body. He had rung her and asked her to come into the university, telling her that Jake needed her help. He had sounded so mature and again now he seemed to have taken the senior role, like that of an older brother.

'Nige,' she asked, 'do you think Dani's death is linked to Vrishti's?'

'Of course it is,' said Phoebe, 'it must be.'

'Not necessarily,' said Nige, his Welsh accent emphasising every syllable. 'Not necessarily. The chances of one event occurring after another unrelated event will, of course be quite small.' He rubbed his chin with his fingers and then stared at his grubby nails. 'If the events were related, then the chances of them happening would be much greater. It's like when you put a series of bets on the horses.'

'For Christ's sake, Nige! It's nothing like betting on horses.' Jake's fists were clenched and his mouth had tightened.

Nige looked alarmed, 'Look, sorry mate. I just was trying, well, you know. Look, why don't I go and get food, eh?'

'That's a great idea, Nige.' Millie reached for her purse and offered to share the cost with him. He gave her a grateful smile and left the house.

When Millie went back into the sitting room Phoebe and Jake were deep in discussion.

'Listen, she was squashed. It could just be a terrible accident. She was between the shelves, they were closed shut. I had to press the button to open them up.'

Phoebe, who had expressed such loathing for Dani in the past, began to sniffle.

'It's a horrible coincidence.'

'Probably,' agreed Jake and sank back on the sofa.

Millie sat down beside him and took his hand.

'Why don't we put the telly on?' she suggested.

When Nige arrived back the three of them were gazing at a game show. He was armed with pizzas, beers and ice-cream. Although they protested they weren't hungry, Millie and Phoebe shared the ice-cream. The boys opened a beer each and shared a pizza. A detective series started and Millie switched channels, rejecting programme after programme, until she settled on a cricket match. She knew it would preoccupy Jake, who was a fan, although she wasn't sure about Nige. Obediently Phoebe sat and tried to follow it, while Nige explained to her in irritating detail what was happening. The empty beer cans gradually formed a heap on the floor and by midnight they were all in a lethargic state.

Phoebe was the first to drag herself up to bed. She waved at Millie and Jake, and pointed to Nige who was propped against a chair with his head lolling on the seat cushion, snoring gently.

'Leave him there,' Millie said to Jake, 'and you're welcome to the sofa.'

'Thanks, I don't think I could face the walk back tonight.'

Millie thought he looked exhausted as she kissed him before climbing off the sofa and up to bed.

The sight of the unmade bed, through the half open door of Dani's room, reminded her with a jolt of the terrible accident. She lay for a long time imagining the sight that had met Jake when he went into the storeroom. She tried to put together the conversation she had had with Dani the day before. What had she said about Vrishti and was it relevant? She slept restlessly and finally at three forty-five got up and went downstairs for a glass of water.

'Can't you sleep either?'

Millie jumped at the voice and her water went everywhere.

'Sorry I didn't mean to frighten you.'

Jake came over and put his arm round her.

'Would you like some water, or hot chocolate, I've got some.'

'Sounds good.'

She moved around the kitchen as quietly as she could, heating the milk, taking care to stop the microwave before the timer made a noise. She used her favourite mug for Jake, and washed up another for herself.

'Nige is snoring for England.' Jake grinned. 'He always does but I don't usually have to share a room with him.'

'You can come upstairs with me if you like.' Millie steadied her voice.

'Are you sure?' asked Jake. 'I don't want you to …'

'It's OK, Jake.'

He followed her up the stairs carrying his mug. They sat in bed drinking their hot chocolate together, Millie in her Mickey Mouse pyjamas and Jake in jeans and college T-shirt. It was just so comforting knowing he was there. Millie slept soundly for the first time in days.

'Hello you!'

Jake was standing beside the bed with two mugs in his hand. His hair was tousled and the state of his clothes confirmed he had slept in them.

Millie squinted in the sunlight and tried to straighten her hair.

'Hi.'

'I've been thinking about what happened yesterday.'

He sat down beside her on the bed and handed her a coffee. For a minute Millie couldn't think what he meant and then the familiar grey feeling reappeared. She waited for him to continue.

'If what happened to Dani wasn't an accident, someone from the department must have done it. It wouldn't be someone from outside because they wouldn't have a key to the store would they?'

'Dani had a key, she could have unlocked the room.'

'D'you think so? It's just that it was Colin who gave me the key to the store. Do you think he could have …?'

'I don't know. We don't know what happened do we? The police have to do all the tests. A post mortem … all that sort of thing.'

Millie didn't want to have to think about it. It was bad enough finding Vrishti. She desperately wanted Dani's death to be due to a horrible accident.

'Sorry,' said Jake, 'I didn't mean to upset you. It must be rough for you.'

He climbed into bed and began to kiss her, at first gently and then more forcefully. Millie responded. It didn't seem right and she felt guilty, almost tearful, but she longed to forget the horrors of the past few days and she found Jake irresistible. When the police rang the doorbell and she dragged on her dressing gown her emotions were a mixture of guilt, irritation and melancholy as she remembered opening the front door to Vrishti the night of the party. This time she knew it could not be the dishevelled figure of her friend but was surprised by the sight of the equally striking policewoman waiting patiently on the step.

'Sorry but I assumed you would be up.' Her tone was matter of fact.

'Sorry, is it late? Do come in. I suppose this is about Dani?'

'Yes I'm afraid it is.' Nina spoke gently. She knew how traumatic these events must be for a young person like Millie and she had worse news to report. 'I need to speak to you and to Phoebe.'

Millie was impressed that the woman had remembered her friend's name but perhaps they were trained for this sort of thing, taught to use first names, to make people feel comfortable around them. There were footsteps behind them

'Hi, Nina.' Phoebe seemed in good spirits.

'Good morning Phoebe. I've just come from the incident room. May I have a word with you both?'

She looked serious and Millie turned to lead her into the sitting room when she remembered that Nige had been sprawled on the floor in there last night.

'Would you like to come into the kitchen?' she asked, leading the way.

They settled down round the table and Nina swept the crumbs from in front of her onto the floor.

'I've come to give you information regarding what happened to your housemate. May I ask first how close you were to her?'

'We knew her but to be honest we didn't get on very well with her.' Phoebe reddened.

'She was a bit difficult to get on with at times,' Millie added wishing that Phoebe had kept quiet.

'Why was that do you think?' the woman asked taking out a notepad.

'Oh just a difference in the way we were, I suppose,' answered Millie trying to sound casual. She didn't want them thinking it was an issue. 'Dani was quite an extrovert and we are rather, well … quieter.'

'Right.' She made a few notes. 'And it was just you two plus Dani living in the house after Vrishti …' She didn't finish the sentence.

'Yes,' they both answered.

'Well, as you know, Dani was found in the storeroom at the university yesterday evening. We are waiting for the post mortem report but it appears she died from the result of serious brain trauma. We are not ruling out an accident but at present it seems unlikely.' Both girls sat in silence. 'The reason I have asked permission to tell you this is because, if I were you, I would want to know what the situation was. Do you understand me?'

They sat nodding but finally Millie admitted, 'No, not exactly.'

'Let me put it this way. My inspector does not feel you are under any threat but I asked if I might come and tell you what the facts are. If I was your mother I would want to know what had happened to your friends. I might be worried about you and I would want to be informed.'

Millie exchanged glances with Phoebe.

'Right,' she said.

She was about to ask for further clarification when Jake appeared at the door, turned and went into the sitting room.

'And that was?' asked Nina, peering past them and into the hall.

'That's Jake,' offered Phoebe. 'He found Dani in the storeroom.'

'Good, I want to have a word with him.'

She jumped up and disappeared into the sitting room. Soon she reappeared with Jake in tow.

'I'm taking him back with me. They need his fingerprints down at the station.'

She was putting her notebook back in her shoulder bag. Jake pulled an anxious face at the girls and followed Nina obediently to the front door.

Once in the car Nina explained. 'Don't worry it's only routine. They need your prints to eliminate them from the crime scene. Did you touch anything?'

'No.' Jake recalled what had happened in the claustrophobic storeroom. When he got to the part where he released Dani from the stacks he remembered. 'I pressed the button to open the shelves.'

'There you are then. They'll need to know they're your prints and not the prints of the person who closed the shelves.'

'Do you think someone deliberately shut her in there?'

Jake had convinced himself that it must have been a accident.

'Don't you?'

Nina was looking straight ahead.

'No, I thought the stacks had gone wrong and trapped her.'

'Does that seem likely?'

She turned to look at him.

'I don't know. I suppose it's a bit unlikely.'

Nina sat in silence and Jake pondered what she had said. If Dani was deliberately squashed in the stacks then it was another murder. Deepal was in custody so it couldn't have been him. Surely a second murder was too much of a coincidence, like Nige had said. Did it mean Deepal hadn't killed Vrishti?

'When we were at the site in Wensleydale you told me that there had been a blade, you know when Vrishti was killed.'

'Yes.'

Nina didn't take her eyes off the road.

'And you said I might look at it to see if I could classify it for you?'

'Is that what you call it?'

'Yes, if it's an artefact.'

'OK then, I'll show it to you when we get down there.'

Before long they were climbing the stone steps into the grand entrance of the old Victorian building that was home to the local police force. Nina introduced him to a young constable who looked no older than he was. He carefully took a print of each finger and thumb before leading him up to an office on the first floor where Nina sat at a desk piled with papers all neatly labelled with words like "pending", "urgent", "next week". She swung round when she heard them behind her and indicated for Jake to sit down. When they were alone she opened a drawer and lifted out a plastic bag containing a hard object. As soon as she passed it to him he recognised the dagger Edie had uncovered at the dig the previous week. It had been cleaned to expose the metal blade and ornamental handle. As soon as he identified it Nina took yet another statement from him. He described where it had been found and how Dr Hammond had taken it off on the Wednesday.

'What time would that have been?' Nina asked.

'About lunch time. He went off soon after because he had a meeting in the afternoon.'

'Are you certain about this, Jake? It could be very important evidence you know.'

'Yes I realise that.'

Jake was concerned about the consequences of what he had told her. Did it really mean Colin Hammond was responsible for Vrishti's death?

'I would appreciate it if you could please keep this information to yourself for now, until our enquiries are completed.'

'Will Vrishti's brother be allowed home? After all, the dagger has nothing to do with him.'

'It's far too early to say. It will be up to my inspector and he currently feels there is a strong case against him. It may be difficult to convince him otherwise.' She turned back to her desk. 'I shouldn't discuss the case with you really.'

'Can I go now then?'

'Yes of course … and tell your friends to be aware of their own safety.'

Ernie stood in the corridor and watched Jake as he strolled out into the street. He had just got back from interviewing the dead girl's parents. It was the second such visit in as many weeks, and each death was as baffling as the other. They had to be related, after all the girls did live under the same roof, but that didn't square with the fact he had the killer of the first girl down in the cells.

He needed a cigarette to think this one through. Gone were the days when he could sit at his keyboard with a fag on the go non-stop.

'Nina, love, could you type out these notes for me while I pop out for quick cuppa?'

Without waiting for an answer Ernie threw his notebook at her and made for the door. When he returned an hour later the notes were typed up and the girl was busy on the internet.

'Did you see the mother's statement?' Ernie asked, leaning on the back of Nina's chair. She looked up.

'Yes, I didn't see anything particular. She didn't have much to do with her daughter once she was at university. She said she had become a bit stuck up.'

'She's a difficult woman, surrounded by screaming brats and distracted most of the time. I did note down a nightclub her daughter frequented called "Selena's" or "Siren's"?'

Nina ran her polished fingernail down the list.

'Selene's.'

'That's the one. I'm a bit old for that malarkey. I thought you could go and have a look.'

'What am I looking for?'

'Anyone who knows her, anyone who can tell us about her. We've got precious little to go on at the moment.' He turned to go. 'I'm off to the university to get to the bottom of this key business.'

He almost ran down the stairs and out into the sunlight, his cigarette ready to light the moment he got through the door. He took the scenic route to the university to savour the comforting haze of tobacco smoke and by the time he reached the incident room he was in good humour.

'Hello young man, how's it going?' Mitch was poring over an exercise book.

'I'm trying to work out who's been in the storeroom over the past few weeks. There's supposed to be a log of people borrowing the key but it's pretty sketchy.'

'Happen I'll go and find that professor woman, see if she can throw some light on it for you.'

Ernie smirked, patted Mitch on the head and set off, whistling a tuneless rendition of "Blue Suede Shoes". He discovered the very attractive Chantelle in the departmental office and decided she would be perfectly capable of telling him who had keys to the storeroom, provided he kept it simple.

'So, Chantelle,' he said with his best seductive smile, 'there are in fact three keys.'

'One of them's a master key, it opens everything in the basement. We keep that here in the office.'

'May I see it, love?'

The girl took a key from her desk and moved over to a key safe on the wall. Ernie watched her hips as she crossed the room, and pondered on whether the miniskirt was making a comeback.

'This is the master key,' she said, waving it from her slender fingers and putting it back in the box.

'So who has the other two?' Ernie followed her figure back to the desk.

'That young detective has the book.' She reddened slightly. 'I think Jake said Dr Hammond had one. I don't know about the other one. The students pass it round and they never fill in the log book.'

'Thanks, love. I'll get the book off my young detective. We call him Mitch Turner amongst other things.'

As he turned to leave, the girl called after him,

'The Dean said I should let her know if you came back. Shall I tell her now?'

'She must have taken a liking to me, eh? Go on then.'

He waited while she made a call and then asked him to make his way down to the Dean's office. Professor McGrath was opening the door as he arrived.

'So how is it going, Inspector? Have you made any progress on these dreadful occurrences?'

'We are proceeding. I was just talking to your girl about who had access to the storeroom. It sounds as though anyone could have got hold of the keys.'

'Well, yes, I agree it is not as secure as it should be. They are asked to sign the book if they borrow the key but you know what students are like, Inspector.'

She sat behind the desk smiling across at him.

'But there are only two keys on loan?'

'Yes.'

'Well, the dead girl had one, it was in her pocket. And the lad who found her had got his key from a lecturer.' He struggled in his pocket and referred to a scrap of paper. 'A Dr Hammond.'

'Ah, Colin.' The Dean's look was enigmatic.

'Could you tell me a little about Dr Hammond?' Ernie asked with his polite smile.

'Well, he's new here, started last term. He's an excellent field archaeologist.'

'I was thinking more of his personal life, Professor.'

'I don't know much about that I'm afraid. He's single, lives in town in one of the new apartment blocks by the canal. He's fairly popular, of course at present he's a bit upset by Joanna's death. You know Dr Armstrong was in a road accident recently. She was on the staff.'

'His girlfriend?'

'I don't know really, you'd need to ask the younger staff about that.'

'I might well do that, thank you.'

Ernie put away his notepad and rose to leave.

'Inspector, Dani's death was just a nasty accident, wasn't it? I mean, there's not any more to it, is there? Your questions … it almost sounds as if …' she stopped abruptly.

'We really can't say at the moment ma'am but we'll keep you informed.'

As he reached the door Chantelle appeared with a tray.

'I thought you might need tea.'

'Too late, love, I've to go but I'll take a jammy dodger.'

As soon as he was back in the office Nina handed Ernie the pathologist's report on Vrishti Bhatt. She had read it carefully and not without emotion. The girl had been beaten over the head with a heavy object. The pathologist had described the circumference of the object and its approximate weight. The girl may have died as a result of the beating but she also had traces of flunitrazepam, or rohipnol, as it was better known, in her body. Later, much later, a blade had been pushed into her chest. Despite the presence of the date rape drug there was no evidence that it was a sexual attack, and there had been no sign of a struggle. It was all rather puzzling. A second sheet had been appended by the pathologist describing the methodology which had been used to look at pollen in her nasal passages. It showed she had been lying in a location quite different from the archaeological site. The seed found in her hair had been difficult to identify. It was definitely not from Wensleydale and was probably from a fig tree.

Ernie had some difficulty following the technical stuff and asked Nina if she could make head or tail of it.

'I think he's saying she wasn't killed in the field where she was found. That she was murdered somewhere else and then moved to where she was buried.'

Ernie didn't respond but stared at the pages for several minutes. Nina waited until he seemed to have finished. At last he threw the paper down and sighed.

'I was talking to the lad who found Dani's body, sir, and he recognised the knife they found in the other girl's body. He says it comes from the site.'

She handed him a neatly typed page. 'It's an archaeological artefact, sir.'

'What's that when it's at home?'

'The blade was discovered at the site in Wensleydale. A student found it but it was taken back to the university by one of the lecturers.'

'Which one? No, don't tell me, let me guess.' He consulted a scrap of paper he retrieved from his pocket. 'Would it happen to be that excellent field archaeologist Dr Colin Hammond?'

'Yes, how did you know that?'

'Just a lucky guess.'

He grinned showing Nina his teeth, yellow from years of smoking

'I just thought if the dagger didn't belong to Deepal Bhatt you might release him.'

'I'll not be rushed into letting him go.'

His smile had disappeared as quickly as it had been revealed.

'Sir, don't you agree that the two crimes are most likely related, with the girls living in the same place.'

'They could be. I'm keeping an open mind.'

'Well, if it's the same killer it can't be Mr Bhatt can it?' Nina tried once more to persuade the irritating old man.

'No, not unless he's rubbed his magic lamp and disappeared through the cell door.' Ernie guffawed. 'I'm off now but don't forget you're going to that nightclub in Newcastle. Best go this evening if you want to meet the punters.'

'But I'm not on duty tonight, sir.'

Nina had been worrying about this order. She hadn't been to a nightclub since she was sixteen and then she was with a crowd of friends. Now she had lots of acquaintances but no real friends in the North-East. They certainly did not go clubbing and she didn't want to go on her own.

'It's not work is it, dear? Bit of fun. I'm sure Mitch would regard it as a treat.'

Nina was tired of the way her boss used her colleague as a threat, suggesting he might be more willing to carry out his orders. She rose to it every time.

'OK, I'll go this evening, after I've been round to Jake's house to interview his friends.'

'Good girl. Enjoy yourself!'

Nina watched him go before she selected the relevant paperwork, gathered her personal belongings and made her way out to the car park. She found Jake's address in the file. The flat was in the student area and it took only a few minutes to reach. The chip shop was doing a roaring trade and the greasy smell reminded her she'd only eaten a bar of chocolate and a sausage roll since breakfast.

The young man who answered the door appeared surprised to see her. She had to invite herself in and clear a space on the sofa before she could sit down. She explained why she was there and began to take notes.

'Name?'

'Nigel Featherstone.'

'And you share this accommodation with Jake?'

'Yes.'

'And how long have you known him?'

'About three years I suppose. He was an undergraduate when I started my PhD.'

'Was Jake a particular friend of Vrishti Bhatt?'

'No, he didn't meet her until the projects started, neither of us did.'

Nina scribbled notes.

'And Dani. What about her?'

'Oh she's been around for a while.'

'She was doing a doctorate as well?'

'No she's finished her PhD. She's a postdoc researcher like me.'

'You must be very clever.'

The lad turned bright red so Nina moved quickly on.

'So did Jake know Dani well?'

'Not so well as me like.'

'So there was no special connection between Jake and either of the girls?'

'No, he's with Millie.'

Nina put her pen in her handbag and stood up.

'One last question, Nigel.'

'Yes?'

'Would you accompany me to a nightclub tonight?'

Chapter 10

Jake had gone straight back to the flat from the police station. He grabbed his kit and went to the university sports centre where he spent an hour in the gym and then swam fifty lengths. The water helped to clear his mind and he had often used the pool to sort things out. As he swam slowly up and down he went over it all. By the time he was towelling himself dry he was certain that Dr Hammond had taken the blade back to his office and kept it there. The lecturer had admitted as much to Ben when they were in the bar the other evening.

When he left the sports centre in his running gear to do a circuit of the park, Jake was convinced Colin Hammond had been using the new Land Rover on the day he came to Wensleydale. It was that evening when Dr Armstrong was killed, struck by a vehicle that left white paint on the stone wall. And as he stood exhausted under the shower, he was certain Dr Hammond was the last person to hold the key to the storeroom before he had discovered the macabre figure of Dani jammed between the shelves.

Finally, on his way to Jubilee Street, he tried to find ways to exonerate his supervisor but the suspicion wouldn't go away and he resolved to discuss it with Millie. But when he arrived there was an estate car parked outside the house, the front door was open and Millie was in the hall.

'It's Phoebe's parents, they're upstairs helping her pack, and they're taking her home. The Dean rang them and told them what had happened to Dani. Apparently she rang Dad as well but I haven't heard from him … yet.' She pulled a face. 'How did it go with the police?'

'OK. Nina showed me the dagger she told us about. It's the one Edie found at the site.'

Millie couldn't bear to think of the ancient artefact being part of her friend's death.

'How's that possible?'

'I don't know but her brother couldn't have had access to it.'

'So who would?'

Jake started to tell her what he had been thinking about at the gym when Phoebe came into the sitting room looking miserable and flung herself on the sofa. Her eyes were red and puffy.

'I've tried to get them to let me stay but they're worried something will happen. I've only got one more resit and my Head of Department has told them I'm excused. I don't understand why your Dean interfered.'

'I suppose she's worried about us.'

Millie sat down and put her arm round Phoebe.

'*I'm* worried about Priti. She'll be on her own if Vrishti's parents go back home.'

Millie tried to reassure her that Priti would be all right and told her what Jake had said about Deepal not being involved. 'I'm sure they'll release him soon and they'll all be together again.' She looked across at Jake and continued. 'I've been thinking it would be nice to have some sort of memorial service for Vrishti. I don't know when her funeral will be but that doesn't stop us remembering her.'

She had the idea when she saw the e-mail about Dr Armstrong's funeral which was to be held on the following day. She realised that Vrishti's funeral might take place without them even knowing, never mind being invited. After all, Vrishti's parents hardly knew them.

'That would be nice. I could come back for it.' Phoebe looked up. 'They can't stop me doing that.'

'You can help me organise it, Phoebes. We can do it by phone and e-mail.'

When Phoebe had gone back upstairs, Jake asked Millie whether she would be going home soon.

'No way!'

'Your dad might feel happier if you did,' he suggested.

'It's too bad. I'm staying here. Apart from anything else I want to carry on with the burial cart project.'

Jake looked pleased and then his face took on a serious expression. 'There may be good reason for being careful. Your dad might want some reassurances.' He thought for a moment. 'What if you come to my parents until Monday?'

Millie hugged him and ran upstairs to ring her father. Fiona answered and made it clear she was not happy.

'Your father is on a sailing trip in Jersey. I've had your professor on to me and I told her I can't get hold of him.'

'Oh dear, I'm so sorry, Fiona. It's a complete misunderstanding, there's no need to bother about it at all.'

'Well, if you're sure.'

'Absolutely, speak to you soon.' Millie cut her off and smiled. 'Yes!' she said to no-one in particular.

When Jake switched on his mobile to call his parents, he found a text message from Nige asking him to ring back. It was an emergency.

'Jake? Thank God you called, mate. I need your help. That policewoman, she's asked me to go out with her.'

'What? Like on a date?'

'She asked me straight out. Would I take her out clubbing? Tonight!'

'Are you sure, Nige? Perhaps it's a mistake.'

'Why? Don't you think she might actually fancy me then?'

Jake was about to suggest it was unlikely but thought better of it and asked whether his friend was going to take her, and if so where.

'Oh she was quite specific. It's a place in Newcastle called "Selene's". D'you know it?'

'Never heard of it.'

Nige paused. 'You haven't got a clean shirt I could borrow, have you?' He sounded desperate.

'I expect so, but you're not having the pink one. Look I'll come back. It's a bit manic here anyway. I'll be about twenty minutes.'

'Thanks mate.' Nige sounded relieved.

It was very quiet once Phoebe was gone and for the first time Millie was aware of being on her own in the house. When she washed her hair she left the bathroom door open so she could hear if anyone came in. She took her only decent dress out of the cupboard and decided on strappy sandals. This sudden decision by Jake and Nige to go clubbing had seemed very odd but she guessed they were trying to cheer her up. She was puzzled when they said they had a lift from a friend of Nige's but even more so when she opened the front door and saw a silver Peugeot with Nina in the driver's seat.

'Don't say a word,' muttered Jake, opening the rear door for her. 'I'll explain later.'

The journey to Newcastle seemed interminable. After the initial polite greetings no-one spoke until they had reached the city centre and they had found somewhere to park. Nina was wearing a simple gold mini dress that showed off her long legs. Nige looked rather strange in his old black jeans with a smart purple shirt hanging over them. His hair looked different and Millie could only assume it had been washed.

'I think the club is across the road and down to the left.' Nina pointed to a side street.

They moved off in a straggling group, Nina leading the way with Nige following and Jake and Millie at the back, sufficiently far behind for Jake to explain Nige's predicament.

'I offered for us to come. The poor guy was petrified.'

Millie was amused and slightly curious as to what the girl could possibly see in Nige. Granted he was a sweet person but he didn't seem Nina's type at all. She was even more curious about why she had chosen this particular club, since it seemed rather run down and definitely not in the smart part of town. The anonymous entrance was down an alley off a side street, with no sign, no neon lights to advertise its existence. They climbed down narrow steps into a dark bar area where the heat was overwhelming. It was not packed out but there were only a few tables and none with space for four, so they all went over to the bar. The girl who was serving Nige had shaved her head and pierced almost all aspects of her face. She was dressed in bondage gear that left little to the imagination and clearly Nige was distracted as he fumbled with his money, spilling the drinks as he handed them round.

Nina cleared her throat and turned to Nige.

'I suppose I should explain why I brought you here.'

Millie wasn't sure whether she and Jake were supposed to hear but the music was loud and Nina was raising her voice to be heard.

Nige looked embarrassed. 'It's OK. I wasn't doing anything anyway.'

'It's just that my boss asked me to come and have a look round. It's where Dani used to hang out.'

Millie gripped Jake's hand. She wanted his attention, not only because of what Nina had told Nige but also because she was beginning to get a feeling about the club. There was something unfamiliar about the décor and the customers. There were no groups of girls dancing round their handbags, no Newcastle chavs showing off after too many lagers. Even the music was a bit strange to her. No, the women were uniformly dressed in jeans or black leather, some in similar outfits to the girl behind the bar. She thought there were men but she wasn't sure whether they were simply women with shaved heads. She discreetly pointed them out to Jake and he remarked that the photographs on the wall were rather interesting and designed possibly for girls who were into girls rather than guys. They agreed they really didn't feel comfortable. However, it dawned on Millie that Dani would have not looked out of place at all, with her piercings, her black leather, and her tattooed friend with the motorbike.

'Was Dani gay?' Jake asked and Millie shrugged.

'What?' Nige had overheard him.

Jake repeated the question and his friend nodded.

'Look,' said Nige, 'it's pretty obvious this is some sort of "specialist" club, yeah? It's pretty weird, don't you think. For example, we are the only blokes here, or hadn't you noticed?'

Millie looked to where Nina was talking to the girl behind the bar. She was showing her a photograph and the girl was nodding and pointing to the corner of the dance floor.

'Her friends are over there,' said Nina, 'I'm just going to have a word.'

'Rather her than me,' said Nige. 'What d'you think of her then?' he asked Jake.

'I think, Nige, that she wanted someone to accompany her to this dive and you happened to be in the right place at the right time. I wouldn't raise your hopes mate.'

'Righto.' He looked disappointed. They stared across at Nina, sitting daintily in her gold dress amongst a group of leather clad women who were smoking and sipping pints. She chatted to them for some time and when she finally left the group several of them shook her hand.

'Can we go now?' asked Jake, who was feeling increasingly out of place.

'Of course we can. And thank you for your help, it has been most informative. I can take you back now.'

'We could find an alternative establishment,' offered Nige.

Millie and Jake both protested, but Nina stopped them.

'Well, we are all dressed up. Perhaps I can show my thanks by buying you a drink somewhere that's a bit quieter and, shall we say, more respectable!'

After wandering about for a while they found a sophisticated wine bar where they could hear themselves speak. They all carefully avoided the subject of Dani and kept to small talk. By the time they were back at Jubilee Street, they were chatting like old friends. Jake wasn't going to let Millie remain in the house alone and she was relieved he offered to stay.

As Nina left, she thanked them again for their help and requested they didn't discuss what had occurred with anyone.

'It's a bit awkward because I probably should have just gone on my own,' she explained.

Back in the car she admitted to Nige that she had really enjoyed the evening and she didn't have any proper mates, having only moved into town a few months previously. Nige said he would have invited her in for coffee if the flat had been half decent and she said she'd already seen how untidy it could look so it didn't matter. By the time she was leaving, Nige had discovered she was a Middlesbrough supporter and had offered to take her to the first home match of the season.

Next morning Millie was up early. Jake had tried to persuade her it wasn't necessary to go to Dr Armstrong's funeral but she insisted, declaring she wanted to pay her respects. She did not admit she had only been to one funeral before, and that was for her mother so it was not going to be easy. Nonetheless she was determined to go, if only to get inspiration for Vrishti's memorial service, since she had no idea how to plan it.

'But we'll have to get dressed up in suits and stuff,' Jake complained.

'No. It says in the e-mail that they want it to be a summer funeral full of bright colours. I think it will be really lovely.'

'Yeah, right, take a look outside, it's pouring with rain.'

Despite his reservations, Jake agreed to join her and set off back to his flat to get changed. By ten forty-five they were sheltering under the porch of the university chapel amongst a crowd of academic staff and students.

When they went in to the darkness of the interior the congregation divided. The staff and relatives graduated towards the front of the chapel while the students waited behind and took up the pews at the back. This created a strange pattern since the older mourners had only paid lip service to the request to wear bright colours, with the odd tie hidden under a dark jacket or a scarf tucked into a grey blouse. The students, on the other hand, had taken the request at face value and a sea of reds, yellows, oranges and blues bobbed about at the back.

Gary alone created a single distinctive figure at the front, sporting a pink T-shirt and white jacket. He sat motionless between Colin Hammond and Joanna's parents. Mrs Armstrong had been responsible for choosing the hymns and prayers but she allowed Gary to select and read a poem and Colin had agreed to say something too. A hush fell over the chapel as the coffin was carried in and the priest began with a prayer. When Gary began "Do not stand at my grave and weep, I am not there, I do not sleep…" he managed to keep going but many in the congregation, including Millie were tearful for him. She had felt in control until that moment. Her grandmother had read the same poem at her mother's funeral and it triggered the feelings of claustrophobia and distress she had felt then. The tears, she realised, were not for Gary or for Joanna but for herself.

As Gary sat down Colin made his way to the pulpit carrying a sheet of paper and stood clearing his throat. Those near the front could see the paper fluttering as his hand shook with emotion or perhaps nerves.

'Gary asked me to speak on behalf of the staff, to express our sadness at Joanna's ... I mean at our loss.' He looked down at the sheet. 'Joanna was a valued colleague and an excellent academic. Her research attracted praise and she was always pleasant.' His head was down and he was mumbling the words. 'I was very lucky to have known Joanna, as we all were. She will be greatly missed by us all.' As he read the last sentence his voice was breaking with emotion. He looked up and round the chapel. 'She didn't deserve it. She didn't deserve to die like that!' He stood in tears without attempting to move until the congregation began to shuffle and the vicar led him gently back to his seat.

'It's all right, mate.' Gary rubbed his shoulder. He was relieved but puzzled there had been no personal remarks concerning Colin's relationship with Joanna.

'No it's not! It shouldn't have happened. Not like that. She should have recovered. She shouldn't have died like that.'

His colleague was still sobbing as the coffin was carried out to be transported to the crematorium.

'I thought Colin was behaving a bit weirdly, didn't you?' Jake asked after they had emerged into the chapel close.

Only relatives and close friends were continuing on to the crematorium so they stood with fellow students in the drizzle until the cars had disappeared.

'Just a bit emotional. I think he fancied her,' replied Millie.

'I can't think why they asked him to speak. You'd think the Dean would have been a better choice.'

'It did make me realise I didn't want it to be like that for Vrishti's memorial service. I think we should just have poems and music.'

'You still keen to do it?'

'Definitely. I think we should do it as soon as possible. I've been thinking it would be nice to hold it in Wensleydale, at the site, because that's where she was found. And the police said we could go back on Monday.'

'It'll take longer than that to organise.'

'No, it won't. It's only for her close friends, I worked it out just now and they'll only be about twelve of us. It will be very simple and, above all, informal.'

'It had better not be raining then.'

Fortunately Millie found Phoebe was much more enthusiastic. She was already fed up with being back in Macclesfield and was happy to exchange ideas by phone and e-mail about how the simple service should proceed. By Friday evening they had planned a rough programme that involved everyone having time for a poem or a song. Phoebe agreed to contact their list of friends.

'What about Priti?' she asked. 'I think we should invite her. I could see if she can get Nina to bring her. She's supposed to be their family liaison officer so it's probably the sort of thing she does.'

Millie refrained from comment. Phoebe was often successful in achieving the improbable through her naïve approach to life. She was therefore unsurprised later when her friend sent a text message which simply said, "Priti coming with Nina and visitor!" Millie assumed she meant the baby. This was soon followed by an e-mail confirming that most of the students on the list had replied to the invitation. One was willing to sing, another suggested a song from a West End show that seemed apt, while a girl in Vrishti's tutor group had asked to read one of her own poems.

Millie did not know what to contribute but she had had an idea which involved tying ribbons on the tree in the corner of the field. She was unsure why this had occurred to her but it seemed a fitting reminder that would stay in position for some time, unlike flowers that would whither away. So, just as the shops were closing, she dashed into town and bought metres of satin ribbon in bright colours. When Jake returned from the department, the floor was covered in strands of yellow, orange and red. He laughed but spent the evening helping Millie prepare a programme entitled "Celebration of the life of Vrishti Bhatt" on the computer. It took them until midnight to get it right and Millie slumped exhausted on the sofa while Jake made coffee.

'By the way, if your father is happy for you to spend the weekend at my parents, my dad said he can pick us up tomorrow on his way back from town,' he called from the kitchen.

'No problem!' she replied, which wasn't exactly untrue, she told herself.

*

Gary had managed to keep going for the entire day, until he got to the reception at the hotel where Iris and Jim Armstrong were staying. He had tipped the men who carried the coffin and spoken to the vicar. He had survived the private ceremony at the crematorium. He had chatted politely to acquaintances of Joanna's that he had never met and remained civil to those friends who had been very rude to him during the divorce. Of course the whisky first thing had helped. Now, with the whole dreadful business behind him, he could drink the entire day into oblivion. He was on his way back to the bar for a third refill when someone tapped his arm.

'Hi there Gary, can I get you a drink?'

Colin Hammond was obviously drunk and Gary pushed him away as he tried to put his arm on his shoulder. The guy can buy me a drink if it means he'll go away and leave me alone, thought Gary. The man had made a fool of himself at the funeral and he was a liability.

'What do want, Colin? Just a chat? Chew over the fat, and put the world to rights, eh?' Gary meant him to hear the sarcasm in his voice.

'What d'you mean, Gary, old mate?' Colin stepped closer, leaning on him.

'Something you want to tell me about you and Joanna? If so, I don't want to hear it.' Gary pushed him away again.

'No, no, you've got it wrong Gary. There was nothing between us, nothing at all.' He lowered his voice and it was difficult to make out his slurred speech, 'But I know you thought there was. I know you were jealous, and I just wanted to say there was no reason to be.'

'Frankly I'm not surprised she wasn't interested in you. Still didn't stop you trying did it?' He turned back to the bar.

'Sorry mate, I know you must be upset.' Colin persisted. 'Listen, I know someone hurt her and I'll make sure that person is punished.'

Gary turned round slowly, 'What are you talking about?'

Colin lowered his voice and moved closer. 'Don't act the innocent with me. I'm talking about murder and I just want you to know I'll make sure that justice is done.'

Gary grabbed hold of Colin's lapels. 'Are you threatening me?'

'Gary! How are you, darling?' It was an old girl friend of Joanna's. Colin made his excuses and stumbled away but not before he leaned towards Gary and mumbled, 'I'll be watching you, Perkins, I'll be watching you.'

Chapter 11

Nina was in a hurry. Her boss had insisted everyone attend a team meeting at four o'clock in the incident room at the university. She wanted to speak to all the girls from Selene's who knew Dani and she had made an early start. Two worked in a supermarket in Sunderland and she had been able to interview them at work, not that they had provided much information. The other two were studying and it had been difficult to track them down. Nina had tried their homes first without success but finding them in the university was not easy. Eventually, after visiting the registry she established that one was abroad until September but the last girl was finally traced to the cafeteria where Nina gratefully sat and had a coffee with her. Sasha, who was a helpful girl despite her belligerent appearance, was quite forthcoming. Although she didn't know Dani well she did identify the friend who Millie had described, the one with the tattoos and the motorbike.

'That's Carmen. They're like really good friends.'

'And where would I find her?' asked Nina reaching in her bag for her notebook.

'I don't know where she lives but she works at the probation office in town.'

And so Nina was speeding away from the university. She had another couple of hours before the meeting and she wanted something concrete to report to the Guv, something to make him acknowledge her for once, instead of Mitch.

Ernie was already in the incident room reading the pathologist's report. Dani had died from massive trauma to her head. Evidence of pottery fragments suggested she had been struck by an amphora several times and fallen unconscious. The shelves had then moved to compress her and prevent her escape. The pathologist had noted that if it was a freak accident the girl had been exceedingly unlucky because even if she had regained consciousness she would not have been able to extract herself to get help. His conclusion was that foul play could not be ruled out unless there was evidence that the stack mechanism had been faulty.

'What have you got in the way of fingerprints?'

'Nothing helpful, Guv.' Mitch replied. 'The young man's prints obliterated anything on the button that operates the stacks. The prints of most of the department are in that room.'

'What about the pottery?'

'Nothing.'

Ernie rubbed his head and swore. 'It says here that murder cannot be ruled out unless it was a freak accident. So what've we got on the freak accident angle?' He was waving the paper at Mitch.

'Nothing, sir. We haven't got the technical report from the estates people yet but the university are adamant that it couldn't happen. Seems pretty unlikely doesn't it, sir?'

Ernie flung the file down on the desk. 'Bloody silly business but I'll bet you fifty quid it's not an accident.'

He sank into his chair. He was tired and fed up. It wasn't supposed to be as difficult as this.

'If it is murder then is it a double murder, Guv?' Mitch looked excited, the way Ernie had felt when he was a young lad with a serial killer on the loose.

'Steady lad, hold yer horses. It could be but we shouldn't rush into any conclusions. Ninety percent perspiration and ten percent inspiration.'

'Like you always say, sir, we should look at the facts connecting the cases. The girls went to the same university, they lived in the same house and they even studied in the same department. That's three connections.'

'No sexual attack, no robbery, so what's the motive then? Different MOs, lad. One was a knifing, one a squeezing to death.'

Ernie couldn't stop himself grinning, in part at the pleasure of showing how his young sergeant lacked experience in solving such a case.

'Actually that's not really correct, is it sir?' Ernie watched the boy redden. 'I mean the report says that the first girl was hit on the head and only stabbed later, after she was dead.' He paused but Ernie kept his silence, enjoying the moment. 'And the second girl was hit on the head too.'

Ernie liked to mentor the boy. 'So that's the MO is it? He hits them over the head then adds something else as a kind of red herring?'

'Yes, sir, that could be it.' He sounded unconvinced and Ernie decided to help the lad out.

'Look, Mitch. I've dealt with serial murders and they have a pattern, the same pattern. There may be coincidences but at the present time we'll treat them as separate cases, OK?'

'Right, Guv.'

'Now get me a cuppa will you? The team will be here soon.'

Ernie wandered round the lecture hall and stopped in front of the photograph of Dani. She was certainly a different sort to the Asian girl. Whoever the killer was he had a varied taste in women that was for sure. He had to accept the fact that the two girls might have been attacked by the same killer. He wouldn't release the brother in a hurry but he would consider the possibility that there was someone else out there who was responsible for his sister's death.

His troops were beginning to gather and Ernie relished the opportunity to show them what he was made of. Several of his men had been questioning staff and students in the department. When he asked them for their progress they had little to offer. He gradually became more irritated with them and was determined to show them how it should be done.

'Mitch, what have you got on the crime scene?'

'Not much, Guv. SOCO reckon all the prints are traceable back to people in the department who use the room regularly. Nothing on the pottery or the shelves.'

'Well, the keys are all accounted for. I checked that myself.' Ernie peered round the room looking for assistance. 'Surely someone's got summat that can help us. We're running adrift here.'

Nina waved a hand. 'I've been talking to the girl's friends, sir.'

'At last.'

'It might be nothing.'

'Heaven help us.' Ernie turned his back dramatically.

'No wait, sir. I spoke to a girl called Carmen. She was a special friend of Dani's.'

Ernie turned and smiled at her, feigning patience.

'And?'

'Well, she was pretty devastated by her friend's death. She was quite emotional so it was difficult at first to get her to open up but eventually she told me that Dani was very stressed about something … or someone.' Nina referred to her notes. 'To be exact she said she had been upset by her housemate's death and she had her suspicions about who might have caused it.'

'Did she say who?'

Now she had Ernie's full attention.

'No, sir, but she's convinced it must be the same person who killed Dani. She's a bit anxious for her own safety.'

Ernie couldn't hide his pleasure, at last something to go on. 'Bring her down to the station, lass. I want a full statement, and keep her here until I've seen her. This might just be the lead we need. Go on then, move!' He felt all powerful again. 'Mitch, those prints at the crime scene, d'you have a full list of whose they are?'

'Why?'

'Not why. Yes or no?'

'Yes, sir.'

'Good. Now think, lad. Is it not a possibility that one of these academicals or students might actually be our man?'

'But they've all been in quite legit, sir.'

'And they might also have been in there when the girl was killed. So get me a list of everyone whose prints were found in the room. Now!'

Ernie watched his sergeant leave. He was really enjoying himself.

'Now listen, the rest of you. Let's assume, just for the sake of argument, that the two murders are related. I want you to look for connections between the girls, apart from the obvious. We know they lived together and studied together but is there anything else? That means going back and checking their stuff back at the station and in the house.'

When Nina arrived back at the probation service offices, Carmen had already gone for a drink with colleagues. As a police officer it was not surprising that she recognised one of the probation staff sitting at a table with Carmen in the wine bar next door. To her surprise he offered her a drink even before she attracted Carmen's attention and told her why she was there. As Nina left the wine bar with Carmen, the probation officer called to her that she owed him a drink next time. Carmen, who had left her motorbike at work, accepted a lift with Nina.

'Is this about what I said earlier?' she asked.

'Yes, it is. We're interested in anything that connects the death of your friend with that of her housemate.'

'What? The princess?'

'Pardon?'

'That's what she called her. The princess. I think it was with her being Indian but maybe also because she was very prim and proper.'

'I heard they didn't get on very well.'

'No. Dani did her best to irritate them all. She enjoyed doing the rebel thing. I think she thought them all rather privileged and from well-heeled families.'

'But she was upset by Vrishti's death?'

'Yes, more than she let on I think. She was worried that she knew who'd done it. I told her to tell the police but she said she needed proof. I told her not to meddle but that was like a red rag to a bull. She loved to do anything she thought I didn't approve of.'

'When we get to the station I'll ask you to tell me as much about Dani as you can. I think you were her closest friend?'

'Yes. You've been to Selene's and met the girls, so you can probably guess how close we were. I'm not ashamed of us but my parents don't know and my workmates aren't aware either. I'd rather it stayed that way.'

'It's not a problem and it needn't be an issue, unless of course it turns out to be relevant to the cause of her death.' Nina hesitated as she parked the car. 'If, for example, Vrishti was also gay.'

'Oh no, I'm sure she wasn't, from what Dani said.'

Nina led the way to the interview room, hoping that Ernie had gone home. Unfortunately he had maintained his energy level by consuming a curry from the local takeaway and came in wiping his chin with the back of his hand. By the time he had introduced himself by remarking negatively on the probation service and made comments about her tattoos, the hostility was clearly evident in Carmen's face. Ernie persisted in referring to her as "sweetheart" and "love", embarrassing Nina more Carmen, who could and presumably would, look after herself. Ernie, who had not asked Nina about her visit to the nightclub, was reminded during the course of the interview and asked if Dani had picked up any men when she was there. Carmen replied politely in the negative but he pressurised her, suggesting that Dani could have started a liaison there. The girl's tolerance exhausted, she pointed out archly that it was not a club where one went to pick up men.

As it slowly dawned on him, Ernie was visibly out of his depth. His attitude was immediately suspicious and his questioning terse as he became increasingly rattled. There was no way that she'll be helping the police while he's in the room, thought Nina. By the time the interview was over, they had no more information than before Ernie had arrived. As she drove Carmen back to where her bike was parked, Nina wanted to apologise for her boss's crass behaviour, but professionalism prevented her. Instead she decided to show her confidence in her another way.

'Carmen, could I could come to Selene's with you one evening? I would like to be sure I've got everything there is to know about Dani and your friends may be more forthcoming if you are there as well.'

The girl was bundling up her hair and stuffing it into her helmet, 'No problem, we can go tomorrow if you like, anything to catch who did it. Meet me here at nine.' She smiled and climbed on the bike. 'And please don't worry about your boss. You forget, I work in the probation service, I'm used to bigoted old farts of policemen.'

Nina waved as the dark figure left the car park with a roar. She followed slowly, feeling the gloom descend as she drove back to her flat for another Friday evening alone.

On Saturday morning Millie felt a weight lifting as she locked the front door and joined Jake and his father. Jake let her take the front seat and there was something comforting about sitting next to Robert as he drove them to Wensleydale. If only her own father was reassuring in that way. But he wasn't dependable like Jake's dad. Someone to turn to in an emergency. More like a pain in the neck, she thought.

Dash rushed out to greet them and Bridget bustled about, leading Millie up to the guest bedroom overlooking the farmyard and beyond to Penhill. Little Toby dragged her across the landing to his bedroom where his toys were strewn across the floor. He insisted on showing her every one, demonstrating each in turn until Jake came up and rescued her.

'Toby, Millie doesn't want to play with Buzz Lightyear now.'

'Maybe later, eh?' she said, giving him a smile.

Toby let out a dramatic sigh. 'It's all very well but I've only got Dash to play with.'

'Later on, then,' agreed Millie. 'We'll come back and play astronauts later.'

'OK.' Toby looked pleased and ran ahead of them down the stairs shouting, 'We're going to play astronauts, astronauts, astronauts, Mum!'

'That's nice dear.'

Bridget was in the kitchen unloading washing from the machine. Millie immediately offered to help. She wanted to be part of this normal family, if only for the weekend and she was really pleased when Bridget handed her the basket of washing and pegs.

'There's a line in the yard. Jake will show you.'

And so Saturday was filled with the routine chores that she had missed for several years. Cooking with Dad consisted of microwaving or takeaways and cleaning was done by a vanload of ladies who descended on the house once a week. Bridget even asked her to pick flowers from the garden and fill vases to dot around the house. Finally Jake drove her into Hawes to pick up groceries. Millie immediately recognised the shop that she had visited when staying with her grandmother in the next dale.

'Does she still live in Swaledale?' asked Jake. 'We could go and see her.'

'No, she's gone to Harrogate now that she can't drive any more. She decided that it was impractical to stay. I go to visit her there sometimes.'

Even so, Millie would still have liked to have gone back to see the little villages snuggled down in the northernmost of the Yorkshire Dales.

'There's an Iron Age settlement in Swaledale,' Jake informed her. 'Maiden's Castle, we could go over there if you like.'

Jake was absently loading his basket with items from the list.

'No, it's all right,' Millie replied.

She wondered if her first boyfriend, Pete, was working at the vet's in the summer holidays again and whether he still walked up to Keld from Muker.

'Are there any good walks in Wensleydale?' she asked, examining a jar of pickled walnuts.

'Millions. Aysgarth Falls, Semer Water, Hardraw, Buttertubs.'

'Are there any good *long* walks? I've got my boots and it would be so nice just to take off for the day.'

'Mum will have some ideas. She knows everywhere round here.'

When they got back to the farm Toby was waiting for them, with his toys lined up in readiness. Millie spent the next hour in an intergalactic battle that left her exhausted from laughing. After dinner Dash curled up beside her in front of the television and she fell asleep while Jake watched the football.

Nina was getting ready to go out. She had chosen her clothes carefully and this time was in jeans. Her makeup was light and she wore no jewellery, she did not want to appear to be "on the pull". She admitted to herself that she was intimidated by Dani's friends and was more nervous now than she had been on her first visit.

When she arrived in the car park at exactly nine o'clock there was no sign of Carmen or her motorbike. She waited with the engine running to keep cool. It was nearly ten past when she heard the sound of the bike and saw the leather clad figure remove her helmet and shake out her hair.

'Sorry I'm late,' she said, without explanation, and climbed in the car.

As she took off her leather jacket and flung it onto the back seat, she revealed a skimpy top and the tattoos that extended across her back. She had a large ring in her nose, another in her eyebrow and with the heavy black eye makeup it was quite a transformation. Nina felt very conventional seated beside her.

Selene's was livelier than it had been on Nina's first visit. The tables were full but Carmen waved her across to the corner where Dani's friends sat. They squeezed along the bench to make room for the new arrivals. Nina quietly offered to buy Carmen a drink but she indicated the notes and coins in the centre of the table, explaining that they had a "kitty". So Nina placed her tenner on the pile and the others followed suit. A woman with spiky blonde hair asked her what she was drinking, grabbed the cash and sauntered over to the bar.

Soon they were on their third round and someone proposed a toast to Dani. As the evening wore on and the group became less inhibited it was obvious that they all knew her better than they had made out to Nina. They discussed how her family had disowned

Dani when she had told them about her relationship with Carmen. How she spent most of her spare time round at Carmen's flat. The fact that she had very few friends at the university. Only Carmen mentioned Dani's concern over Vrishti but the others agreed that she had been very distracted over the last week or so.

On the way back Nina asked Carmen if she would come to the memorial service that Millie and Phoebe were holding for Vrishti.

'But I didn't know her. I wouldn't have known who she was if I'd met her,' Carmen protested.

'I thought that there could be someone or something that jogs your memory. It might help.'

'Won't her friends mind?' she asked.

'I'm sure they won't but I'll let them know.'

Nina began to describe how Carmen could find the archaeological site in Wensleydale but eventually suggested that she drive her down herself.

'I'm taking Vrishti's sister-in-law, there'll be room for you.'

'If you're sure.'

It was three in the morning by the time Nina was climbing the stairs to her flat. She was tired but admitted to herself that she had actually enjoyed the evening. Sunday was her day off and she planned to lie in bed until very, very late.

Toby was always up early and Sunday was no exception. He was in Millie's room before eight o'clock, asking to play astronauts again. Jake came in to tell him to be quiet and the three of them ended up having a pillow fight. The sky was clear blue and the sun hot by breakfast time when Jake announced that he had found a suitably strenuous walk up Penhill. He moved the marmalade and spread the map out on the table. Bridget leaned over and pointed out West Burton.

'Such a pretty village, you'll love it.'

'Nice pub,' added Robert.

Jake traced the walk with his finger and Millie followed the route up to Penhill Beacon.

'But there's no path marked.'

'That's all right, it's an easy route,' Jake said. 'And it takes us to West Witton. Now that's got a nice pub.'

'And very busy on a July Sunday,' said Bridget. 'I've packed a rucksack for you.'

When Jake picked it up he pretended to drop it again, saying, 'Must be lead sandwiches.'

Despite Millie's protestations, Jake refused to take the dog so Dash lay on the doorstep and watched them leave.

Even the short walk down to West Burton was hard work in the hot sun and Millie insisted on spending some time looking round the village. Eventually Jake dragged her up the lane marked "To the waterfalls". There they sat in the shade and enjoyed the relaxing flow of the water into the deep pool. After a long uninterrupted spell of silence Jake hauled the rucksack on his back and hand-in-hand they made their way slowly up towards Hudson Quarry. Jake insisted on describing the settlement and field system at Burton Moor that Millie had seen on the map. Later she proudly pointed out the cloudberries amongst the heather and he said that round these parts they were called knoutberries.

Jake marched on at a fair pace and Millie was tiring in the heat. She was convinced that they must be lost as they ploughed on through tall bracken and stinking bog. But finally they reached the summit and Millie was able to rest as they admired Wensleydale spread out before them. But not for long. Jake seized her hand and pulled her along, protesting at every step until they reached a stone cairn.

'This is Penhill Beacon. It's supposed to be the resting place of the last Iron Age chieftain.'

'Wow, really?'

'Well, probably.' He sat down and started unpacking the food. 'Help yourself.'

Millie munched in silence.

'West Witton is down in that direction.' Jake pointed. 'They'll be burning "Old Bartle" there next month. We should go.'

'What's that?'

'Don't you know? It's like Guy Fawkes. They make like an effigy of Old Bartle and there's a procession through the village. Then they burn him.'

'So who was he?'

'I've no idea.' He bit into his sandwich. 'There's a rhyme we learned about it: "In Penhill Crags he tore his rags, at Hunter's Thorn he blew his horn, at Capplebeck Stee he brake his knee, at Grisgill Beck he brake his neck …" I can't remember the rest. It's something to do with Penhill, there are lots of legends about it. Like the Giant of Penhill.'

'The Giant of Penhill?'

'Yes, he was a gruesome character. He had this dog called Wolfhead that was right fierce and the Giant goes out and sees a girl tending sheep. So he sets the dog on the sheep but when she asks the Giant to call it off he tries to rape her.'

'How horrible!'

'No it's all right because she gets away but the dog catches her and she beats it over the head with a stone.'

'Good for her.'

'Ah, yes but I remember now. The Giant gets really angry then and he beats her to death.'

His voice dropped and he covered his mouth.

'That's horrible,' Millie said slowly.

She shivered and dropped her sandwich. The sun was still shining, the view was the same but the spell was broken.

'I'm sorry, Millie.' Jake put his arm round her. 'That was really stupid of me. I just didn't think.'

'What happened in the end?'

'He fell down a crag and was never seen again.'

They packed up and continued, trying to revive the earlier holiday mood but it never really returned. They didn't bother to go to West Witton but carried on along the lane towards a disused quarry marked on the map. By contrast to the first part of the day it seemed a gentle stroll back through the fields, beside the quarry and along a green lane. Here it was cooler in the shade of the trees. Millie could see Bolton Castle in the distance and on another occasion would have confided in Jake how she had gone there with her first proper boyfriend but today, when Jake pointed it out and explained what it was, she pretended that it was new to her and let him continue with a history lesson. A little further on Jake beckoned her into a field to what he described as the site of an old chapel that had belonged to the Knights Templars and showed Millie the tiny coffin of a crusader. She was just glad to rest before they set off back down the cool lane to West Burton.

'Time for a pint I think,' announced Jake, leading the way to "The Fox and Hounds".

*

Millie spent that evening in restless anticipation of the memorial service for Vrishti. She accessed her e-mails on Jake's computer and rang Phoebe three times. There was nothing left to prepare so she checked the weather forecast. It was going to be fine. She made her excuses and went to bed early, lying awake for hours going over the plans for the next day. She planned to be out early so that she was on site before anyone else. Everything was to be perfect.

She was up and dressed by seven but Bridget had to take Toby to school before Jake could take the car. Finally he offered to drop his little brother off on their way, which meant that they would be on site by nine.

'That'll give us a ages before people start arriving,' protested Jake.

'I want to make sure that everything looks nice.'

Consequently they waited for nearly an hour, occasionally talking but mostly sitting in silence or wandering around the site peering into the test pits.

Phoebe was the first to arrive with her mother who was staying to drive her back home afterwards.

'She's taking me back to Jubilee Street to pick up the rest of my things,' she told Millie.

'Can I get a lift with you? I ought to go back and see whether everything's OK.'

Her friend nodded.

'What's it like being back at home, Phoebes?'

'Horrible. They're treating me like a five year old. I don't know when they'll let me come back … if they let me. Next term I suppose.'

More students appeared and stood around awkwardly. The Dean came with some of the senior staff from the department. The friends were getting ready to start the service when Millie recognised the silver Peugeot with Nina at the wheel.

'Hey, it's Priti!' exclaimed Phoebe, running over to the car.

Millie watched as Priti emerged with Sunil in her arms, closely followed by Deepal and, even more surprisingly, the girl with tattoos.

'Who's she?' muttered Jake as the group walked towards them led by a beaming Phoebe.

'Dani's friend with the motorbike,' mumbled Millie.

'Isn't it wonderful? Deepal is back home now!' Phoebe's smile was triumphant. 'You must be so pleased, Priti.'

'Of course.' Priti was looking up at her husband, who was quiet but smiled back.

The Dean came over and drew the Bhatts to one side, sympathetically taking Priti's hand.

'Have you met Carmen?' asked Nina, looking from Millie to Phoebe and Jake.

'You're Dani's friend,' said Millie and immediately felt embarrassed by the baldness of her statement.

'Yes.' The girl also looked awkward. 'She told me about Vrishti. Before ... well, anyway *she* asked me to come.' Carmen motioned towards Nina.

'Well everyone's here now I think.' Phoebe smiled.

She was in her element and Millie was happy to let her shepherd the visitors towards the corner of the field by the tree.

In the distance Millie could detect the sound of a diesel engine and soon a white Land Rover sailed into view. Nige was driving and he had brought Dr Hammond, Dr Perkins, Chantelle and Ben. It was too late to chat and so the group was ushered towards where the others were sitting on the grass. They made an odd sight, a mixture of young men and women dressed in jeans, T-shirts, long skirts, and short-sleeved shirts. In contrast, Deepal was in a suit and tie, Priti and Nina wore brightly coloured saris, and Carmen was entirely in black.

Phoebe distributed copies of the programme and, in turn, each contributor did their piece. There was a young man playing guitar, a girl reading a prepared speech, another reciting a poem that she had written. Vrishti had been a quiet, sometimes shy, young woman but she had made many friends in the department and they were obviously affected by her death. To Millie's surprise Phoebe had actually written a poem herself entitled "Vrishti cared about the world". It referred to her friend's love of the natural environment and how she was considerate to everyone she met. It spoke about how much more she might have done and Phoebe was not the only one in tears by the time she finished.

Despite lying awake worrying about what she could contribute, Millie had nothing prepared when it came to her turn. She stood up and faced the group. All she could think of was the poem that Dr Hammond had read on Friday, the one she had heard for the first time at her mother's funeral. She knew every single word because she had memorised it and repeated it again and again to herself after her mother was gone.

'Do not stand at my grave and weep ...' she began and she kept going, tears streaming down her face but her voice getting stronger and stronger. Several anxious faces peered back at her but she didn't care and anyway she could hardly make them out through her tears. She felt calm as she sat down again.

Nina and Priti asked if they could sing a song that they had learnt from their mothers as small children.

They stood together and held hands, singing in beautiful harmony. Even though Millie couldn't understand the words, she felt the comfort that the lullaby imparted. Finally Deepal stood up and asked if he might say a few words. He spoke of his little sister and how proud he had been of her, how clever she was, how beautiful and kind. He would carry her in his heart always. At this point his voice began to crack.

'And if Priti and I are blessed with a daughter, she will be called Vrishti.'

Millie waited until Deepal sat down again before she initiated the final tribute. In turn each of them tied their ribbon to a branch of the hawthorn tree and, as an unexpected breeze moved across the field, they watched the strips of silk in yellow, red and orange leap in the air, as if Vrishti's spirit was acknowledging them for one last time.

Chapter 12

Millie knew something was wrong the moment they drew up in Jubilee Street.

'The front door's open!'

'Maybe the police have come back,' suggested Phoebe.

Millie didn't answer but rushed inside, Phoebe's mother shouting to her to stop. Once in the hall her excitement or anger or whatever it was that had propelled her forward disappeared as rapidly as it had come. What if someone was in the house? And not the police as Phoebe had suggested. Gingerly she walked round the ground floor but there was no sign that anyone had been in. She went upstairs creating as much noise as she could. The doors to the bedrooms were open, although she was sure that she'd shut her own. She peered in but it was as she had left it. Phoebe's room was across the hall and it seemed normal. Next was Dani's bedroom and she hesitated, peering from the doorway. It looked as though it had been struck by a hurricane. There were clothes, books and papers everywhere. She went to step inside but something crunched underfoot and she moved back to the door. Turning she went across the hall to Vrishti's room, hoping that it had been left in peace. But no, the chaotic scene was repeated. There were footsteps behind her and she turned to see Phoebe coming up the stairs.

'Mum says we should call the police.'

'Yes,' Millie said, taking out her mobile.

Phoebe's mother wanted them to wait outside until the police arrived but Millie persuaded Phoebe back into the house.

'Must have been a burglar who knew we were all away,' suggested Phoebe.

'No, don't you see? They didn't touch our rooms, only Dani and Vrishti's.'

'Perhaps they were disturbed in the middle of it.'

'I don't think so. I think they were after something particular, maybe something to do with their deaths.'

'You mean it was one of their killers?'

'I think they were killed by the same person. It's too much of a coincidence.'

'In that case you can't stay here. He may come back.'

'I doubt it. He waited until we were away didn't he?'

They had several hours to sit and ponder who might have broken in and all their suggestions sounded ridiculous. Phoebe eventually convinced her mother to come inside but she was obviously nervous and relieved when the uniformed police finally arrived, swiftly followed by Sergeant Mitch Turner who was accompanied by a "scene of crimes" officer. They spent an hour or so up in the jumbled rooms and then came down to ask where the girls had been over the last few days. The sergeant was puzzled that there was no evidence of any forced entry and asked who had keys. Millie and Phoebe were aware that the university accommodation office had a spare set but they didn't know what had happened to the other girls' keys.

'Do you agree that they shouldn't stay here in view of what has happened?' asked Phoebe's mother.

'Probably best to get a new lock, just as a precaution,' said Mitch. 'May just be an opportunist burglar found a set of keys. I don't suppose they'll be back.'

As they watched the police car disappear down the street, Phoebe's mother made Millie promise to have the lock changed immediately. As soon as Phoebe had collected her belongings and gone, she visited the accommodation office. The administrator was used to the problem of lost keys but when she heard about the burglary she showed genuine concern and immediately rang the estates people to fit a new lock that same afternoon.

Back at the house Millie surveyed first Vrishti's bedroom and then Dani's. Her initial interpretation of the scenes was one of chaos but as she studied the rooms in turn she could see a pattern. Clothes were strewn across the floor quite evenly and papers were distributed in the same way. It was as if the perpetrator had intended the place to look dishevelled. Surely if someone was searching the wardrobe they would push the clothes to one end or leave them in a pile on the floor, not throw them round the room. The papers must have come from Dani's desk but they were spread on the floor as if by a fan. The books must have been hurled from the shelves to reach the corners of the room where they lay. It was the same in Vrishti's room. Whoever did this wanted it to look random. The mystery was what had they been searching for and did they find it? She felt spooked and went into her own room, looking around for evidence that the person had been in there too. Had the cover been half off the bed like that? Had she left that drawer open a bit? She couldn't remember.

When the bell rang she looked down into the street before opening the door. A van with the NYU university logo was parked outside. The handyman worked quickly and soon he was off, leaving Millie with a bunch of shiny keys. Feeling more secure she stood on the landing wondering whether she should tidy up. The police had said that they'd taken everything they wanted so she started in Vrishti's room by hanging up her dresses and folding her jeans. Everything reminded her of her friend and Millie was finding it increasingly difficult to carry on. When the doorbell rang again she shot across to her room and peered out. This time she was looking down at the top of a fluffy white head.

'I saw you was back love,' the old woman said. 'I live at number forty-three, across the street. I saw the police were here and I said to my Jack this morning, I said that door's been open all night, it has. And when I saw you come back I thought summat's not right. Anyway I thought I'd pop over and have a word like.'

'Thank you,' said Millie. 'I think we were burgled.'

'You see!' The woman was triumphant. 'I knew it weren't right. When I saw that girl I said to Jack, she's not one of them students. None of them rides a bike like that.'

'A bike?'

'Big powerful thing for a girl to be riding.'

'And she was here?'

'Aye, she roared up, that's why I noticed her. I look out and in she goes. Few minutes later she zooms off again right past my window.'

'So she came in here?'

'Yes, love. I saw her.'

'And did she leave the door open, do you know?'

'Now that I can't rightly say but she must've mustn't she? It were open all night.'

'Well, thank you, Mrs …'

'Call me Vi, dear. Remember, number forty-three.' She pointed along the street.

'Thank you, Vi.'

'That's all right, dear. Let me know if you need owt else.' She turned and waddled back across the road.

Millie closed the door and went into the sitting room. Dani's friend with the tattoos must have been in quite a state to trash the rooms and to have left the front door wide open. Millie snatched up her mobile and began to press the code for the police station. She stopped mid-way and cancelled the numbers. Perhaps she should talk to Carmen first, find out what she wanted and why she left everything in such a mess. She didn't know how to contact her but she knew someone who did.

'Nina? Hello, it's Millie here. It was so nice of you to bring Priti and Deepal this morning, and it was good to meet Dani's friend, Carmen. I wanted to thank her for coming but I don't know how to reach her. Could you call me, please?' She finished the message by leaving her mobile number.

When Jake arrived early that evening, Millie told him what had happened and he insisted that she inform the police.

'I have. I rang Nina straight away.'

'And?'

'She hasn't got back to me yet.'

'That's because she's out with Nige.'

'What on a Monday?'

'He's taking her to a film this evening.'

'Seriously?'

'Yep. They're going to a "Star Wars" spectacular at the uni.'

'When does it start?'

'I don't know. Do you seriously want to go?'

'No, you dope, but I want to catch Nina.'

They half walked, half ran, slowing only when they saw the Peugeot parked outside the fish and chip shop. Nige looked surprised and slightly embarrassed when they burst into the flat. Nina was sitting watching television and he was obviously in the middle of drying his hair.

'We're just going out,' he said.

'It's OK, mate. We just wanted to catch Nina.'

Millie tried to sound casual as she explained that she wanted Carmen's contact details. Fortunately Nina didn't find the request odd but she didn't have a phone number for her personally, it would be in the files at work. However, she did tell her that Carmen frequented Selene's and they might try there for her or her friends.

'It was nice of you to drive the academics over this morning,' said Millie to Nige, quickly changing the subject before Nina asked her why she wanted to see Carmen so urgently.

'Chantelle knew why I'd booked the Land Rover and she told Colin Hammond and Gary Perkins. I asked Ben so it wasn't just me and them.'

'Well, it was nice of you to bring them.'

Nige blushed and looked at his watch. 'We'd better go or we'll miss the introduction. It's a special showing in the Student's Union,' he explained, 'with a talk from a "Star Wars" authority from the Mechanical Engineering Department.'

Nina caught Millie's eye and grinned.

'Enjoy!' shouted Jake as they left.

'Right, that's it! I'm going to the club to see if I can find Carmen,' Millie announced as soon as they were alone.

'Don't be daft, it'll be closed today.'

'It might not. Come on, we can get the train on the hour.'

Jake was switching on the television. 'There's no point, it won't be open.'

'Oh come on, it's worth a try.'

'Nope. You go if you want but it'll be a waste of time.'

Millie felt a pang of disappointment quickly followed by irritation. If he wasn't going to be supportive she would carry on without him.

'Fine, I'll be off then.' She picked up her bag and left, slamming the door behind her.

Most of the big clubs that Millie passed in Newcastle were firmly shut and so by the time she was walking down the narrow side street she was pretty sure that she'd made a fool of herself. She pushed at the door, expecting it to resist and staggered forwards when it flew open. It was quiet inside except for the sound of a slow ballad sung in a thin reedy voice. She hadn't expected to see Carmen standing on the tiny stage holding the microphone. She was wrapped up in her song until the end when she looked surprised at the burst of loud applause from her friends, giving a cursory bow before making her way back to their table.

Millie took a deep breath and walked over, waiting until Carmen noticed her.

'Sorry, but can I have a word?' Millie tried to keep her voice friendly.

Carmen seemed relaxed and, to Millie's relief, suggested they went outside. They stood side by side on the pavement, leaning against the wall of the club in the warm evening air.

'So what d'you want?'

The girl took a pack of cigarettes from her bag.

'I want to know what you were doing in our house yesterday.'

She flicked her lighter, then inhaled deeply, blowing the smoke out slowly without looking round.

'Nothing.'

'What d'you mean "nothing"? You admit that you were there then?'

'Yeah. I went to get my things back. Dani used to borrow my stuff ... DVDs, CDs, books, all sorts.'

'So you admit that you broke in then?'

She turned to face Millie and blew smoke out of the corner of her mouth.

'I didn't break in, I knocked. No-one answered. The door was open and so I went in. It was a mess. Dani's stuff was everywhere. I didn't know what to think.'

The girl stopped, drew on her cigarette, waiting to exhale before continuing. 'I was so upset I just ran. I realised afterwards that it must have been burglars but at the time I was really scared. I thought that it might be the person who killed Dani.'

'Why did you think that?'

Carmen leaned back on the wall. 'Well she knew something, didn't she?'

'Did she?'

'She died because of it. If I was you I'd be careful. Are you still living in that house?'

'Yes. Why?'

'Because it didn't feel right. Whoever messed up those rooms is well mad.'

'I think it was deliberately made to look like that.'

'Could well be. There were two rooms destroyed – who did the other one belong to?'

'Vrishti, but that could have been a coincidence.'

'Yeah, right!' Carmen threw down her cigarette and stamped on it. 'Is that all?'

'Yes.'

Millie watched Carmen turn and disappear back into the club.

On the return journey Millie tried to imagine who could be behind the phoney burglary but was no further forward by the time that she got off the train. To her delight Jake was sitting waiting for her as she left the platform. He admitted that he had been there for over an hour.

'You look shattered,' he said.

'I am.' She snuggled up to him.

'Well I thought that we'd do something different tomorrow,' he announced as they walked back to Jubilee Street.

Millie yawned, 'And what's that?'

'We're going with Nige to look at the chariot burial near Driffield.'

'Wow! Really?'

Jake looked smug, 'I knew you'd like it. Nige says he'll drive and we can see the new exposed part. It's really exciting because they found a piece of bone yesterday, and it could be human.'

Millie kissed him. 'Thanks,' she whispered.

That night, she lay awake listening to him snoring gently and felt really relieved that he was there for her.

*

Nige's driving was erratic at times and Millie wished that she had sat in the back with Jake. When they reached the site she jumped out to breathe in the fresh air. The site was full of activity with several large groups operating in different parts of the excavation. Nige proudly led them over to his patch and introduced them to a group of third year students who Millie recognised but had not spoken to before. The excavation amazed her in its size and depth. The main pit went down several metres and standing above it she could determine the outline of the chariot. There were wooden pieces in a rough square and indications of where the wheels would have been.

'Is it a grave?' asked Millie.

'Not sure,' answered Nige, 'it's difficult to tell because of the disturbed ground.'

'So is this what we might expect to see in Wensleydale?' Millie turned to Jake.

'Not likely,' laughed Jake, 'wrong terrain.'

'Could happen,' argued Nige.

'Don't start that again.'

'Well, I think this is amazing,' Millie said to keep the peace.

Nige excused himself to go and look after the students, allowing Millie and Jake to wander round the rest of the site. Although they weren't allowed to take part in the work, they watched fascinated by the meticulous way that every inch of the ground was investigated. There was an air of importance that pervaded every aspect of the site and when, in the early afternoon, someone picked up a tiny object covered in soil, there was no question of washing it. It went straight into a bag to be transferred to the conservator back in the laboratory.

'So why is it so different down here?' Millie asked.

'Colin is only interested in this work at present. He doesn't really care about the Wensleydale site.'

'Can we go back there soon?'

'I thought that you'd never ask,' he said with a smile, putting his arm round her. 'I do need to get work done on my PhD this summer.'

'Well I can help, can't I?'

'Of course.'

As they climbed back into the Land Rover at the end of the day, Jake rubbed his finger along the wheel arch.

'They did a good job on this.'

Nige went round and peered at it. 'Yep, it was the garage in town. They were told to get it fixed as quick as possible, no expense spared apparently. An insurance job I suppose.'

'Hmm, I suppose so.'

The moment Nige had dropped them off, Jake turned to Millie, 'You know, nothing was ever sorted out about the damage to that Land Rover. You saw the damage and I showed you the paint on the wall where Joanna Armstrong was run down. It matched the Land Rover paint, Jeff said so. I think I should say something.'

'Couldn't you ask Nige to mention it to Nina, sort of informally?'

'That's just it. I don't know whether to mention it to Nige, if you see what I mean?' Jake was looking at the ground.

'Hey, you mean that he might have been driving?' Millie tugged at his sleeve.

Jake didn't turn round. 'No, of course not … more likely to have been Colin Hammond. But he is one of the drivers.'

'And so are you, as well as Dr Hammond and Dr Perkins.'

'I know. Nige said he's sure it was one of them driving that day.'

'Well then, best go to the police directly,' suggested Millie.

She wanted to add *if Nige is a suspect*. He knew Dani better than any of them and he had been the last person to see Vrishti before she disappeared, as well as being the only driver in the log book the day Joanna Armstrong died.

They stood looking at the ground between them and Jake rubbed at a patch of dirt with the tip of his boot.

'Yeah, right.' He took her hand and pulled her gently along to the bar without another word.

The summer vacation had left the place strangely quiet now that most of the students had left. Those remaining were mainly postgraduates and staff, and even they were depleted with many of the archaeologists abroad on fieldwork. Ben was sitting alone at the bar and seemed pleased to have company. He leapt off his stool and offered to buy them a drink.

'Quiet in here now,' he said, sipping his beer. 'Gary Perkins was in earlier drinking pints in quick succession and then whisky chasers.'

'He seems in a bad way since Dr Armstrong died.' Millie was thinking about what Jake had said, that he was one of the drivers of the white Land Rover. 'Still I suppose Dr Hammond was just as bad last week wasn't he?'

'You mean when I had to separate them?' asked Ben. 'That was scary. I thought they'd gone but after you left he came back.'

'Who?' asked Jake.

'Colin. He came storming in and insisted on having another drink. In the end I had to take him home. He was in no state to walk even, never mind drive!'

Millie caught Jake's eye but he obviously hadn't registered the significance of what Ben had just said. She sat quietly while they chatted about nothing in particular until she decided to go back to the house.

'You have another drink. I've got things to do anyway,' she said.

But Jake wouldn't let Millie stay in the house alone.

'You're beginning to sound like my dad,' she complained.

On the way to Jubilee Street he gave her an ultimatum, she could either go home to her father …

'And Fiona? No way!' Millie exploded.

'OK. Come back to the farm or let me stay here.'

'I don't mind either,' Millie smiled, 'but it might be cosier here.'

'Right then.' Jake sounded matter-of-fact but he was grinning at her, 'I'll get some of my stuff later. I'll help you clear up.'

They worked until late, sorting and putting things away. First in Dani's room and then in Vrishti's. Neither spoke as they carefully, almost reverentially, lifted, folded, ordered and stacked the girls' possessions.

'We ought to pack it all up in boxes. Their parents will want to collect it.'

'No!' Millie couldn't bear to think of such a final act.

Her mobile rang and she looked at the screen. It was her father ringing for the third time that evening. On this occasion she answered.

'Hello Dad.' She listened patiently while he ordered, cajoled and then demanded that she return home immediately.

'No Dad, I'm staying here. I'm perfectly fine and there's no problem with me carrying on.' She looked across at Jake. 'I've got my project to do and my friend will be around.' She pulled a face at him.

'Your Head of Department has been on the phone again today. *She* doesn't think it's safe. She says that you've been burgled, that doesn't sound OK to me.'

'I promise you I'll come home the minute there's any problem. Bye.' She cut him off.

'Your dad?'

'Yep.' Millie carried on straightening the soft toys on Vrishti's bed.

'Look, it might be best if you do go home.'

'Nope.'

She turned her back to him and stacked books on the shelves. They worked in silence until the room was spotless. Millie wished that she had flowers for the window-sill. A foolish gesture she decided.

As they sat without speaking downstairs, Jake tried again but Millie shut him up.

'OK then,' he said, 'let's sort out what we're going to do now.'

'What d'you mean?'

'I mean, let's get some order back into our lives.'

'What about getting back to work for a start?' suggested Millie. 'Let's go to Wensleydale and get some excavating done!'

'Don't forget Dr Hammond's seminar tomorrow lunch-time.'

'So?'

It's about the chariot burial near Driffield. He's talking about Nige's work.

'And Dani's?'

'Yes I guess so.'

'In that case we'd better go.'

Millie yearned for normality and suggested they ordered a takeaway. She looked forward to an evening sprawled in front of the television as if everything was back to normal and what had happened in the last fortnight was just one of those weird dreams you have when you've tried too many vodka shots.

Millie woke Jake with a toasted cheese sandwich and a mug of coffee.

'It's not my birthday!' he exclaimed, sitting up and grabbing the plate.

Millie sat in silence watching him eat greedily.

'What's with you this morning?' he asked, wiping crumbs from his beard. 'It's only twenty past ... nine?' His voice lifted the sentence to a question as he consulted the clock.

'I let you sleep. It's a lovely day and I want to get out of here.'

'Really? So where do you want to go - as if I didn't know?'

'What?' Millie put on an innocent expression.

'Back to Wensleydale I suppose.'

'Only if you want.'

'You know we'll have to visit Mum and Dad?' Jake grimaced. 'Damn! It's Hammond's lecture this morning, we can't go.'

'Oh.' Millie was disappointed. She really was looking forward to being with Jake's family again.

'Unless we go later today and stay over at the farm.'

'Oh Jake, can we?' She gave him a kiss and then struggled up. 'Come on, we'd better get a move on if we're going to leave straight after the seminar!'

Millie told Jake to collect his things from the flat while she sorted her own stuff out. She was deciding what to take when the doorbell rang.

'Dad! What are you doing up here?'

Chapter 13

'I came to take you home, Millicent.'

Her father pushed past her into the hall and slammed the door dramatically behind him.

'Your Head of Department has told me what has been going on and we agreed we can't let you stay here on your own.'

'I'm all right. See, look I'm fine.'

He moved into the sitting room and seemed to fill the place. Millie was quite shocked by how concerned he appeared to be. Through the window she could see Fiona reading a magazine in the front of the red sports car and she wondered whether they had come especially or were just passing by.

'… so that's final!'

'Look, I'm sure the Dean doesn't want me to miss my fieldwork this summer. You ask her, Dad.'

'Oh I will. We're going there right now. She's expecting us. I've got the car.'

'What? Go in that thing? You must be kidding!'

'You can fit in the back.' There was something in his voice that stopped Millie short of resisting. She was sure the problem would be quickly solved by seeing the Dean and persuading her that she could stay. Reluctantly she crawled into the back of the car and nodded at Fiona without a word.

'Millie, darling, how are things? Your poor father has been so concerned about you, haven't you darling?'

She smiled across at him with her head on one side. His response was inaudible as they roared off down the street.

It was a long and excruciatingly embarrassing meeting for Millie. The Dean and her father discussed her as if she wasn't there and her overwhelming desire to walk out was only restrained by the fact that she was in her Dean's office. Finally the older woman turned to Millie with a smile.

'It's obvious that your father is concerned for your welfare,' she said. 'We all are but it is, of course, your decision as to what you do now.'

Millie could have kissed her. Instead she thanked her, rather too profusely, and explained that she wanted to continue her fieldwork in Wensleydale.

'Well, in that case we must find a way for you to do so.' Again she smiled serenely.

'I'm not letting her stay in that house on her own and that's final.'

Millie wondered whether to point out that Jake was staying with her but she wasn't sure of his reaction, since he didn't know about him and university rules didn't actually allow "subletting".

'I have a suggestion, Mr Sanderson, if I may. What if Millie was to stay with me at the "Deanery"? It's a big house, plenty of room and she would be safe there.'

Millie watched her father's face transform into a strange smirk that suggested he liked the idea of her in the "Deanery". She thought quickly while they both looked expectantly at her. She hadn't planned for this and she couldn't see what else to suggest. It would be a pain stuck out in the country on the other side of town but she'd be working in Wensleydale most of the time. Eventually she smiled politely and said that it would be wonderful. Her father's grin broadened, the Dean shook his hand and offered them coffee.

'No, sorry, we can't stop, I've got Dr Hammond's seminar ... and Fiona is waiting for you,' she hissed at her father.

'In that case I'll leave a key with Chantelle. You can come back after the lecture.'

Millie agreed without mentioning her planned trip to Wensleydale. She'd sort that later, once Dad had gone.

Fiona, who was waiting outside, was excited by the idea of the Deanery.

'It sounds so sweet.'

Millie assured her father that she would be moved out of the house by the end of the day.

'I'll know if you're not,' he warned, 'She'll ring me like she did before.'

'Yeah right,' she muttered as she sprinted off to the lecture theatre.

The hall was nearly full and Millie was pleased to see that Jake had kept her a seat. She spotted Nige down at the front, connecting the projector to a laptop computer while Dr Hammond fussed with his notes.

'Where have you been?' asked Jake as she sat down but Millie could hardly speak, she had been running so fast to get there in time.

'Dad ...' she gasped, '... the Dean.'

'Something wrong?'

'No, I'll tell you later,' she whispered as Dr Hammond clapped his hands for silence.

He had only just started introducing his talk when the door at the back slammed open and he stopped mid-sentence. Everyone turned round to see Dr Perkins swagger in clutching a large paper cup. He walked deliberately down to the front row and made a fuss of edging past several students to a spare seat.

Dr Hammond stood in silence watching his progress and, in a sarcastic voice normally reserved for students he said, 'If Dr Perkins is comfortable, I'll continue.'

He turned to look at the slide and then quickly back in surprise as Perkins responded with a wave of his hand.

'Go ahead. I'm sure we'll all be riveted.'

Hammond chose to ignore him and continued to describe what they had looked for at their site on the outskirts of Driffield. Millie took out her notebook. There would be no wood left after two thousand years but the metal rims of the wheels, things called terrets, which were metal rings, linch pins and strap unions had all been found in similar burials. They had identified the site by a rectangular area of soil, which was a different colour where the cart had decayed. He was just getting into his stride when Millie noticed that Dr Perkins was making a pantomime of taking the lid off his cup. He was pulling and tugging at it with exaggerated actions until finally it gave way and coffee flew across the front of the desk and onto the floor.

'Oh sorry mate,' he said loudly and insisted on getting out of his seat to mop the floor with his napkin, causing merriment among the audience.

Hammond waited for a few moments before marching over to the crouched figure and demanded that he stop immediately. He pulled at his arm and Perkins lurched back to his seat.

'Do you think he's drunk?' whispered Millie but Jake just shrugged.

'Are you trying to bore us to death?' called Perkins. 'Trying to kill us *all* this time?'

A few people began to shush him but without success. He continued to interrupt until he could no longer be ignored. Hammond strode over to the front row and Perkins tried to take a swing at him. Nige leapt up from his seat and bravely held them apart. The students in the audience began to cheer, stamping their feet, and chanting "fight!". There was no option but to call a halt to the proceedings.

'I will try again next week,' called Hammond above the uproar and swept out of the hall, leaving a few of the postgraduates, including Nige, to escort Dr Perkins away.

'Unbelievable.' Jake was laughing.

'Well I think it's rather sad actually,' said Millie.

'So where have you been?' asked Jake ignoring her.

As they walked slowly across the lawns to the main gate she explained what had happened. The campus was quiet and it seemed as if they had the place to themselves.

'... so I've got to move my things over there tonight otherwise Dad will be on to me again.'

'That's all right, I can help you move and then we can go and stay at the farm, at least until after the weekend.'

Millie went into the department to pick up the key while Jake searched for a vehicle that he could borrow. Millie was waiting outside in the sunshine when Jake drove up in the white Land Rover and proudly announced that he could have it until Sunday. It took them less than two hours to reduce all Millie's possessions to a pile of cardboard boxes, a few carrier bags, one suitcase and a rucksack. The Land Rover wasn't even full when they slowly drove down Jubilee Street. Millie twisted round in her seat to take a last look at the house, wishing that she didn't have to leave the final thing connecting her with Vrishti and Dani.

The Deanery was a large Edwardian house at the smart end of town. It was set back from the wide leafy avenue and so it wasn't until they turned down the curved gravel drive that they could see the front porch. The departmental party had been a barbeque and Millie hadn't seen much of the inside of the house. When she opened the front door and stepped into the hall she was taken aback by its size. There was a note in the envelope with the key which told her to make herself at home. Her bedroom was to be the one on the landing opposite the stairs and she should make use of the kitchen and lounge. Angela, she signed herself Angela, would not be back until late.

'Wow, this is very grand,' remarked Jake as he dumped her bags on the bed. Millie went to the window and looked down onto the drive.

'Yes, it's a bit old fashioned,' she muttered, turning to survey the room and pull the chintz curtains straight. 'I don't suppose I'll be allowed to change it.'

There was a table in the corner where she could put her laptop and cupboards on either side of the fireplace for her books and files. Perhaps it wouldn't be too bad.

She had packed everything she needed for the rest of the week in a small bag and she wanted to be off. They left a message for Angela on the table in the large contemporary kitchen to say that Millie would be at the Sweeting's farm until Sunday, adding their telephone number in case her father wanted to check up on her.

*

Ernie was beginning to feel out of his depth and he'd had this feeling before, many times. The local paper had picked up on the fact that the two girls were students together and they'd even suggested a connection between them and the woman lecturer who been killed in the hit-and-run. The report from the university stated that everything in the storeroom was working perfectly but what did that prove? It was a freak accident? In fact although he now had three unlawful killings, only one could be classed as a murder. According to the pathologist the murdered girl had been lying on her back on a hard floor, probably concrete, until the time that she was moved to Wensleydale. He had suggested a garage floor but then said there was a very high pollen mix in her nasal cavity, whatever that meant. The seed found in her hair was, according to the expert, from a fig. Well, there were no botanical gardens at the university, so the lads would have to search every garden and allotment in town to find the source of that particular clue.

'No, we won't,' said Mitch grinning, 'I've seen it done before. I'll contact the specialist suppliers and find out who in the area has ordered a fig tree in the past few years.'

'Well you do that, if it makes you happy, sunshine. Meanwhile I want you to check that girl Dani's mobile phone records. See who she's been ringing.' He paused. 'Actually while you're at it, check the Asian girl's phone too.'

'Righto, Guv.'

He sat down at his desk and started tapping his keyboard furiously. He looked round to check that Ernie was gone then opened the search engine and busied himself noting down contact numbers for nurseries.

Soon Ernie was back in the office. 'One of the problems with this case,' he complained, addressing no-one in particular, 'is that there are too many legitimate prints on everything. They have all been accounted for by staff or students in that Archaeology Department.'

He was studying a list of names starting with the Dean and ending with the cleaners.

'Footprints?' suggested Mitch.

'Bit of a mess really. There's nothing distinctive that we can work with, unless we ask all twenty three of them to bring in their shoes.'

'It would only be the shoes they wore that day,' said Mitch.

'Most of them academics don't know what day it is. Look, we don't have the resources, right?' Ernie was getting irritable and Mitch knew when to keep quiet.

'I've got a list of specialist nurseries,' he offered.

'What's that for?'

'Vrishti Bhatt, sir. I've contacted the three biggest so far and they're sending me a list of customers who have ordered fig trees.'

Ernie was walking slowly towards him, 'You are kidding me aren't you?' He was grimacing. 'And the phone list?'

'Oh that's done, sir,' he lied, reaching over to his desk and handing Ernie a few sheets of paper.

'I want the results not the list, the results of any matches.' He was already on his way to the door.

'I'll do it straight away Guv.'

Soon Nina was hunched over her keyboard doing what she liked best, detective work. So much of it was leg work but this was interesting. She liked to be systematic so she had listed all the Bhatt girl's calls first, since there were far fewer from her phone. She grouped them according to number and located the name of the recipient. Then she did the same for Dani Vincent. It took considerable time but at the end of the morning she had neat columns for each of the girls. Most of them were made to the university, mainly to other students in the department. Dani had made many more calls and none of them were friends in common. There were no odd calls that stood out.

Nina wrote a brief report and placed it in front of Mitch, who looked up absently and thanked her with a wave of his hand. She replaced the itemised calls in the appropriate files and then hesitated over the Vincent file. It contained copies of photographs taken from the girl's mobile phone. As Nina flicked through them she recognised her friend Carmen and other girls that she had met at Selene's, as well as some of the university staff, apparently at a party. There was one of Dr Perkins glaring at Dr Hammond, his hand in a tight fist. One was of Dr Hammond and a woman lost in each others gaze. Groups of friends with raised glasses, posing for the camera. She recognised the slight figure of Vrishti in a couple of them, standing chatting with her lecturers.

She wandered over to Mitch. 'These people with the dead girl,' she asked, 'this one's Dr Hammond, yes?'

'Yep, and he's with Dr Joanna Armstrong here, and here he's with her ex-husband Dr Gary Perkins.'

'So this is Perkins with Vrishti Bhatt? He seems to be getting a bit close there, doesn't he?' Nina handed Mitch the photograph.

'Yeah, a bit of a lad by all accounts but they all seem to be having a good time don't they?'

'Judging by her face, I'd say she's had a bit too much to drink. I think they're holding her up here.'

Picking up the next photograph Mitch waved it at Nina, 'Look at this one, the Dean is supporting her, she's almost falling over.'

'I wonder what the connection is between the two girls, and why would Dani Vincent take so many photographs of Vrishti when they weren't really friends?' asked Nina, putting everything back into the file.

Mitch was taking his jacket off the back of his chair. 'I'll go and have a chat with the staff. They may be able to tell us something about the party … if they weren't all too drunk to remember!'

The Dean was sitting at a desk covered in folders. Mitch noted the similarity with Ernie's pile of paperwork. He wasn't going to become a pen pusher. He enjoyed getting out and talking to people and he liked to think that he was rather good at it. Invariably he could get them to give him useful information which they didn't think was important.

'Hello sergeant.'

She smiled up at him and immediately he was back at school in front of Miss Meredith, his form teacher for three years at middle school. He could feel himself reddening.

'Do have a seat,' she continued, waving him into the high backed chair across the desk. 'What can we do for you?' she asked, putting down her pen and removing her glasses.

'I was looking at the photos, photos taken by one of the dead girls on her mobile phone.'

'Oh yes?' she replaced her spectacles.

'Ah no, I haven't brought them but I wanted to ask you about some pictures that were taken at a party. It looks like a departmental do where both staff and students were present.'

'That would be the end of term party at the Deanery. I hold one every year. It was quite a jolly do.'

'I wonder if you could give me a list of everyone who attended.'

'Of course.'

'And did you see Vrishti Bhatt there?'

The Dean smiled, 'Yes I do remember. She was quite tipsy.' She sat and waited. 'Is that all?'

'Yes just the list of guests.'

'Certainly, my personal assistant can print one out for you.'

She took him down the corridor to Chantelle's office where she left him hovering while the girl stood at the photocopier.

'Can I ask you something?'

She looked round, 'Yes?'

'Are there any botanical gardens round here, you know, part of the university?'

'There are flower beds round some of the buildings but that's all. Maybe more at the halls of residence. What exactly are you looking for?'

'A fig tree. It would probably be in a greenhouse.'

'No, nothing like that, not like Kew Gardens. Have you been there? It's really nice.' She handed him the photocopied list.

'Thank you.' Mitch was disappointed but decided to go back via the halls of residence anyway.

*

There were thirty-one guests and Mitch was quick to hand the names to Nina with a request to compare the guests at the party with the list of prints found in the storeroom.

'What's the connection?' she asked.

'Not sure but it might just be that the Vincent girl had made an association between Vrishti Bhatt and her killer. We should leave no stone unturned, as they say.'

She watched him leave and muttered under her breath that slimy things emerged when stones were lifted. She enjoyed this sort of job when she could see the sense of it but only when there was a hypothesis to work on. Both lists contained about thirty names and quite a few appeared on both, which was not surprising since they all came from the department. Among the students she recognised Jake Sweeting, Nige, Edie Spencer, Ben Hughes and Dani Vincent plus three more that were new to her. The staff included Joanna Armstrong, Gary Perkins, Colin Hammond, John Standing, Nancy Burns and Harry Green. If Mitch's hunch was correct then the list of possible killers had been reduced to eleven people … no, nine because Joanna Armstrong and Dani Vincent were already dead.

She was disturbed by a polite cough.

'Dr Carter, do come in.'

He had a large folder under his arm.

'Do you have something for us?'

'Yes I have.' He looked pleased. 'I've had a most interesting time with this case of Miss Bhatt's. Come up with some very intriguing findings. May I?'

He pointed to Mitch's desk and Nina nodded.

'Most interesting,' he repeated as he unloaded his paperwork. 'Look!' He extracted photographs of the young girl's body. 'Here, this is her back – as you can see there are the usual markings caused by her lying face up after she died. Nothing unusual there, except that her arms were down by her side, like she was standing to attention.'

'Mmm.' She couldn't help but stare at the photograph.

'If we look carefully you can see the skin is unbroken and smooth as if she was lying on a floor rather than rough ground, do you see?'

'Yes, but what's that line down the middle.'

'Well spotted. I wondered that myself. It could be due to a floor board or a joint in something. It is unusually prominent, which suggests quite a ridge. To be honest I have no idea.'

'But I thought you'd already given Guv a report. Mitch has got quite excited by the fig seed. He's trying to locate the tree now.'

'Yes, that's why I asked an expert to look at them but what he found most fascinating was the unusual amount of dust in her nasal cavity.'

'But hadn't she been in the soil for days?'

'Yes but this is different, she'd been lying in thick dust, and she'd been breathing it in, along with the pollen.'

'It's amazing what you can find out about a body.'

'My dear, that is nothing. That is quite routine. This is the interesting part.'

He produced a thin document which he opened at a page covered in figures.

'Let me explain. The mixture of dust and pollen seemed odd so I asked my colleague who knows about these things. He suggested that it wasn't normal house dust or the sort you get from the city. This is the analysis of the dust. It shows it is a mixture of debris, mainly derived from plant material and wood.'

'What does that mean?'

'It means she was lying somewhere where there is vegetation, not surprising in the circumstances you might say.'

'No.'

'But it is when you learn the age of it.'

'I don't understand.'

'My colleague thought the pollen looked old and suggested I got the dust carbon dated. I've never tried that before so I thought I'd give it a go. Well, it's fascinating. I went to see how it's done and I was very impressed.'

'And what did it show?'

'It proved,' he produced another document with a flourish, 'the dust has an average age of five hundred years. They say that part may be modern dust and the rest could be much older.'

Nina waited for Dr Carter to explain what the analysis meant.

'Wherever this poor girl was lying before she was taken to Wensleydale, it was very old and very dusty. Somewhere like a castle … or a church perhaps.'

Nina considered. 'What about an archaeological site?'

His face lit up. 'Ah no. But a good question. You see I took samples over in Wensleydale, if you remember. Nothing there of that age and the pollen is quite wrong.'

He took off his glasses and polished them, replacing them carefully on the end of his nose.

'Well, thank you Dr Carter.'

'I just thought I'd drop the papers by. I'm sorry to have missed your boss but I'll be back again with the results of the other poor girl soon. It is a most unfortunate pair of deaths.' He paused, and then added, 'Do we think they were related in any way?'

'I was going to ask you that.'

He shook his head slowly. 'No, nothing I have seen although I understand they shared the same accommodation and that does seem too much of a coincidence.'

'That's what I think but it seems to be the only connection. The girls seem to have been as alike as chalk and cheese.'

The doctor considered for a moment and then smiled. 'Well, they both contain calcium of course.'

He tidied his papers into the large folder and extracted a report, which he handed to Nina.

'All yours then. Let me know if you have any questions after you've read it all.'

He smiled at her and wandered back out into the corridor.

Nina studied the report on the carbon dated dust, making notes to help her understand the technical details. It took her most of the afternoon but when Ernie reappeared she was able to explain the results to him. He did not share her excitement, telling her to put the report in the file. She had to admit it didn't get them any further forward with the investigation.

Now Ernie was back she presented Mitch with her list of matches so her boss knew who had been doing the paperwork. When Mitch explained why he was comparing the lists, Nina could tell that Ernie was sceptical.

'Why should being at the party be relevant to Dani Vincent's murder?' he asked scathingly.

'Because she had photos and it might have been why she was murdered, you know … evidence.' Mitch replied.

'In that case,' said Nina, 'we should narrow the list down to those people in the photos.'

'Yes, of course!' exclaimed Mitch, 'Didn't you do that?'

Nina sighed and took back the list. Her pen hesitated over Nige's name then she moved down the list circling Jake, Ben, Gary and Colin, before offering it back to Ernie.

'OK,' said Ernie slowly, studying the list, 'so Dani Vincent takes a photo putting the murderer with his victim. She tries to blackmail him, so he kills her. Is that the idea?'

'Maybe.' Mitch didn't sound sure.

'If that is the case,' said Nina, 'what was the motive for the first murder?'

Mitch didn't answer.

'Right lad, it looks like you better get out there, talk to these four and find out their relationship with the victims. Remember, motive and opportunity. See what they were up to on the evening when Dani Vincent died.'

'Yes sir!' Mitch jumped up and left.

'Meanwhile, petal, let's get the kettle on shall we?'

Nige had been waiting patiently in the departmental office until the Dean had finished her meeting with the young detective sergeant who had obviously impressed Chantelle. She described in detail the conversation she had with him about fig trees.

'Why did he want to know about them?' Nige asked, more out of politeness than with a genuine interest.

'I don't know exactly,' she said, lowering her voice, ' but he said it was to do with the murders.'

Nige eyed the young policeman enviously when he came into the office with the Dean. He worked with Nina all day every day, although from what she had told him, she had little time for him.

'Oh, Detective Sergeant,' began Chantelle, playing with her hair, 'why was it you were asking about greenhouses, again?'

'I'm looking for a fig tree,' he replied, self-consciously. 'It could be at the site of a murder.'

Chantelle looked knowingly at Nige.

'Nigel?' The Dean was staring at him. 'Did you want to see me?'

'Yes Professor McGrath.' He could feel himself turning pink. 'I would like to talk to you about the Land Rover.'

She looked serious. 'You'd better come to my office.' She peered at him over her glasses, studying him as he took the hard seat opposite her. He gulped and began the speech he had prepared the night before, repeating it without stopping for breath.

'Are you saying that you are not responsible for the damage?' She looked sceptical.

'No, I'm not responsible and I consider it an injustice that I'm being accused of doing it. I'm a scapegoat. Yes, a scapegoat,' he repeated indignantly.

'But your name is the only one in the logbook, Nigel. Who else could have driven it?'

'I've worked out it was done on the eleventh and the only people who could have used it are Dr Hammond or Dr Perkins.'

'But they haven't come forward and they've had plenty of time to respond to the notices I've sent out.'

'Yes.'

There was nothing more Nige could say. He was effectively accusing his supervisor of lying. His Head of Department appeared to be considering what to do.

'Right. I'll speak to them and sort this out.' She pulled the phone towards her and lifted the receiver. 'Leave it to me Nigel,' she added, nodding at him.

'Ah, yes, right then.' He realised he was being dismissed and headed for the door, content in the knowledge that justice would be done.

Gary Perkins was not surprised to receive a call from Angela McGrath. He had missed a couple of meetings and some of the students were complaining about him. He was ready to tell her to her face how unimportant it all seemed now. But when he approached her office he could hear Colin Hammond's voice and hesitated at the door.

'Come in, Gary, come in,' called the Dean.

'I can come back later.'

'No, I want to see you both, come in.'

Gary lowered himself into the only free chair, folding his arms and glaring at his colleague. Hammond sat placidly smiling into the distance.

'Thank you both for coming. I'm trying to find out, once and for all, who damaged the new Land Rover. Nigel Featherstone has come to see me to complain that he is being made a scapegoat, insisting that it was not his fault. So I am asking both of you, as the only other possible culprits,' she smiled in an apologetic way, 'to let me know who it was.' The two men sat in silence. 'It appeared to have been damaged on the eleventh.'

It was like a punch in the chest for Gary. The day when Joanna was run over. 'It wasn't me,' he responded, trying to remain dignified.

Colin Hammond shook his head. 'Not me.'

'But someone must have been responsible,' the Dean insisted. 'Did either of you drive the vehicle when it was first delivered?'

'I drove it on the Wednesday after it arrived, to test it out,' admitted Hammond, 'I went over to Wensleydale with it before the staff meeting.'

'When was that?' demanded Gary.

'The staff meeting was on the eleventh,' said the Dean quietly.

'But it wasn't damaged when I brought it back,' protested Colin.

'Are you sure?' the Dean asked sharply. 'I really would like to know the truth. It doesn't affect your ability to drive College vehicles you know.'

'Are you calling me a liar?' Hammond rose, leaned on the desk and said slowly, 'because I've had enough of this. Read my lips, *I did not damage your precious Land Rover.*' He slammed the door on his way out.

'I'm sorry you had to experience that, Gary,' the Dean said with a sympathetic look.

He nodded while his mind was racing. Hammond had dented the vehicle on the night Joanna had been run down. Was it possible the two incidents were connected? He had to think about this and he had to talk to Nige Featherstone about it. He could do with a quick swig from the bottle in his desk drawer.

'Thanks, Angela. Got to go. Something to do.'

Back in his office he felt more like his old self, in control, analysing the situation. He looked up the number for the postgraduate office and made the call.

Nige was expecting to hear from his lecturers after what he'd said to the Dean. He knew he'd be in trouble the moment she suggested speaking to them. He didn't want to drop anyone in it but he wasn't going to carry the can for someone else. Perkins wanted to have a chat, all friendly like. Could he pop down?

'Hello Nige old chap. I just wanted to get the facts straight over this damage to the departmental vehicle. Wondered how you knew when it happened, that's all.'

'It must have been in the first week we got it because it was fine on the Tuesday when I took it to Wensleydale and by the Thursday there was a damn great scratch along the side.'

'Like it had hit a wall or a tree?'

Nige hesitated, worried about where this was leading. He recollected the conversation in the bar when Jake had told him about the paint. At the time he'd been quite convinced.

'Would you like a drink? I've got some scotch here somewhere.' He rooted about in his desk, produced a bottle and poured a tot into a paper cup, offering it to Nige, who sipped politely.

'I just wanted to get to the bottom of the mystery,' continued Perkins, drinking directly from the bottle. 'Do *you* think it hit a wall?'

Nige was trying to work out whether Perkins thought he was responsible for damaging the vehicle. If he was then he might be connecting him with Joanna Armstrong's death.

'I didn't hit a wall,' he insisted.

'No, Nige, I don't think you did,' he said slowly.

Now he was confused. If Perkins knew he wasn't the culprit, did it mean that he had done it himself?

'I think I know who did it,' he continued, gesticulating wildly with the bottle, 'and I think I know where!'

The scotch was beginning to have an effect. Nige couldn't understand how the man knew about the paint. 'I don't think the paint from Redmire proves that the Land Rover was there, Dr Perkins. Jeff told me it wasn't conclusive when I asked him about it.'

Perkins stared across at him for a while and then struggled up from his desk. 'Well thank you for being so helpful, better get on now, eh?'

Nige followed Perkins out of his office and saw him disappear into the lift. The lights indicated that it stopped on the second floor and Nige took the stairs, reaching the laboratory in time to see his lecturer in deep conversation with Jeff.

Nige waited until he had gone. 'Jeff, what was that all about?'

The analyst was standing with his hands in the pockets of his grubby white coat. 'He wanted the results of the work I did for Jake. I told him it was just a white paint sample. It only proved it was from a white car.'

'You told him the paint on the wall where his wife was run down matched the paint from a white vehicle?'

'Yes. Is that a problem?'

Chapter 14

Once Millie was settled in at the farm she felt both safe and relaxed. She slept so well she only woke when Toby came in to see her before going to school. He seemed delighted that she had come to stay and made her promise she would play with him at the weekend. She dressed quickly and hurried down stairs, where Jake was helping Bridget sort out his young brother's packed lunch. Toby left reluctantly with his mother and Jake cooked breakfast on the Rayburn. It was a bright day and the kitchen door was open to allow the heat from the stove to escape. Occasionally a hen would wander in and Jake would shout at it, flapping a tea towel until it retreated.

When Bridget returned from the school run, she made them a picnic lunch and they set off for the site. This time Millie worked alongside Jake as he carefully exposed the next layer of the main pit. He was an excellent teacher, explaining everything he did as he went along and encouraging her to attempt the different techniques he demonstrated to her. Millie tried to remember what Nige had said about the clues that would indicate a chariot burial. Metal rings, stained soil, beads, human remains. So far their finds had been limited to a dagger but that must suggest an important burial site surely?

'Not necessarily.' Jake was carefully dusting off a stone and examining it. 'It could just be a weapon dropped during a conflict. You shouldn't get too excited by that.'

They were squatting side by side working on a corner of the main pit.

'D'you think the soil in the middle is a slightly darker colour than the rest?' she asked, sitting back on her haunches.

'Possibly but that's probably because it's damp.' Jake didn't look up.

'Don't you want it to be a chariot burial site?' She was exasperated by his indifference.

'Only if it is. It's my PhD at stake here and I can't make it something that it's not.' He handed her the pebble. 'Now stick that in the water and give it a good swish round.'

They worked in silence, stopping to examine the sieve, ensuring Jake checked before Millie disposed of anything. They rarely conversed except to discuss an aspect of the work but Millie enjoyed the fact they didn't need to speak all the time that they were together.

She surveyed their work with pleasure as they ate their sandwiches and casually asked, 'Wouldn't the soil in the middle be dried out by now?' Jake pretended to aim a punch at her but she continued, 'It's been hot all morning and it hasn't rained for days.'

'Maybe. I don't know for sure.'

'Fine researcher you are!' She ducked as he threw an apple core at her.

'We'll see what happens when the next layer comes off.'

They were still on the last corner when a Ford Focus appeared at the gate.

'Great! It's Hammond. What does he want?' muttered Jake, standing up and stretching.

Millie sat back on the edge of the pit and waited.

'Hi there!' he called, picking his way over to them. 'Working hard, I see.'

'Thought we'd get on,' replied Jake.

'So how's progress?'

'We're down to the next layer, with nothing to report. We're finishing off that corner and then we'll start again.'

Millie could not resist the opportunity to ask, 'I was wondering about that darker patch in the centre, do you think it might be some sort of discoloration?'

The older man immediately jumped down into the pit and examined the soil. First he took a sample between his fingers, he sniffed it and rubbed it, then he took a trowel and scraped at it.

'You might have something there.' He pulled off his jacket and threw it to one side, rolling up his sleeves. 'Let me carry on with this. Perhaps you could check on the other pits for me, Jake?'

Jake didn't answer but strode off to the nearest pit with Millie in pursuit.

'Sorry, I didn't mean him to take over, I just thought he might know whether it was important or not.'

He continued to poke about without comment, peering across to see what Colin Hammond was up to. Finally he said, 'Yeah, well that's typical of him, keeping anything interesting for himself. You know that Nige wrote the entire lecture for him, the one that was such a shambles. Anyway we might as well get work done on this one now.'

An hour or so later a shadow fell across their pit.

'I'm off now, got to get to a meeting. You carry on if you like but let me know if you find anything. I'll be back tomorrow.'

'Yes, sir, of course,' answered Jake, making a rude gesture at his supervisor's back as he walked to his car.

'So where are his records?' asked Millie when the car had left and they were back at the main pit.

'I don't suppose he's done any, he's a lazy git. Look at the state he's left it in. It'll take the rest of the day to sort it out and record it.'

They worked hard until Millie reminded Jake that he had promised to be home by six. Toby, being young, had his dinner early, so they were seated at the large kitchen table by six thirty, enjoying an informal family supper.

'Are you back there tomorrow, like?' asked Robert, piling his fork with meat and vegetables.

'Yep, it's getting a bit more interesting now.'

Millie kept quiet, conscious she was responsible in part to the increasing interest but also the unwanted interference from Dr Hammond.

'Toby told me it's his last day at school tomorrow,' said Millie, changing the subject. 'Are you looking forward to the holidays, Toby?'

'Don't!' said Bridget. 'He's a nightmare when he's at home under my feet.'

'I am not!' objected Toby. 'I'm going to help Dad with the animals.'

'Is that right?' Jake asked his father, who shrugged.

'If he says so, happen he is.'

The rest of the evening they watched television. Jake didn't say much and Millie could tell that he was still smarting from being dismissed from his excavation, and it was her fault.

She was dreading the next day but he seemed in good spirits over breakfast and teased Toby about the present he was taking for his teacher.

'You be careful she doesn't get the wrong idea, our Toby. She might think you fancy her, giving her chocolates.'

'But everyone gives her sweets,' and then he added seriously, 'anyway she's married.'

Millie was still laughing as they set off for the site. It was sunny again and promising to get hotter.

'Millie, I'm sorry I was a bit of a misery yesterday. I shouldn't have let Hammond get to me.'

'It's all right.'

'Is that it?'

'What d'you mean?'

'Well, that was supposed to be an apology. I thought that the making up was supposed to be the best part.'

'You!' Millie nudged him and he pretended that she had forced him to swerve into the middle of the road.

'Careful!'

When they arrived Millie automatically studied the dark stain in the pit. Jake stood beside her.

'I think you're right,' he sighed, 'and it could be rectangular.'

'Does that mean what I think …?'

'Hold on. It could be but without anything else it would be difficult to prove.'

'In that case, we'd better get moving.'

They worked systematically, with Jake sieving and examining while Millie recorded every detail meticulously. Several hours passed without incident until Jake picked something out of the sieve.

'What's that?' asked Millie. His fingers traced a circle as he tried to remove the soil.

'It looks like a ring but it could be a bracelet.'

'Or a terret?' suggested Millie.

'What?'

'It's a circular piece of metal to join harnesses together. Shall I wash it for you?'

'No, no, no! I think that we had better wait until Hammond arrives.'

He suggested lunch but Millie was so excited she could hardly eat and kept asking to have another look at their find. It was about five centimetres in diameter and so covered in soil and debris they couldn't tell what it was made of. She wandered about impatiently while Jake ate his sandwiches and was about to suggest they carried on when she heard an engine and saw Hammond parking his car at the gate. When Jake showed his supervisor the ring, he took it and turned it over, rubbing at the rough surface.

'Very interesting, very interesting,' he repeated to himself. After a pause he looked up at Jake and told him that no further work should take place until he was able to study the find properly.

'I thought it might be a terret,' offered Millie.

'Did you? Well, we'll see in good time. I suggest that you two take the afternoon off. And we'll see what we've got on Monday.'

Millie read the disappointment in Jake's face although he said nothing. His mouth tightened as he picked up his things. Millie followed him to the Land Rover.

'Bloody typical,' he began, 'as soon as there's anything interesting he takes over again.'

'It's only till Monday. It'll be exciting to see what it is then. What do you think he'll do with it?'

'I dread to think,' answered Jake, climbing into the driver's seat. 'After all, look what happened to the dagger that Edie found.'

Colin Hammond waited until the diesel engine was just a faint sound from the main road. He wanted to savour the moment and take his time. His interest had first been aroused by the dagger that Edie had found on the site. It was definitely Iron Age and it meant there was a good possibility that someone important had been buried here. If the metal ring was also identified as that period, then it could be the first evidence for such a burial so far west in Yorkshire. Now he wanted to find a chariot. He smiled to himself as he worked on the centre part of the pit, gently clearing the area where Jake had discovered the ring. There would be a good eight hours of daylight left and if the weather held he would stay in the car, catch a few hours sleep and start again at dawn. The weekend stretched out before him as he stepped back and took a swig from the coke bottle. The vodka gave it a pleasant kick. He bit into a cheese sandwich and then continued with the sieving and sorting, stopping only to take another mouthful and a drink from the two litre bottle.

'So what are your plans for tomorrow?' Bridget was busy ironing after supper. 'I only ask because your father and I thought we'd take Toby into Richmond. He needs new trainers.'

'It's OK, we're going for a walk, aren't we, Millie?'

'If you're sure? You're welcome to come. And then I thought we'd invite Joan over for tea,' added Bridget.

'No, sorry, we planned to be out all day.'

'Oh well, another time.' She struggled through the door with a pile of clothes in her arms.

'I wouldn't have minded going to Richmond,' said Millie.

'It's not that, it's Aunt Joan. She never stops talking and she's got a horrible little dog that's really old and pees on everything. You don't want to be there.'

'So where *are* we going then?'

'Not sure, depends how energetic we feel.'

They studied the map during the evening and Jake persuaded Millie to try a circular walk that would take them from Wensleydale to Coverdale and back via Bishopsdale. She didn't admit to Jake that she had never walked fourteen miles before and he didn't ask.

Toby didn't let Millie lie in on Saturday morning. Opening one eye, she was greeted with his rosy face squinting at her, asking if she was awake. Breakfast was a chaotic affair with Bridget trying to organise her family while Toby sought attention and Robert read his paper. Eventually the door closed behind them and the house fell still.

When they stepped out into the sultry morning Millie was grateful that she had decided to wear shorts, even though she was worried that woollen socks and walking boots accentuated her skinny legs. Jake insisted on carrying everything in his rucksack including jumpers, waterproofs and enough food for several days. So Millie was left with the map and a compass, even though Jake knew the way. They drove through Aysgarth and turned down the hill past the church to the river Ure. The car park was already filling up with walkers and they followed an older couple as they went back over the bridge, stopping to watch the water cascading over the rocks below.

Jake pointed out Yore Mill on the other side that had been used for cotton in the old days and led her up the steps into the churchyard, behind the church and across fields into a wood. Although it was shady the air was still and Millie was glad to be out in the open again and walking through fields above the river. The path was leading them away from the water and onto a road but Jake soon pointed out a stile that took them back in the direction of the Ure.

'Stony Stoop Lane,' he announced.

'What?' Millie consulted her map.

'Stony Stoop Lane,' he repeated. 'It takes us down to Slapstone Wath.'

Millie laughed as she traced the lane and identified Slapstone Wath on the map.

'You can get to Redmire from here.'

Millie was tempted to cross on the stepping stones but she didn't want to spoil their day with thoughts of Dr Armstrong's cottage on the other side of the river.

It was easy terrain and Millie was enjoying the walk, except for the flies that followed them relentlessly. Their progress was punctuated only by ladder stiles until finally they went down the man-made steps to Redmire Force. Jake suggested they stopped for a while.

Millie listened to the sound of water tumbling down the rocks and dispersing back into a gentle river. A dipper was moving quietly along the water, hopping from stone to stone. There was no-one around and Millie would have happily stayed there all day. A splash downstream made her start.

'A fish,' said Jake stroking her hair and she looked up at him and smiled.

Colin Hammond tried to turn away from the bright sun that was shining through the windscreen. His legs, bent double while he slept, ached when he tried to straighten them and he could hardly walk as he struggled out of the back of the car. He rifled through the glove compartment and found a bar of chocolate, biting into it appreciatively, despite the fact that it had melted into the wrapper. He washed it down with warm cola and made a mental note to buy more. His head was strangely light as he made his way back to the pit but soon he was engrossed in the job. Progress had been good, although he knew he was cutting corners. He wasn't keeping proper records and his finds were heaped in the corner of the pit. So far he had uncovered several pieces of metal that could be part of a harness and he was brushing at an object that he was hoping would prove to be a decorative stud. He mused on the impact that his find would make. He imagined himself presenting his work to a large international convention, receiving praise and perhaps an award. Soon he was compiling his acceptance speech for the Duxbury Medal.

By mid-day Hammond had uncovered a piece of metal that was clearly bigger than the other artefacts. He was fairly certain that it was part of an iron tyre and he worked on, knowing he should not continue without proper assistance from conservationists. He just wanted to be sure, to be certain this was a chariot burial and that the press would interview him about it. Certain that he would appear on the local news and "Timewatch" and he would be involved in the reconstruction when it was televised. Finally hunger forced him to drive into the village to buy more drink and biscuits. It took him no more than twenty minutes but by the time he started work again he was not alone.

Reluctantly Millie left the waterfall and they carried on until the path led them away from the river and up an overgrown lane. It took them towards West Witton, where Jake was keen to show her one of his favourite pubs. The bar was cool and they sat inside sipping their pints of Black Sheep bitter. Millie studied the map and was disappointed to see they were only about a quarter of the way round the route.

'At this rate we won't get back until about seven o'clock!'

'Good,' said Jake. 'That means we'll miss Aunt Joan and her mutt.'

They left the village and started up a narrow lane to Melmerby. They walked uphill steadily until Millie begged that they stopped for lunch but Jake insisted that they waited until they were over the summit. The climb seemed interminable but finally they were at the top and joining an unfenced road leading downhill. The views over Coverdale were spectacular and, as they ate their sandwiches, Millie used the map to identify the peaks of Flamstone Pin and Roova Crags, in the distance. There was a gentle breeze on the fells and they were soon striding down into Melmerby and along to Carlton. Leaving the village they joined the track that Millie traced on the map right across Carlton Moor back to Bishopsdale. It was rough country and Millie was getting tired, finding excuses to stop and admire the view as they climbed up past an old shooting lodge. Jake suggested they had a good rest at the top, opening the rucksack to find the cake that Bridget had promised to put in for them.

When they finally continued down the track they were met with clear views over Wensleydale. Crossing a small river they walked into West Burton for a pint at the "Fox and Hounds". Millie wished this was the end of their walk, as it had been on their previous visit but now she had to steel herself for the final couple of miles. Her legs ached and her feet were hurting inside boots that felt like lead weights. By the time they reached the car park at Aysgarth Falls it was almost empty and Millie fell into the Land Rover, closing her eyes with a sense of achievement tempered by exhaustion.

'Where d'you want to walk tomorrow?' asked Jake with a laugh as they drove back to the farm. Millie just shook her head.

Revived by the sugary drink laced with vodka, Hammond worked all afternoon to uncover the almost perfect shape of a wheel in the soil. His mind seemed sharpened by the adrenalin and he stopped to consider his next move. Based on the burial at Wetwang, the wheels would be away from the body and over in the area where the soil was stained, just as the girl had said. He straightened his back and climbed up on the side of the pit. Sure enough he could see how it might be laid out now and he jumped back down, working frantically on the darkened earth. Several hours passed while he worked at the soil until finally the miracle happened, he found a bone, a human bone. He was convinced of it. He was certain he had found the grave. Another two hours and he had uncovered three finger bones. Although he didn't want to damage the skeleton, and he knew that he should stop, he was determined to expose it all before anyone else saw it.

He stopped to rest, unaware he had been watched for hours, on and off, by someone hidden behind the hawthorn hedge beyond the field gate. The observer had left his car a mile up the road and crept purposefully along the far side of the wall that divided the fields. He watched with disdain while the man he had come to kill sat back on his heels and grinned down at something in his hand. If he kept to this side of the wall he could creep round to the far gate and climb into the site unobserved. The clown would have his back to him and anyway he was so absorbed in his pathetic little finds that he wouldn't even notice him coming up from behind. A curlew's cry attracted Colin Hammond's attention. The watcher bobbed down behind the wall and began edging round the site. At the gate he could see his victim, sweeping and scraping like a man possessed. He climbed the gate quietly and jumped down into the field.

Hammond glanced round, leaping up when he saw the dishevelled figure bearing down on him. He instinctively ran to the other side of the pit and the two men stood facing each other across the void.

'I've come to chat about Joanna.' Gary's voice wavered on the name he had used so often in the past.

'Oh yes?' Colin was white-faced, his appearance unhealthy and dishevelled. He was gripping a trowel in both hands and crouching, as if to protect himself.

'I know you killed her,' Gary shouted, standing rigid at the edge of the pit.

'I didn't.' Colin remained still, ready to run.

'Oh yes you did. You took the Land Rover and you drove over here and you ran her down in cold blood.'

He bent his knees and slowly reached one hand down to pick up a spade.

'Why would I do that Gary?' He attempted a smile.

'Because you couldn't have her!' He swung the spade but it didn't even reach half way across the pit.

Colin was glued to the spot, transfixed with terror. For Gary it proved his guilt.

'Admit it!' He jabbed towards him with the spade. 'Tell the truth.'

But the other man was silent, his legs were shaking, he thought he would vomit at any moment.

Gary hurled the spade and to his satisfaction hit the man on the side of his face. His knees crumpled, his hands went up to his head and he was falling in a heap into the pit. Gary stood over the motionless body while all the anger, frustration and despair overcame him. He picked up the spade and let it fall hard on the twisted torso, and then raised it again ... and again ... and again ...

Chapter 15

'What have you got for me, Henshaw?'

Ernie had been woken from his Sunday lie-in by the local police. To give them their due they'd had the decency to let him know as soon as they realised it was on the site of his murder. It was only an hour ago that they'd been alerted by the farmer who was puzzled by the sight of Colin Hammond's car in the field all weekend. He'd spotted him from his tractor across the lower field on the previous day but when the archaeologist wasn't around in the morning, he took a closer look. The sight of the body spread-eagled in the pit sent him rushing to the phone box down the road. Ernie could sympathise. It wouldn't have blended well into the Dales countryside.

He consulted his watch. The pathologist was due any time now and so he walked briskly over to view the body before Doc Carter took over the scene. The pit was taped off and he had to walk along a narrow piece of scaffolding to look down into it. The man's face was battered beyond recognition, his body twisted, as if in pain.

'Not a pretty sight, eh?'

Ernie turned to find a young woman standing behind him. She was wearing cut off jeans and a bright pink top with thin straps that showed her freckled shoulders.

'Who the hell are you, a bloody reporter?'

'I'm your bloody pathologist,' she said holding up a white body suit. 'It's Sunday, remember?'

She walked back along the plank and started kitting up.

'How come I don't get a day of rest then?' Ernie shouted, watching her slim figure wriggling into the coveralls.

She turned round and asked him what he knew about the victim.

'Nowt yet, although the local uniform have identified the car as belonging to a lecturer from the university.'

'Do you know him?'

'Yes, happen I do. He was one of my chief suspects for the other murders. The first body was found buried here under that tree.'

'Well that is interesting.'

She pulled on purple gloves and edged past him back along the plank. Picking up her case, she disappeared into the pit. Ernie watched as she began a meticulous search of the body. At one stage she prised something from his hand and dropped it into an evidence bag. Ernie peered down, trying to see what it was.

'What's that?'

'Not sure but it looks remarkably like a piece of metacarpal.'

'What's that when it's at home?'

'A finger bone.'

He stood in silence as she continued her examination.

'Do you have a time of death?' he asked when she finally stood up and stretched, rather provocatively he thought.

'He's been dead about twelve hours, I would say between six and ten last night.'

'And how did he die?'

Her hands were shielding her eyes from the morning sun. She studied him seriously.

'It's very difficult to say but judging from the position of the body, the state of the face and the large spade covered in blood lying beside him, I'd say he was battered to death with a blunt garden implement.' Then she grinned.

Ernie gave her a withering look but he could hardly hide his admiration. It was just the sort of answer he would have given as a youngster. 'It should be easy if there are any prints on the handle.'

As it turned out he was soon proved correct, there were blood stained prints which were immediately identified on the database as those of Dr Gary Perkins. What's more, when Ernie and Mitch went to his house, he quickly admitted his guilt. At least, the words that came out through the alcoholic haze sounded like "I meant to kill the bastard".

Ernie knew better than to interview him under the influence of drink. He made sure that his suspect was plied with coffee and fed until he sobered up. Only then did he tell his sergeant to bring him to the interview room. Ernie was looking forward to hearing how Dr Perkins had planned the third murder, and to find out why he had killed the two girls.

After three hours he confided to Mitch that he was disappointed. The man was now subdued and he still admitted to savagely attacking Colin Hammond with the spade and beating him to a pulp. However, he denied having anything to do with the other murders.

'You know, Mitch, I thought we would be finished by this evening. I reckon he thinks he can get away with it by pleading diminished responsibility over his ex-wife and pretending he thought the poor sod had killed her in the hit-and-run!'

The young man nodded.

'More like he was bothering those students and they threatened to tell on him and so he killed them. Perhaps Hammond found out and was going to give the game away!' he added, waiting for his boss's approval.

'You're not wrong there, lad. We'll need corroboration but you can work on that, build up the picture so to speak. I'll leave it to you, I'm off home now to finish my weekend in peace but you can go through it tomorrow morning. It'll give you a few hours to piece it all together like.'

Mitch stood by the window watching for Ernie's car to leave the car park and then he called Nina. She had only just woken up but when he mentioned the latest body she said she would be in straight away. They worked until late, picking up a Chinese takeaway and eating it at their desks. The sun was rising when they gave up and went home exhausted, but by then Mitch was ready to present his case to the boss.

Millie requested a quiet Sunday to recuperate and rose only in time for Bridget's roast lunch, sitting in the garden and reading the papers all afternoon. Jake wanted to see what his supervisor had done to the site but Millie reminded him that Hammond had told him to come back Monday. In the end he was persuaded to play rounders with his brother, using a tennis ball and a cricket bat, while Millie watched. Later, Bridget came out with lemonade and sat next to Millie, watching her sons playing together.

'Something's happened at the place where Jake is digging,' she said quietly. 'There's been an accident. Martin's just rung.'

'Martin?'

'He owns the field where they're working. He says he found a body. Police and newspaper men everywhere he says. He's been interviewed by the BBC.'

'Jake!' Millie instinctively called for him. She needed him there. Her stomach twisted. There was a thudding in her head. 'Jake!' she almost screamed.

'It's all right, Millie,' he said softly.

Bridget had fetched her a glass of water and they both were looking at her anxiously.

'If you're all right I'll let you sit for a bit,' she said and went back to the house.

'Millie, it was Hammond. He was working there all day yesterday, Martin said.'

'But what if it had been you? Maybe they meant it to be you or me!'

The horror of another death was too much for Millie. They had moved away from it and it had followed them again, and each time it seemed to move closer. They sat in silence for a long time until Jake seemed to make a decision.

'We might as well go back to uni. Let Nige know what's happened. See if there's anything we can do.'

'Such as?'

'I don't know but there's no point in staying here.'

Bridget and Robert were disappointed they were leaving and Toby begged them to stay, but Millie even began to wonder if they might not be putting Jake's family in danger if they remained. She felt relieved when they had put some miles between themselves and Wensleydale, driving straight to the flat and staying there until Nige appeared. He was surprised to see them and shocked to hear the news that his supervisor was dead.

'That explains why Nina's working tonight,' he said. 'She didn't tell me the reason.'

He took out his mobile and began texting. Jake turned on the television and they sat dismally drinking beer and watching the early evening programmes. The local news had a brief item with shots of police cars coming and going at the Wensleydale site. They called him Professor Colin Hammick, an eminent archaeologist and showed a view of the front of the university. When Nige's mobile played a cheery tune he grabbed it and checked the message.

'She's not giving much away but it sounds like she's on the case.'

'I'd better get back to the Deanery,' said Millie, without enthusiasm.

As they were leaving, Nige suddenly said, 'I'm supposed to be doing Colin's seminar tomorrow. He didn't want to have another scene like last week. He said I'd written it so I might as well give it.'

'Perhaps you should present it then,' suggested Jake.

'Wouldn't that seem a bit bizarre?' asked Millie.

'Possibly,' said Nige, 'I'll think about it. But we've already ordered the food and everything.'

Mitch was preparing a flip chart early Monday morning when Ernie arrived to announce that the victim had been positively identified as Colin Hammond. He was swiftly followed by Nina with the "Super" close behind. Finally they were joined by several uniformed colleagues.

'Right then, lad, give us what you've got.'

Ernie leant back in his chair with a grin and folded his arms. Mitch turned back to the front page of the chart, which he had entitled "Vrishti Bhatt".

'Right then.' He stood upright and confident. 'Vrishti Bhatt, she was found in Wensleydale on Monday the sixteenth of July. Her body had been moved from the place where she was killed and our theory is that Gary Perkins was having an affair with her or he wanted to. Either he panicked when she threatened to tell or ...' he looked across at Nina, 'more likely she resisted his advances and he was angry. Whatever it was, he killed her with a blow to the head and dumped her in Wensleydale. The use of the dagger and the choice of where to leave her body was designed to make it look like Colin Hammond did it.'

'How do we know he wasn't responsible?' asked Ernie.

'Who, Hammond?'

'Aye'.

'Well we don't but we're assuming it's down to Perkins, sir.' He emphasised the "sir".

'Evidence?' asked Ernie.

'We have a photograph of him with his arm round the girl and she rang him just a day before she disappeared.'

He turned over to reveal the next page, entitled "Dani Vincent".

'The next victim was killed in the storeroom in the basement at the university. Perkins had access, his prints were all over the room and it was the same MO, a blow to the head.'

'Motive?' asked Ernie.

'Either he was having it off with her and she was going to the authorities, which seems unlikely, or ...'

another nod from Nina, 'she found out that he had killed the other girl and threatened to tell. The evidence for that,' he added quickly, 'is it was Dani that took the photograph of him and Vrishti.'

'And Dr Hammond?' Ernie asked.

'Ah yes.' said Mitch, turning over the chart again. 'He finds out about Perkins and threatens to spill the beans. So he gets the chop as well.'

Ernie sat in silence for a while studying the ceiling.

'Well lad, we need to be sure that Hammond wasn't responsible for the girls' deaths. We need a watertight case and at the moment I see a few drips seeping out. Hold fire till I've spoken to one or two of them university people. I need to be sure about this Hammond guy.'

Ernie privately couldn't give a damn whether Perkins was responsible for one murder or three. He'd admitted battering Hammond and that would put him away for long enough. Whether it was him or the victim that killed the others was neither here nor there to him but he knew that his superintendent would expect him to care. As he dialled the number of the university he planned his encounter with the Dean. He would seek her opinion of the two men and get her view on whether either of them would be capable of killing the two young students. Then he would put that forward as supportive evidence. Chantelle informed him that Professor McGrath would be free at eleven and so he sat impatiently at his desk, half-heartedly dealing with paperwork until it was time to go.

The moment that Ernie left, Nina launched a verbal attack on her sergeant. He had not once mentioned the work that she'd done for him to find photographs and make lists of calls, nor had he acknowledged the time she had spent during the previous night throwing around ideas and responding to his suggestions, picking holes in his arguments and providing alternative reasoning. The young man reddened but he could not bring himself to apologise. He simply said that he recognised her help.

Ernie felt, once again, the familiar sensation he experienced every time he went into the Dean's office. She was forever charming and he always felt awkward in her presence.

'I'd like your help,' he began and went on to explain how Colin Hammond's body had been discovered at the archaeological site in Wensleydale and that Gary Perkins had been arrested for his murder.

She looked shocked and sat for a few moments.

'Are you sure that Gary is responsible?'

She was obviously finding it difficult to believe. With anyone else Ernie would have offered sympathetic words, asked if she needed a few moments, but this was an influential woman and he knew his place.

'Yes ma'am, he has admitted to it.' At this stage he knew that he couldn't say more.

'I find that difficult to believe.' She was shaking her head slowly.

'And we think he may have killed the young girls as well.'

'No, surely not?'

'It's fairly certain … unless Colin Hammond did.'

She seemed to be considering for a moment.

'Gary was always, shall we say, fond of younger women.' She paused. 'And to be honest there has been talk regarding Vrishti and a matter of sexual harassment. She spoke to poor Joanna about it, I know. In fact now you mention it I wonder if that might be something to do with the dreadful accident that she had.' She looked at Ernie. 'Is that possible?'

Ernie leaned forward. He could smell her flowery perfume across the desk. 'Are you saying that Vrishti Bhatt made a complaint to Dr Armstrong about a member of staff?'

'Yes.'

Ernie used the excuse of making notes while he pondered the significance of what she was saying. 'Do you think Dr Perkins would be capable of running over his own wife?'

'His *ex*-wife, Inspector. He was very jealous of her being single again, she told me so.'

'And Dani Vincent. Do you know anything that might connect her with Dr Perkins?'

'She was a strange girl. She might have known something about Vrishti's death. She did live in the same house after all.' She sighed and rested back in her chair. 'You know, Inspector, I don't envy you, working with such horrible situations.'

Ernie noticed that her eyes were blue and full of compassion.

'It makes my own life seem so tranquil.' She smiled and he smiled back.

There were very few women who understood his stressful existence. He accepted her offer of coffee and stole a few more minutes in her company.

Down in the lecture hall Nige began his seminar with a description of the most important chariot burial in Yorkshire, discovered in Wetwang. Millie was surprised to find she knew most of what he covered, recognising the slides of the Roman coin that depicted a war chariot being ridden in action. He showed them the pieces of metalwork from the horse's bridle and the wheel rims. She had studied the BBC website that showed a reconstruction of how it was built and proved it was used on the battlefield. Nige quoted the description by Julius Caesar, and his diagram showed how it was designed for the horse rider to sit in front of the standing passenger. He had the video of the reconstruction that had been made by the BBC, demonstrating exactly how it worked.

Millie smiled at how absorbed Nige was in his research. Carried away with enthusiasm, he had his back to the audience, looking at the slides and waving his arms as he described each one in turn. And then he came to a shot of some of his colleagues with Colin working on the main pit. As if he suddenly realised his mentor would be doing no more work, he went quiet and turned to the audience.

'At this point I would like to acknowledge the work of my supervisor, Dr Colin Hammond and my colleague, Dr Dani Vincent. Neither of them is … well, that is, they are … I just wanted to say that …' he hesitated for a moment or two, trying to recover his composure.

Millie started clapping, nudging Jake to do the same. Immediately the hall was filled with applause. Some figures stood and soon the entire audience was on its feet in a sombre and dignified ovation. Nige flicked past a couple of slides to a final photograph of the research group, pints in hand, standing outside the union bar. Colin Hammond was at the centre surrounded by his students, enjoying a joke. Nige's hair was much shorter then and Dani was blonde but otherwise it could have been last week.

Millie had wanted to ask about the discolouration of the soil but the lecture had reached its natural conclusion so they spilled out into the sunshine of the atrium, where wine and crisps had been provided.

'Nige! Nige!' Millie called as she fought her way to the table of drinks. 'Nige, that was brilliant!'

He reddened, 'Don't be daft, it was terrible,' but he appeared pleased with the compliment. He downed a glass of wine in one gulp and took another.

'I wanted to ask you about the wood, the way it decays. I know the soil changes colour but does it change chemically as well? You see I was thinking …'

'Millie, get me a drink, I can't get through!' Jake was calling across the crowd. Nige grabbed another glass and they made their way back to meet him.

'Well done, mate,' said Jake taking a glass from Nige.

'That's OK, I was getting another for myself.'

'I meant well done for the lecture, muppet. It went really well.'

Nige laughed, 'I'm glad it's over, that's all. I don't want to go through that again, not for another few years.'

'Disappointed there aren't more staff here,' Jake commented, looking round the atrium.

'Pretty much in disarray I shouldn't wonder, finding out Perkins is our murderer. Anyone for another drink?'

As he headed back to the table, Millie looked at Jake. He seemed as puzzled as she was. 'Dr Perkins?' she asked.

'Don't ask me, I know as much as you do.'

They waited impatiently for Nige.

'What d'you mean, Perkins?' Jake asked him as soon as he returned.

'How do you know?' added Millie.

'He's admitted killing Colin.'

'No!' they both exclaimed.

'Yes, he's in police custody.'

'Nina told you?' asked Millie

'Obviously she did,' Jake interrupted, 'and has he admitted to any others?' He looked at Nige.

'No, not so far but it's only a matter of time, Nina says.'

'Why on earth would he kill Dr Hammond?' asked Millie.

'He says it's because Colin killed Dr Armstrong.'

They stood in silence, jostled by the other students as they were making their way noisily back and forth to the table. Both of them were weighing up the significance of what Nige had said.

'So Dr Hammond was driving the car that killed Dr Armstrong?' Jake finally asked.

'I suppose it was the Land Rover then?' Millie added, motioning them to move into a quieter corner of the hall.

'Probably,' agreed Nige. 'Unless Perkins did it.'

'Is that likely?' said Millie, 'His own wife?'

'Ex-wife.' Jake and Nige said at the same time.

'Yes but even so.' Millie paused to think. 'What if he's right and Dr Hammond did kill her? It ties in with what Dani's friend said about suspecting her supervisor. That would be Dr Hammond wouldn't it? Carmen said that Dani had something on her supervisor.'

'Maybe Dani told him that she knew and he killed her to keep her quiet,' said Jake.

Nige looked puzzled, 'Does that mean he killed Vrishti as well?'

'He did have the dagger. Ben confirmed that.'

'It's almost unbelievable but it fits, doesn't it? Perhaps Gary Perkins did the best thing.'

'Not for him. He'll get life,' said Nige.

'Manslaughter. Diminished responsibility. He didn't know what he was doing, that's for sure,' said Jake, draining his glass.

'Perhaps it was all for the best then,' added Millie, 'I know that I'll feel more comfortable now, whichever one of them turns out to have killed Vrishti and Dani.'

Jake gave her a hug. 'Does that mean you'll be moving out of the Deanery?' he asked.

'Can I come and see it before you leave?' asked Nige.

Millie thought about the empty house in Jubilee Street and hesitated. 'I think I'll stay a bit longer, if I'm allowed to. Although I suspect my dad will insist.'

'Are you going down to Driffield tomorrow, Nige?' asked Jake.

'Yep, I reckon so.'

'Shall we go too, Millie? They won't let us into Wensleydale for a bit.'

'I think I'll have a day at home, well at the Deanery. I've got loads of washing and stuff to do.'

She couldn't face the sight of a field full of pits just now. She would rather sort herself out. Contact Phoebe. Perhaps write to Priti and go to see Carmen. Even ring Dad. It now seemed the right time to draw a line under the whole distressing episode.

Chapter 16

Millie opened her eyes slowly and lifted her head far enough off the pillow to survey the bedroom. Books and files were neatly stacked on the shelves and the rest of her belongings were hidden in the cupboards. All her clothes had fitted onto hangers or lay folded on the shelves in the wardrobe. Jewellery hung from the mirror and on the table was the stereo and her laptop. Yes, it was definitely looking more like home. She lay quietly listening to the sounds of the house, waiting for some activity downstairs. She'd only seen the Dean fleetingly the night before when she'd knocked gently and asked her if she needed anything. Millie had been half-undressed and opened the door very slightly to say no thank you Dean, she was fine. "Do call me Angela" the woman had said. Thinking that she must have left for work hours ago, Millie padded downstairs in her pyjamas to make coffee.

'Hello there, did you sleep well?' Professor McGrath was standing at the bottom of the stairs dressed in track suit trousers and a T-shirt. 'I've just been for a run and I got soaked,' she added, combing her hair back with her fingers.

'Sorry, I thought you'd be gone by now,' said Millie, turning to climb back up to her room.

'No problem, I was going to make breakfast, would you like some?'

'I'd better get dressed,' mumbed Millie.

'Later, then,' the Dean called after her.

By the time Millie had showered and dressed hurriedly, the smell of bacon was drifting through the house. The glass table in the kitchen was covered with boxes of cereal, cartons of fruit juice and a pile of toast.

'I hope you eat bacon. I just love bacon after a run.'

Angela McGrath at home was very different to the one that Millie saw at the university. This one looked younger without any makeup and she seemed bright and breezy. Millie found it disconcerting at first but relaxed as they chatted over bacon sandwiches and coffee.

'Usually I would be out by now but I thought I would go in later today,' she confided. 'I've been very busy recently, with all the upheaval in the department.' She was spreading marmalade onto a piece of toast. 'Anyway, do you have any plans today?'

Millie didn't explain why she wasn't working on the site, simply saying that she preferred to work at home today. But the older woman immediately understood.

'Ah yes, of course. You were working over in Wensleydale, weren't you?'

Reluctantly Millie agreed and explained that Jake had gone off with Nige to the other site.

'Well, I've got internet here so you can use it if you've brought a laptop. You make yourself at home. You're very welcome to stay here as long as you like. I told your father I thought it would be best to remain here at the Deanery until the start of the autumn term, if you're agreeable.'

'Have you spoken to him?' asked Millie, wondering how embarrassing he had been.

'Only on Friday. I rang to let him know where you were. By the way, did you have a nice time with your boyfriend's family?'

Millie was pleased with the change of subject and described her weekend in detail, including the fourteen mile walk. Then she realised that she was going over the top with her description of Bridget and she fell silent again.

'I guess it's nice to have a bit of mothering occasionally,' suggested Angela. 'My mother died when I was young so I missed that.'

'Me too,' said Millie, 'I mean my mum died a few years ago too.'

'Yes, I know dear, and I can sympathise. It's hard to be without a mother at your age. But your father has a girlfriend, I think?'

'Yes.' Millie answered cautiously.

'I detect you are not enamoured with her?' Angela smiled. 'I had the most awful rows with my stepmother when I was growing up. She was horrible to me and I hated her.'

'I don't hate Fiona, I just have nothing in common with her.'

'Well it's good you've got your career to concentrate on now.' She smiled and offered Millie more coffee.

The conversation flowed easily and before long Millie was talking about her school and the friends she had left behind. Then Angela asked about the future.

'I'm not sure but I think that I'd like to do research like Jake.'

'It's hard work doing a PhD, Millie. There will be lots of problems on the way particularly if you are doing fieldwork. There's the weather, permits, equipment and all sorts of unexpected things. Just look at what happened in Wensleydale.' Finally the subject had been broached and Millie was stunned that the Dean should mention it. 'Who could have imagined that the work would be stopped by a police investigation?' she continued and stared questioningly at Millie until she felt uncomfortable. 'It must have been a terrible experience for you, Millie … finding your friend like that.'

She was only trying to be kind but Millie couldn't look up from her plate. 'Yes it was.'

'You know you can always talk to me about it, don't you? I promised your father that I would keep an eye on you and it's the least I can do. After all, at present I am the departmental tutor until there is a new appointment.'

Millie was still looking down but there was something she wanted to know. 'Can I ask you a question? Did Dr Armstrong mention anything to you about Vrishti? Only I think she was worried and she might have asked Dr Armstrong's advice.'

'It's funny that you should say that because Joanna did come to see me.' Now Millie was looking up at her. 'She told me Vrishti had made a complaint about a member of staff.' Angela looked serious. 'She told me that Vrishti had complained about Dr Hammond.'

'Really, do the police know?'

'Of course, I told them.'

Millie sat quietly, playing with her knife, absorbing the information. 'And did Dani say anything to her, or to you?'

'Not in so many words but I can see it now. She implied something was wrong but I didn't realise at the time.' She gave a sigh. 'It's difficult to believe a man like Colin Hammond could kill three women in the way that he did. I shouldn't say this but in many respects Gary Perkins did us a favour putting an end to it all. I feel sorry for him, he deserves better.'

Millie nodded. 'But the odd thing is that Ben was with Dr Hammond the whole evening when Dr Armstrong was run over.'

Angela got up from the table, looking puzzled, and began loading the dishwasher without a word. Millie tidied the table. Finally the older woman straightened up and turned round.

'I've got to go into the department this morning, would you like a lift?'

'No thanks, I'll just work here.'

'Well, I'll get changed then. I will be going down to London later to a meeting at the Society of Antiquaries. I probably won't be back until tomorrow evening.'

Half an hour later, Millie was seated at her laptop when the blue Audi turned out of the drive. She picked up her mobile and called Jake to tell him that the Dean was going to be away. He called her back a few minutes later asking if Nige could come over to see the Deanery, and would she mind if Nina was with him because he had already arranged to see her this evening. Millie agreed on condition he brought something to eat and drink. After that she spent a good part of the day talking to Phoebe.

First she sent an e-mail and soon received a reply: *Just got back from London, the Rath Yatra festival was on down there on Sunday and I told Priti I'd meet her and Deepal there. It was brilliant!* She had included photos she'd taken on her mobile and Millie replied. She followed it with another message and this went on during the afternoon until Millie decided it would be easier to call her. She updated Phoebe with what had happened in Wensleydale and relayed what Angela had told her about Vrishti.

'Angela?' Phoebe giggled. 'Do you mean Professor McGrath, Millie?'

They chatted for some time, until Millie heard a car on the gravel drive. She could see Jake and Nina climbing out of the Land Rover with carrier bags. Nige appeared from the back waving a small barbeque above his head, announcing that he was going to be cooking sausages and burgers for everyone. She let them in and showed them through to the kitchen. The boys had bought cans of lager while Nina had thoughtfully provided wine. Jake and Nige took the meat and charcoal through to the garden, while Millie opened a bottle and handed a glass to Nina.

'Thanks very much for inviting me. I was so pleased when Nige said I could come.'

'No problem.'

Millie found it difficult to think of anything to say. She was very conscious that the girl was a police officer involved in the investigation of her friend's murder.

'This is a fantastic kitchen.' Nina was moving slowly round the room, her long silk skirt swaying as she walked. She stopped by the cooking range and then moved on, running her fingers along the stainless steel surfaces. 'Must have cost a fortune.'

'I guess the university pays for it all,' suggested Millie.

'I'd love a place like this,'

'Why, do you like cooking?'

'Oh yes, I used to help my mother when I lived at home and now my flat is so tiny I can hardly cook toast in it.'

Millie didn't comment but sipped her wine.

'Millie, can I ask you something?'

'Of course.' She was puzzled and slightly nervous.

'It's about Nige … do you think he likes me?'

Millie was so relieved by the question that she grinned.

'I knew it!' cried Nina. 'He's quite indifferent to me and now you've confirmed it. I'm sorry, I've embarrassed you.'

Millie laughed. 'Nonsense, that's just Nige. He's very shy.'

'He goes red very easily and he hates it if I tease him.' She giggled then resumed a serious expression, 'I do so like him, he's such an honest person, don't you think?'

Millie agreed that he was honest, and then that he was shy and later that he was sweet. She was relieved when Jake joined them.

'It's started raining, we're coming back in.'

Millie watched in admiration as Nina took over control of the cooking. She was in her element, grilling and frying while she mixed condiments from bottles that she had lined up beside the cooker, including tomato ketchup, brown sauce and tabasco. The boys had found the television and were snapping cans of lager. Nina's occupation was never far from Millie's mind and she wandered in to ask Jake who was driving.

'Nina said that she'd drive,' he replied.

'What?'

'Nina's taking Nige back tonight.'

'And you?'

'I thought it'd be all right to stay here. You said McGrath was away.'

Nina called them to say that the meal was ready.

'This is just like a proper dinner party,' exclaimed Nige, as he surveyed the glass table set for four.

'And how would you know?' asked Jake.

Nige went pink, 'I meant proper plates and glasses, like.'

They all laughed. It was certainly a contrast to the way he usually ate, slouched on the sofa.

'Well, I think that we should have a toast.' Jake raised his glass, 'To the Dean!'

'Don't be silly, we should toast Nina. To the chef!' Nige waved his glass, spilling drops of the deep red wine on the table.

'You are an idiot, Nige!' shouted Nina, leaping up to fetch a cloth.

He blushed and Millie whispered. 'She was telling me how much she liked you.' He went even redder and it was Millie's turn to be embarrassed. 'Sorry, too much wine,' she added.

'What's that?' asked Jake, 'More wine?' He filled her glass and his own.

Millie made coffee when the meal was over and the boys went off to watch television again. Nina started on the washing up.

'It's OK, there's a dishwasher,' Millie pointed out.

'Millie, you can't put these glasses in a dishwasher, or these pots. It won't take long.'

'You know, Nina, you're like the complete opposite of Nige. He's so untidy and you're so …'

'Fussy? I can't help it. It was the way I was brought up. I was Mummy's girl and my sister was the clever one. She trained to be a lawyer. I suppose that's why I joined the police force, to try to be like her.'

'It must be really exciting.'

'Not usually. I spent three and a half years as a beat patrol constable and that wasn't much fun. It's only since I've been attached to CID that it's become really interesting.' She paused to fold the tea towel neatly and hang it up. 'Nige has a really clever brain and clever people don't always remember to brush their hair or wash up the pots.'

'That's true,' agreed Millie, thinking of Dani.

'Look at the things that Nige has told me about archaeological excavation. What do they say? It's like being a time detective.'

'But not important like the work you do.'

'It could be, Millie. Think of the knowledge you have that could be used for police investigations.'

'I guess so. When Jake had the paint analysed from the Land Rover where it hit the wall …'

Nina was looking at her quizzically.

'Yes?'

'Oops! It was just that Jake had this idea about the Land Rover so he asked Jeff to analyse paint from the wall where Dr Armstrong was hit.'

'And?'

'And it was white paint that could have come from the Land Rover. But I said that it could be any car it didn't have to be the Land Rover, but the Land Rover was scratched.'

'I see. Well Jake should have told us this but it isn't surprising. Gary Perkins certainly seems pretty convinced that Colin Hammond hit her with the Land Rover. The evidence would have been helpful but it won't stand up in an inquest court without police corroboration and it's too late for forensics now.'

'The only thing is, Ben said that he had to take Colin Hammond home the night that Dr Armstrong was run over because he was so drunk he couldn't drive.'

'Really?'

Nina looked serious and marched into the other room, turning off the television. Millie had to smile at the startled look on the boys' faces. She asked them to explain exactly what they knew and quizzed them about Ben.

'Surely it doesn't change anything, even if Dr Perkins was wrong in thinking that Colin killed Joanna Armstrong,' said Nige. 'The outcome is the same.'

'Yes, Nige, but it changes the facts as we understand them, if it's true. If someone else killed Joanna we should find out,' Nina said sternly.

'Presumably it was Gary Perkins,' offered Jake.

Nina looked thoughtful, 'That would mean that he's lying about the motive.'

'Exactly,' said Millie, 'and he is, if he killed Vrishti and Dani as well.'

'Does that mean he killed them all?' asked Jake.

'I should think so, even if he is denying it.' Nina stood up. 'I'll need to let the boss know early tomorrow. I think we should go back now Nige.'

Outside it was raining hard and Nina insisted that Millie and Jake stayed indoors, after thanking them profusely for a wonderful evening. She spent several minutes fiddling with the position of the driver's seat and adjusted the mirror carefully before setting off in the dark and rain. She woke Nige gently when they arrived at his flat, refused to stay, and left him with a goodnight kiss. As she got into her Peugeot, she told him to make sure that he rang her the next day.

The cleaners were still in the office when Nina arrived at work in the early morning. She switched on her computer and pulled out the notebook from her bag. She had spent a restless night going over whether Gary Perkins killed his ex-wife, looking for other suspects and finding all her avenues were cul-de-sacs. But she had made copious notes and planned to spend the quiet hour before the others arrived to compile her thoughts. However, confusion soon turned to frustration and she went to the kitchen for a coffee.

'You left your computer on all night,' accused Mitch on her return.

'No, I've actually been in since seven, clever-clogs. Some detective, eh?' she added, trying to hide her irritation.

'Bit keen.'

'I had some information I wanted to sort out.'

Now Mitch was showing interest and he listened carefully as she explained what she had been told about the Land Rover.

'You do realise that none of that can be used as evidence,' Mitch warned.

'Yes, but it does suggest that someone other than Hammond was involved in Joanna's murder.'

'First of all we don't know that it was murder, secondly we don't know exactly when the vehicle was damaged and thirdly it makes no difference to anything because Perkins will go down whether it's for one, two, three or four murders.' He raised a finger for each one as he spoke.

'Isn't it just as important to know the truth?'

'In this case not really, we'll get a result whatever.'

'But what if there's still someone out there who might kill again?' Nina could hear her irritation coming through.

'Unlikely.'

'But possible?'

'Look, who else could be involved? You checked the list of who was at the party, who had keys to the storeroom, and whose prints were picked up at the crime scene.'

'Perhaps I should find out who can drive the Land Rover?'

'If it makes you happy.' Mitch smirked and shook his head.

When Nina rang Chantelle, she offered to get the list of drivers but with the Dean away it would take a little while to find it. She would fax it as soon as she could.

When Ernie arrived, Mitch took obvious delight in relaying the details of Nina's "discovery". He scornfully explained how she'd got the information from Nige. His boss listened politely enough but soon began picking holes in her argument.

'Seems to me the most likely candidate is that boyfriend of yours, love.' He winked at his sergeant. 'He was at the party, he was the last person to see the Bhatt girl alive, he had access to the storeroom, and his prints were all over it. He also seems to be the main driver of the Land Rover.'

'That's nonsense.' Nina felt her cheeks burning but she could see that he was right.

Ernie was not looking at her now. 'Let's get on with questioning Perkins. Once he's admitted he killed his missus it'll all fall into place. C'mon, my lad, let's get cracking.'

Nina watched them go and paced the office, stopping at Mitch's desk. She opened the file containing the pathologist's report and went back to her notes on the dust and pollen that had been dated and to the conclusion that Vrishti's body had lain in an environment full of ancient wood. It must have been a confined space to have generated such a high concentration of dust in her nasal cavity and ear wax it said. She tried to imagine the victim lying on her back, her arms at her side, enclosed in wood. All she could see was a wooden coffin. It would have to be very old and she guessed they had wooden coffins then. She tried to envisage it but could only see a body-shaped coffin like an Egyptian mummy's tomb. Would that be so odd in a university department full of archaeologists? She rang Nige's mobile but there was no answer so she sent a text and waited.

Nige had three students to pick up from the department that morning before collecting Jake. He climbed wearily into the Land Rover, cursing Nina for adjusting the seat. He had to fight with the mechanism in the old vehicle to move it back. It had been much easier on the white Land Rover. As he fiddled with the rear view mirror he tried to remember when he had done the same in the new vehicle. It wasn't the first time he drove it, but soon after. Could it have been on the Thursday when he went to Driffield? He couldn't be sure but it might be relevant. Someone shorter than him must have been driving it and that ruled out Colin Hammond and Gary Perkins. It was still bothering him while he waited in the atrium for the students. He tried ringing Nina but her phone was switched off so he quickly left a garbled message as the undergraduates arrived, not noticing that there was already a text waiting for him.

Jake answered the door at the Deanery and asked Nige to wait. He quickly carried a mug of coffee up to Millie and shook her gently.

'I've got to go, Nige is waiting and he's got students with him.'

Millie opened her eyes, her head was throbbing and her mouth was dry.

'Here.' He thrust an envelope at her, 'This was on the doormat this morning. It must have come by hand.'

Millie opened her eyes again and waved her hand, 'See you later,' she murmured.

She could hear Nige's unmistakable accent urging Jake to hurry up, then the crunch of gravel and the sound of the diesel engine disappearing down the road. Disappointed that Jake had not suggested she went with him, but admitting to herself she would not have wanted to go, she pulled herself to a sitting position holding her head. The coffee helped and soon she became curious about the letter. It was addressed to Miss M Sanderson and was in an official university envelope, probably a bill. She ripped it open and saw a sheet of typed A4 from the Archaeology Department. *Dear Millie,* it began, *I would like you to help me with a small job. If you meet me at noon today in the archive store, I can show you what needs doing and, obviously, I will pay you for the work.* It was signed by Angela McGrath.

It was already past ten and she had no transport. She jumped out of bed and then sat down quickly, thinking that she would be sick. Moving more slowly, she washed and dressed gingerly. Downstairs she nibbled some toast and took some painkillers. Finally, checking that she had keys and an umbrella, she left for the university.

The fresh air did her good, so she began to walk more briskly, lifting her head and breathing deeply. The ground was still damp and trees that hung over the pavement from the big gardens dripped as she walked. On the main road Millie looked in the shop windows as she passed, at first there were butchers and bakers, several restaurants and delicatessens. Then charity shops, a library and small supermarkets open all hours. Finally by university were the kebab shops, tattoo parlours and launderettes.

It was after eleven when she finally reached the department but there was just time for a coffee and a doughnut before she saw the Dean. It was only when she was sitting quietly sipping a cappuccino that she remembered what Angela had said about being back late today. She'd presumably meant that she wouldn't be at the Deanery until evening, since she was clearly in the department. Millie hoped that she was correct because there was still a pile of damp charcoal in the garden to be cleared up before she returned.

She left the café at five to twelve and took the lift to the basement. The door of the store was open but the room was in darkness and there was no sign of Angela. After a few minutes Millie decided to wait inside. She was fumbling for the light switch when she was pulled into the room and the door slammed behind her. Something hit her with tremendous force and she was falling down a deep, deep well.

Chapter 17

When Nina came back from making herself a coffee there was a missed call. She checked her messages and heard Nige mumbling about the Land Rover. She shut her eyes to concentrate but the background noise was too loud. She wanted to ask him about the mummy idea but his phone was still not responding so she began flicking idly through the file again, looking for where she had missed a significant link. At last, the fax machine started whining and she tugged impatiently at Chantelle's list of authorised drivers. There were four names under "staff" and four under "students". They looked pretty much the same as her previous lists and she compared them as she went down: Hammond, Perkins, Armstrong, and Standing. She stopped. Why wasn't Standing on her list of suspects already? He had been a party guest but he didn't have access to the storeroom and there were no undentified prints there. Well, that made sense, so she continued. The students were all on the list already: Jake, Nige and Ben. Dani no longer counted. She reached for the phone and called the university.

'Hi there, Chantelle, it's Nina from CID. Can I ask you about one of the drivers on the list that you faxed through? It's a John Standing.'

'Professor Standing?'

'Yes. Can you give me his contact details? I'd like to have a chat with him.'

'He's in Egypt at the moment. He went out to a conference and he's staying to do field work until …'

there was a pause and Nina could hear Chantelle flicking pages. 'Yes, he's back in September.'

'When did he go?' asked Nina.

'On Monday the ninth of July.'

Nina put the phone down with a sigh. Her list contained three dead people and someone who was out of the country when the murders took place. The only explanation was that either Hammond or Perkins was responsible and that was that. She picked up her handbag to go and find a sandwich when her mobile rang. Nige was calling from the site, the signal was not good and she had to ask him to repeat himself several times until she got the message.

'There's a coffin in the department, I can show you when I get back.'

'Meet me here!' shouted Nina. 'Come here at six!'

The phone went dead and she threw it on the desk in frustration.

When she came back from lunch Ernie was sitting on her desk laughing loudly, while Mitch leaned back in his chair looking pleased with himself.

'Guess what?' he said to her.

'What?'

'We've virtually got Perkins on all four murders.'

'I reckon you've done well, lad.' Ernie was beaming at him. 'He's a broken man, he just wants to get put away and be done with it. A pretty good result I'd say.'

Nina watched the two men without speaking for a while and then asked them what evidence they had for the girls' murders.

'He's as much as admitted it, love.' Ernie looked irritated.

Nina waited for him to heave himself off her desk and amble to the door. 'I reckon it's time for a bite to eat – fancy a pint to celebrate, son?'

'I'll be along shortly, Guv. Just a few things to sort out first.' He watched Ernie leave and turned to Nina. 'What d'you reckon? Not bad, eh?'

'I'm surprised he's admitted to all of them.'

'Don't knock it, girl. Everything sorted in a quadruple murder, I don't reckon I'll be DS much longer, if you know what I mean.'

Nina listened patiently and then said, 'Can I ask you about the pathologist's report on Vrishti Bhatt?'

'Why? Can't you leave it alone now?' Mitch was making for the door.

'It's just the old dust and pollen. I thought I'd look at possible sites where she may have been held before she was moved to Wensleydale.'

'There's no need now, we've sorted it. It's over.'

He left the room whistling to himself. Mitch, a detective inspector? Did that mean she should be looking at sergeant? She laughed out loud and sank down on her chair, deciding to clear her desk and finish her report on a series of break-ins that had been put to one side when the first body was found. She knew that once the boss was back from lunch, he would be passing her all the paperwork to type up.

Millie was aware of a light so bright that it made face burn and her head hurt. She shut her eyes but there was no difference. She tried to raise her hands to her head but she couldn't move them … It was still very hot and her head was throbbing but the bright light had subsided. She couldn't move her legs or her arms, although she could feel them. She tried calling out but she couldn't open her mouth and then she was falling back down the well …

Jake was becoming increasingly irritated with Millie for not responding to his calls. He'd left a message at lunch time to see how she was and then again several times during the afternoon. He assumed that she was ignoring her mobile while she slept off her hangover and decided to forget about it until they had finished for the day. The work had gone well. The burial site was beginning to take shape, with two circles containing fragments of metal indicating where the wheels had been placed carefully side by side. Nige became quite emotional as he surveyed the scene, expressing his regret that Colin Hammond was not present to witness it. When Jake reminded him that it was time they were heading back to the flat, Nige announced their imminent departure to the other students and soon they were speeding northwards on the A1M, jostling with the evening traffic while Jake tried to contact Millie again.

When they had dropped the students off, Jake insisted on going straight to the Deanery. There was no answer when he rang the bell and so he peered through the letterbox but the place seemed deserted.

'Don't worry,' said Nige, 'she's probably gone shopping. I'm supposed to be meeting Nina at six.' Jake dropped Nige off at the police station, waved at Nina who was waiting out in the sunshine and drove back to the flat to wait to hear from Millie.

'So where is this coffin, Nige?' she asked.

'Hang on, aren't you going to say hello properly?'

'Not here, my car's over there.'

They walked across the car park to the Peugot and as soon as they were settled inside she gave him a kiss.

'Is it in the university?'

'It depends what you mean. There's a wooden coffin that would have contained a mummy years ago. It was donated by some old boy who lived locally.'

'How big is it?'

'About normal coffin size, perhaps a bit smaller. It just looks just like an old wooden box, not painted or anything elaborate.'

'I'd like to have a look at it.' She started the engine, putting the car into reverse gear. The air conditioning began to cool the interior. 'Where is it?'

'In the storeroom, but why do you want to see it?'

Nina began to explain about the carbon dating but Nige knew more about it than she did and soon he was giving her a lecture on how to determine the age of archaeological artefacts.

'A proper professor, you,' she teased. 'We'll have to have you as our expert witness to explain all about it to the jury.'

She swung the car through the entrance gates of the university and drove slowly round the perimeter road to the Archaeology Department. She stopped the car in front of the building as a blue Audi pulled into the space marked "The Dean". Professor McGrath climbed out and waved.

'Just the person!' cried Nina as she caught up with her. 'I need to get into your store, Professor. Do you have a key that I can borrow?'

The woman looked puzzled. 'I don't have one personally but I'm sure we can get you one. Come up to the office.'

Nina followed her into the lift and called to Nige to meet them down there.

'You were lucky to catch me, Constable. I've only just got back from London. Am I allowed to ask why you want to get into the store? Is it about Dani Vincent?'

She unlocked the door and went into the back room while Nina waited in the stuffy office.

'Yes and no. I'm looking for something. I believe there's an Egyptian coffin in the store. Nige told me there was.'

The woman came back smiling. 'Well, he's a clever boy so I expect there is. Here.'

She offered Nina a key, carefully locking the office before following her back to the lift. Nige was waiting in the sweltering heat of the unventilated corridor. Nina waved him aside as she unlocked the door and switched on the light. The wooden coffin was in the corner, piled high with dusty old cardboard boxes which were labelled haphazardly with names and dates.

'Is this it?' She was expecting something more ornate, shaped and carved.

'I think so,' said Nige.

'Are you sure?' The Dean was peering at the corner.

Nina began to move the boxes aside, while the others stood watching her.

'Give me a hand, Nige, these are heavy.'

They helped her clear the boxes and then stood back as she examined the coffin. She could see it had been tested for fingerprints; the powder was visible on the side of the box. Gingerly she tried to open it but it was wired closed. Nige examined the top and, pulling at the edge of the lid, he managed to raise it a few inches.

'Hold on,' he said, reaching across for a metal trowel that was lying on a shelf nearby. He pulled the lid up and used the trowel as a lever. Then he stood back, wiping the sweat off his face.

'This should do it,' he said.

He leaned on the handle of the trowel and groaned with exertion. The wire snapped and the lid flew back, hitting the wall with a crash. Nina had been expecting to see the ridge that had formed the mark on Vrishti's back, the dust and pollen that had filled her nose and ears, maybe even a sign that Vrishti had been incarcerated in the coffin. She had not expected to find the body of a girl, mouth taped and hands tied.

'Millie!' Nige shouted.

'Don't touch anything,' ordered Nina, panic overcoming her. What had she done? She hadn't sought her governor's permission for this and she had jeopardised a crime scene.

'But her eyes moved. I saw them!'

'Is she breathing?' asked the Dean, moving forward.

Nina switched into automatic, ripping the tape off the girl's mouth and checked her airways. She was breathing but she appeared to be unconscious. Asking the others to stay with Millie but not to touch anything, she ran upstairs to get a signal and contacted the ambulance service. Then she called her boss and explained what had happened. At first he didn't seem to comprehend her but eventually she managed to make him understand. He said he'd go straight to the hospital and ordered her to stay with the victim at all times. She hurried back to the basement and sent Nige to wait for the paramedics.

Nina was grateful for Professor McGrath's company while they waited. There was nothing that they could do once they had untied her hands and checked she was breathing effectively but sit beside the unconscious girl lying in the coffin. Her training told Nina she should be looking for any indications of how the crime had been committed but she was so shaken that she could hardly hold back the tears. When she heard Nige directing the ambulance crew downstairs she broke down and the Dean gave her a handkerchief, putting an arm round her and gently leading her out into the fresh air.

'Looks as though she's coming round, she's had a nasty blow to the head,' said one of the men as he strapped the stretcher into the ambulance. Nina instructed Nige to go home as she climbed up to join them. Once they had set off, the paramedic put in a line and carried out tests, suggesting she might just be concussed. Ernie, who was already at the hospital, began by asking Nina what she was doing in the store in the first place. She was still explaining when Professor McGrath joined them and the three sat waiting to hear news of Millie until Ernie announced that he was eager to go home and left. Angela McGrath offered to stay with Nina and so she was by her bed when Millie opened her eyes several hours later.

'Mum?'

'It's all right Millie I'm here.'

She closed her eyes again and the older woman took her hand and talked to her gently.

Millie was floating in a deep still pool while her mother sat at the side. She lay on her back and watched the dragonflies skimming the water. Her mother was calling her and she swam back to the edge of the pool. She was clutching onto the side but it kept giving way and she had to get out …

'Millicent! Millicent! Can you hear me?' There was another rougher voice now. A nurse had come down and was trying to rouse her. Millie opened her eyes and stared at them.

'Hello darling, d'you want a drink?'

Nina rang Nige to let him know that Millie had regained consciousness and to reassure him that she was going to be all right. She suggested that he and Jake come in at visiting time the following day. She had been shown the kitchen by the nursing staff and occupied herself making tea and taking a cup along to Angela, who had remained with Millie while she was washed and given liquids, eventually falling into a peaceful sleep. When the nurse suggested that she remained undisturbed until the morning, Angela offered to give Nina a lift to the university to pick up her car.

The young detectective was back on duty at the hospital by six the next morning and the nurses were busy giving patients their medication and getting them ready for the change of shift. Millie had slept well but was having a CT scan as a precaution. So, while Nina waited, she rang Ernie to tell him the news. He picked up the call, saying irritably that Mitch would be down to question the girl; she just had to wait there until he arrived. She was clearly in for a severe reprimand next time she saw her boss face to face. The smell of breakfast wafting along the corridors was overwhelming and she set off to find comfort food before her sergeant arrived.

By the time Mitch had joined her, the nursing station was busy with doctors preparing for their rounds. They spoke to the staff nurse, who showed them down to the girl's bed and pulled the curtains round before leaving them alone with her. Nina noticed how pale she looked and there were dark rings under her eyes.

Millie was feeling better after her sleep but she still felt rather confused about what had happened.

'I got this letter from the Dean asking me to meet her in the storeroom.'

'The Dean? Do you have the letter?' he asked.

'It's in my bag.' She looked round at the bare locker. 'It might be in the cupboard. It's a black canvas satchel.'

Nina looked inside but it was empty.

'He must have taken it,' she suggested.

'Can you remember what it said?' Mitch asked.

Millie tried to visualise the page but she couldn't remember. 'It just told me to come to the storeroom.'

'Can you remember what happened when you went into the room?'

'No. It's a blank. I'm sorry.'

He smiled. 'That's fine, Millie. Don't worry. It'll probably come back in time.'

Millie wasn't sure that she wanted to recall what had happened, it might be too horrible.

'We'll ask you again later but let us know if you do remember anything,' he said.

'Do you know when you'll be leaving here?' asked Nina.

'They said they'd see after the results of the scan. If it's OK I'll be let out today.'

As they left Nina expressed concern for the girl's safety.

'She's in good hands at the Dean's place. She'll look after her and her parents will know what to do. Angela McGrath is contacting Millie's father.'

'That's all right then.'

Ernie was waiting for them down the hall and Nina immediately began to apologise.

'Save it for the office, I want to know what's going on here. Who's responsible for this attack?'

'She can't remember, Guv. She got a note asking her to the storeroom, purporting to be from her Dean.'

'How d'you know it wasn't?'

'It couldn't have been. She was in London until I saw her coming back after six last night.'

'Bloody hell! We're running out of suspects here. Who's left?' Ernie was addressing his sergeant.

'I'd need to look at the lists again, sir.'

'You and your ruddy lists.'

'Any ideas, Constable?'

'No, sir.' She knew the list by heart and it left only Jake, Nige and Ben.

'Well I need you to find something for me. We're beginning to look stupid.'

'There is the missing bag, Millie's handbag is missing.'

'Well get onto it then! I'm off to make my excuses to the Chief Super.'

Mitch insisted on going back to the university to look for the bag and to get the crime scene investigators in, leaving Nina wondering where to start. She had been in the office for less than half an hour when Mitch called to say that the bag was in the storeroom but there was no sign of the letter. He remarked, pointedly, that the room had been left open overnight so anyone could have been in and tampered with the evidence.

At first Jake didn't recognise Millie, she looked so pale and tired. He put a bunch of flowers on the locker and perched on her bed. She smiled at him and put out her hand to cover his.

'Hi.' He leant over and kissed her on the cheek.

Millie burst into tears and hung onto him, shaking with loud sobs.

'Hey, it's all right, you're all right now, Millie.' He pushed her away gently, far enough to look at her face, she was smiling.

'Sorry, I'm just glad to see you. I want to go home. They said I could when the doctor's seen me later this afternoon.'

'That's good. Millie, what happened? I was trying to call you all day.'

'I can't remember. I went to the store. You remember that letter you gave me? It was from the Dean. At least that's what it said. It asked me to meet her in the storeroom. So I went and that's all I remember.'

'Where will you go when you leave here?'

'Back to the Deanery I hope. I don't want to go home. They won't send me home will they?'

'I don't know. Nina said that the Dean was letting your father know what's happened.'

'Damn!'

'Millie, you've got to take this seriously.'

'I got a bump on the head, that's all.'

'Millie, you were found tied up in a coffin. If Nige and Nina hadn't found you God knows what would have happened.'

'What?' Millie could recall the restriction of that enclosed space, the bright light ... but that was all.

Jake recounted what Nige had told him when he burst into the flat with the news. He was almost hysterical and Jake could hardly understand his strong Welsh intonation. When he calmed down he described how he'd forced the lid off the box and found Millie. Neither of them slept while they waited for updates from Nina and only collapsed on their beds when she told them that Millie was sleeping and she was going home for a few hours rest herself.

As they chatted quietly Millie felt more normal. She could remember bits of the previous day and when Jake reminded her about the abandoned barbeque on the day before and how he had gone off to Driffield, she was able to piece together parts of the early morning. The Dean appeared after an hour and Jake excused himself, saying that he would come back to see Millie later.

'No need. I've spoken to the doctor and he says that she can come out this afternoon, provided that she rests for a while. He'll be coming to see you in a few minutes and then I can take you home Millie.'

Chapter 18

Millie was in bed, propped up on several plump feather pillows, wearing a white embroidered nightdress that Angela had given her. She had washed Millie's hair and was drying it for her.

'There, is that better, Millie?' she asked, as she turned off the hairdryer.

'Yes, thank you.'

It was so comforting to be fussed over. She had missed the closeness of an older woman, caring for her. It made her feel like a little girl again.

'I'll make some toast, would you like honey on it?'

Millie nodded and the woman disappeared downstairs. The windows were open and a warm breeze was blowing the flowery curtains about. It was a different room to the one she had moved into when she came to the Deanery, smaller but prettier. Millie sighed and closed her eyes, there was an exhaustion that hadn't left her since the hospital and she was drifting off when Angela returned with a tray. This was so like her real home, when Mum was alive.

'Does Dad know what's happened?' she asked as she ate.

'Yes, dear, I rang him. He said to give you his love and say that he'd be in touch soon.'

Millie was initially disappointed that he wasn't rushing up to see her but then relieved, in case he took her back with him. She preferred to stay here with Angela than have to be down there with Fiona.

'This is really good. I always used to have honey on my toast at home.'

'I expect your mother used to make a fuss of you when you were a little girl.'

Millie smiled at the memory. 'She used to bring the portable telly up to my room if I was ill, and buy me my favourite comics or magazines when I was older.'

'Well I'm sure I can find a small television …'

'No, I didn't mean …'

'And I'll get you some magazines when I go into town this afternoon. Which ones do you like?'

Millie was nearly in tears, Angela was being so kind.

'I'll leave you to rest now and you might like to get up for a while at lunch-time. It's very warm in the garden today. You have a sleep and I'll wake you when it's time to eat.'

Ernie had called the team for a meeting to update them all on the latest attack. He asked Nina to tell them what had happened when she went to the storeroom. Mitch chipped in to add that the handbag had been left behind until he found it but she insisted that the bag had not been in the room when she went in.

'OK, OK, break it up, let's move on,' shouted Ernie. 'The important thing is that another student from the same house has been abducted, suggesting that our Dr Perkins, who is in custody, may not have been responsible for the other attacks. If that's true, we must get out there and find who is. Detective Constable, you had a list of suspects before, can we see those on the board please?'

Nina stepped up and wrote the names in green felt tip pen. Jake Sweeting, Nigel Featherstone and Ben Hughes.

'So, we have three students who had the opportunity to commit the attacks on Vrishti Bhatt, Dani Vincent and now Millie Sanderson. We don't have a motive yet but it would seem quite a reasonable possibility that one or more of these three are involved.'

He looked across at Nina but said nothing about her connection with Nige. She wondered if she would be taken off the case.

'Mitch, I'd like you to take a couple of colleagues and see them individually. Don't let them speak to each other until you've interviewed them.'

'Yes, Guv.'

'Guv, I know that Jake Sweeting and Nigel Featherstone were both near Driffield all day yesterday.' Nina was blushing.

'Do you now?'

Turning to the team he said, 'Bring Ben Hughes in first. See if he's got a good alibi for yesterday lunch time.'

Ernie came over to Nina and spoke quietly, looking over his shoulder to check no-one could hear.

'Best keep out of the way until the interviews are over. Check the CCTV footage. See who was in and out of the Archaeology Department yesterday. And no contacting the boyfriend. Got it, petal?'

She bit her lip and went into the cubby-hole they called the video room with the cassette he had handed her. The camera gave a clear view of the entrance and the car park along the front of the building. At six o'clock the cleaner's van arrived and then it was quiet until around eight, when staff and students started to appear. She could identify some but a number were unknown to her. At half past she saw the Land Rover in the car park and Nige disappearing through the entrance. He reappeared soon afterwards with a gaggle of unidentified students in tow. People wandered in and out with no apparent pattern and the occasional vehicle parked briefly in front of the building. She stopped the tape and noted down that Millie had arrived at eleven thirty-one precisely. A couple of people left the building and then, at eleven forty-three a dark car drew up immediately outside the entrance. Before the figure emerged Nina knew it was the Dean. She stopped the tape, rewound and ran it again. It was definitely Angela McGrath. When she had appeared in her car later that day she had told Nina that she'd just got back from London, hadn't she? Nina pressed continue and watched carefully, after thirty-two minutes she re-appeared, climbed into her car and drove off. Nina ran the tape backwards and forwards to compare the two images of the woman but everything was identical, not a hair out of place. She continued to monitor the tape until it reached the point where she and Nige arrived. It showed them meeting up with the Dean and all three of them entering the building, the ambulance arriving and there she was standing in tears with the Dean comforting her.

As she removed the tape and picked up her notes she hesitated. She wasn't sure that she could fully understand what she had seen but she knew that if it had been Nige that had appeared around mid-day when he was supposed to have been elsewhere, they would be bringing him in for questioning.

Back in the office she described what was on the CCTV to Mitch. His first reaction was to tap his pen on the desk and look into the distance, his lips tight.

'Look, I'm waiting for them to bring this Hughes guy in, he fits the MO better, eh?' He leant forward and smiled at her. 'I'm not sure how to put this, Nina, but why don't you back off for now? The boss is none too pleased with you at the moment. Take a tip, make yourself scarce. Go shopping or something.' His smile faded.

Nina stared, not believing that she had heard him correctly. She went back to her desk and wrote up her notes, folded them carefully putting an elastic band round them and the tape. She placed it on the desk in front of him.

'I will go, Sergeant Turner,' she said stiffly, 'but I think you should also look at the CCTV tape for the period when Vrishti Bhatt went missing. I'm sure she was hidden in that box before she was taken to Wensleydale.'

She walked out, slamming the door behind her.

Jake had been restless since Nige had left for Driffield, refusing to go himself, insisting that he had to see Millie. But her phone was switched off and he had spent the last hour trying to get hold of the Deanery number. He was switching channels on the big old television that dominated the small flat and jumped up when the land line rang. He assumed that Millie had finally got his message and the voice was familiar but at first he didn't recognise Nina's excited tones.

'Jake? It's Nina. Is Nige around?'

'No he's gone to Driffield. Has something happened?'

'No, but I wanted to talk to him. He left a message but I couldn't understand a word.'

'The signal's hopeless down there, no wonder you can't get hold of him. He'll be back this afternoon. They leave early on a Friday to avoid the traffic.'

'Jake, can I come over now? I need to talk to someone and they won't listen to me.' Her voice was becoming emotional.

'Sure.'

'I'll see you soon.'

The line went dead. Jake was replacing the receiver when his mobile started ringing.

'Jake? It's me.' There was no mistaking the Welsh accent.

'Nige?'

'I'm on my way back. It's Ben, they want him to report to the police station. I'm bringing everyone back now. I've tried Nina but she's not answering.'

'She's on her way here. I'll tell her. That's probably why she's coming.'

When Nina arrived at the flat she had regained her composure. She was angry but no longer stinging from the insult of being told to go away when she had important information. But she wasn't going to be stopped by misogynists who were too obsessed with their own glory to ensure that all bases had been covered. The news that Ben was being questioned didn't surprise her.

'Is that why you came?' asked Jake. 'Nige will be back after he's dropped Ben and the others off.'

'I've got a load of questions that don't make any sense. I need to bounce them off someone. I've made a list.'

'I don't think I'll be able to help.'

'Let's try, shall we?'

She smiled weakly and perched on the edge of the sofa, her knees and ankles together, hunched over her notebook.

'The wooden box that we found Millie in …' Jake noticed that she avoided the word coffin. 'By the way, how *is* Millie?' She looked concerned.

'I don't know, I couldn't get hold of her by phone and I've got no transport with Nige away so I haven't been able to get to the Deanery.'

'The Deanery?'

'Yes, she's staying with Professor McGrath.'

Jake expected her to be pleased by the news but her expression didn't change. She looked down at her notes.

'The wooden box, Jake. Would it have contained dust and pollen that was hundreds of years old?'

'Probably, it's supposed to have held an Egyptian mummy at some stage. Why?'

'Because they found old dust on Vrishti's body and I think she may have been put in there as well. If that's the case, the person who attacked Millie was probably also responsible for Vrishti's death.'

'And Dani's I suppose, since she was found in the storeroom as well.'

'Very likely.' Nina was looking at her notebook again. 'How well do you know Ben, Jake?'

'Pretty well, we were undergraduates together. He's quite straightforward, very reliable.'

'Do you know of any reason why he would harm Vrishti or any of them?'

'No, I don't think he even knew Vrishti.'

She turned to the next page.

'The Dean told my inspector that Vrishti had complained to Dr Armstrong about sexual harassment. Would you know who she could have been referring to?'

She looked up at him.

'Hmm, no prizes there, my guess would be Gary Perkins.'

'Not Colin Hammond?'

'Possibly but he was all over Joanna, I mean Dr Armstrong.'

'Now, the Dean. Did she ever get involved with the work? I mean did she visit the sites, drive the vans, or put things in the store.'

'Not really. I expect she used to do research before she became Head of Department and Dean but she's always in her office or out at important meetings.'

'So she wouldn't be in the storeroom for example?'

'No way. That letter to Millie must have been sent by someone else, to fool her into going down there!'

'But who would have her headed paper?'

'Anyone. All you need is a computer and the logo.'

'So it would be someone in the department?' Nina continued writing.

'Probably. Look, you don't think he's still out there? I'm worried about Millie. It's very quiet around that big house.'

'If you want we can go over there now and see how she is. Would you like to do that?'

'Can we?'

She rang Nige and left a message.

Ring me when you've dropped Ben off, Nige, please.

Angela had put a reclining chair out on the terrace, close to the house. The garden fell away and in the distance Millie could see tennis courts and greenhouses, the tall trees and hedges that surrounded the garden, screening the adjacent properties completely. She watched a blackbird collecting worms from the lawn and blue tits flying back and forth to the bird feeder hanging from a tall ornamental tree. Angela came out with a bowl of soup for Millie and sat watching her while she ate it greedily, even though it was rather spicy.

'That was delicious,' she said. 'It's so nice out here, the garden is huge.'

'Several acres,' agreed Angela. 'There's a tennis court down there and a vegetable garden in the corner.'

'You must have a gardener.'

'Yes, the university provides one. He comes twice a week and the produce is used for entertaining in College House. There's a lot to do. There are the vegetables in the summer and the greenhouses are full of fruit. You should go and have a look round when you're better.'

Millie tried to answer but instead yawned loudly. The fatigue was returning.

'You lie back and have a sleep while I go into town. Here I can move it further down.'

She lowered the back of the reclining chair and put a rug on her legs. Millie closed her eyes gratefully.

Nina parked the Peugeot in the road and they walked up the curving gravel drive to the front door. They heard the bell echoing round the hall as they stood on the red tiles of the ornate porch. Jake tried again.

'No-one in,' suggested Nina. 'Her Audi isn't here.'

'Millie can't have gone out. I'll try one more time.' He pressed the bell and stood back, impatiently. Finally he could bear it no longer and walked round to a side gate. It was padlocked. A garage blocked access on the other side of the house. When he peered through the gap between the doors he could make out the shape of a car inside.

'I can't get into the garden but there's a car in the garage.'

'Well there's no-one in the house, that's for sure,' said Nina turning back down the drive.

They sat in the car for a few minutes while Nina worked out what to do.

'Right!' she said decisively. 'We're going back to the station and I am going to demand that someone listens to me.'

As she turned the car round at the end of the drive, Jake peered up at the window of Millie's room. It might have been a reflection but he was almost sure that something moved inside. Before he could comment he was jerked back suddenly as they accelerated away. He was quite alarmed by Nina's driving and held on to the side of his seat as they flew along the main road back to the police station.

'Stay in the car,' she instructed as she jumped out and took the steps two at a time.

Inside there was the usual air of excitement associated with a suspect being interviewed and Nina noted that the team had gathered like a pack of wolves.

'Where's the Guv?' she asked.

'Out the back having a fag.'

'And Mitch?'

'Interviewing the Hughes boy.'

She ran down the stairs, past the desk and out to the tiny back yard where Ernie was standing, his sleeves rolled up, blowing smoke in a contented way.

'Hello, love. Everything all right?'

'No, it's not. Did Mitch tell you about the CCTV footage?'

'No, what about it?'

She explained how she had seen the Dean enter the building just before Millie was attacked and leave soon afterwards.

'So what? The woman works there!'

'But she said that she was in London that day.'

Ernie sighed. 'Look, petal. I'll be going to have a word with her later. I'll check her movements then. Is there anything else?'

She turned away and then swung back. 'I'm concerned about Millie Sanderson's safety, sir. I went to the Deanery just now and there was no sign of her. May I check it out?'

'No you may not, Constable. I will not have Professor McGrath harassed. You will stay away from her. Now bugger off!'

He was grinding his cigarette end into the ground, red in the face. Nina swiftly left the building and joined Jake back in the car.

'Where's Nige now, Jake?'

'On his way back to the department I guess. I'll call him'

Nige answered immediately and Jake could hear the engine in the background.

'Are you driving?'

'Yes, mate, so be quick, I'm dropping the undergrads off in town.'

'Meet us at the department, and hurry up.'

'Righto.'

'Was he driving?' Nina asked.

'No,' lied Jake, 'he was at some traffic lights.'

The Land Rover arrived a few minutes later and disappeared round to the parking area at the back. Nige reappeared from the main entrance.

'How did he do that?' asked Nina.

'He used the side entrance. It goes in at basement level,' said Jake

'I definitely don't want to have to go to the police station again in a hurry,' said Nige, climbing into the back seat.

'You may have to,' said Nina. 'I didn't say anything before, Jake, but when they've finished with Ben they may want to question you two.'

'Why?' Nige looked puzzled.

'Because you're the only suspects my inspector has. Have you got enough leg room, Nige?' she added, turning round.

'Yes thanks. Hey, that reminds me! Did you get my message?'

'I couldn't understand it. It was gobbledygook. Was it important?'

'I don't know. You see I was in the Land Rover, and I had to move the seat because you'd been driving it. You've got little legs compared to mine, see. And I started to think about the week that the new one was involved in the accident ...'

'We don't know that it was the same vehicle, Nige. My boss isn't interested in that.'

'It was just that the seat had been moved forward and I've never had to adjust it that way before. Jake, Hammond, Perkins, they're all the same height really. It's only Ben that's different.'

'Ben?' Nina jerked her head round to look at him.

'Yes, he's much taller, see. This person who had been driving was much smaller. A bit mysterious like. What do you think?'

What Nina was thinking was so implausible that she had difficulty putting it into words. So she simply said, 'We're going back to the Deanery and this time we'll get inside and make sure that Millie is safe.'

Chapter 19

Millie was sleeping fitfully in the sun. She would wake suddenly from nightmares that were weird fragments of her ordeal. Drifting into dreams where Angela was her stepmother, trying to poison her. The familiar perfume took her back to that hot stuffy room and she shuddered. She opened her eyes slowly but everything was out of focus but she could make out Angela was standing over her. Millie felt dizzy and her arms flopped as she tried to push the woman away.

'There's no point in doing that, Millie. You won't be able to move in a few minutes and in a short time you'll be out like a light. Wonderful stuff, rohipnol. You didn't remember a thing after I gave it to you last time, did you?'

She could not stop Angela from tying her hands together. She was dizzy again and tired, very tired. 'What?' was all she could manage.

'Don't answer, you won't be able to. Just stay still while I tie your feet.'

Millie was sure that she was hallucinating … a horrible dream … the result of concussion.

'I put you in the recliner with the wheels so it would be easy to move you. Rather clever, don't you think? It's nothing personal. You do know that, don't you? In fact I was beginning to get quite attached to you during your stay with me, in a maternal sort of way. I think I would have made rather a good mother don't you?'

Millie felt herself being lifted and the surroundings were moving past her slowly. It made her feel sick.

'I think you like me. Your friend was different. She didn't understand about my feelings towards her. Rather a sheltered upbringing, now I think about it. She reacted rather foolishly, so it needed sorting out.'

Millie wasn't listening. The ground was rough and sloped so she was gradually moving backwards towards the top of the chair. She was suddenly jerked roughly back into position.

'Should have tied her onto it.'

Millie could hear Angela muttering and see her peering into her face. She tried to ask where she was taking her, but it came out as a long moan.

'Quiet or I'll have to put the tape on your mouth, and I don't want to do that.'

Millie could see the tennis court moving in and out of focus. Angela's voice came and went.

'I didn't want to hurt her … Joanna, I liked her but … Dani Vincent deserved … scheming ... don't want to hurt you … thought I …. but I couldn't find … letter … final piece …'

Then she must have passed out because when Millie opened her eyes she was looking up at a glass roof. She was lying on a tarpaulin on the floor and the air smelt earthy. If she turned her head to one side she could see Angela fiddling with the plants.

'Needs watering.' She moved out of sight. 'This one's bone dry. Must tell the gardeners when they come.'

Millie couldn't tell how long Angela stayed but eventually she heard the door bang and after that nothing. With a sigh of relief Millie travelled back through the long dark tunnel into unconsciousness.

*

'I've been thinking about the Dean and it makes a lot of sense,' said Nige. 'She's the only person who has unlimited access. She can get keys to anywhere.'

'If Vrishti was complaining about sexual harassment from a member of staff she would talk to Dr Armstrong. She's the tutor,' added Jake.

'But why would she complain about Professor McGrath?' Nina asked.

'Perhaps she was the victim of McGrath's advances,' said Nige.

'What?' Nina slowed the car to a crawl. 'Professor McGrath?'

'Didn't you know she was gay?' Nige sounded surprised. 'Dani told me. She saw her at one of the clubs.'

'I think Dani may have known about Vrishti,' said Nina slowly, pulling the car up to the kerb. 'That would be motive enough.'

For God's sake, Nina, get a move on. We've got to get to Millie quickly,' shouted Jake.

This time Nina pulled straight into the drive and Jake jumped out before she had finally stopped the car. He was hammering on the door and running round to the side gate. When there was no answer, he began to climb over into the garden.

'Hang on, I've got a tyre lever in the boot,' shouted Nina.

Jake jumped down and grabbed it off her, forcing the flimsy padlock apart. They raced after him into the garden and stopped short at the sight of the Dean seated in a reclining chair.

'Hello, there.' She waved. 'Did you find the gate open? I keep telling the gardeners to lock it. Never mind, It's a good thing because I didn't hear you ring.'

'We came to see Millie,' shouted Jake. 'Where is she?'

'Oh you've just missed her, Jake. Her father came to fetch her this afternoon.'

'She would have told me,' Jake shouted indignantly.

'She was still very tired and woozy. I expect she'll call you in the morning.'

There seemed no option except to leave but as they turned to go, Jake muttered to Nina that he didn't believe her.

'Hang on a minute. I've got an idea.' Nige turned back and smiled at his Dean. 'Professor McGrath, I'd really love to have a look round the Deanery, if I may. It's architecturally very beautiful.'

She looked nonplussed and appeared lost for words.

'It's not that impressive.' She paused. 'But if you want to look round, go ahead.'

She remained on her seat but they stood resolutely until she was forced to join them. Once inside she became more relaxed and voluble as they moved from room to room. Nige hung back and whispered to Jake to search the garden, especially the greenhouse. Angela didn't notice that Jake was missing until they were upstairs in the bedroom overlooking the garden.

'Where's the other boy?' she demanded.

Nige pointed to the front of the house,

'He's gone out the front for a cigarette,' he lied.

The woman made for the door and Nina gave him a questioning look.

'In the garden,' he mouthed.

They followed the Dean onto the landing and began to admire the paintings that hung there. She was looking agitated and started down the stairs. She was opening the front door when Nige felt his silent mobile vibrating. The message read: *found m.*

'He's in the garden!' he shouted and Angela ran back indoors, pushing Nina aside and dashing past him to the kitchen.

The back door was open and she flew outside, coming to a halt at the sight of Jake walking up the steps with Millie in his arms.

'She's alive but she's not conscious. I've called the ambulance.' He looked pale and his voice was shaky.

Nige grabbed Angela's arm but she shook herself free.

'Leave me alone. I'm not going anywhere.'

Nina spoke to the colleague who answered Mitch's phone. 'Tell him that he should get down here immediately. I'm arresting Professor McGrath for attempted murder.'

Jake placed Millie gently on the sofa. Nina sat the Dean down at the glass topped table and Nige stood sentry until they heard a siren. The paramedics arrived first, and swiftly transferred Millie to a stretcher. Jake went off in the ambulance as Ernie and Mitch appeared, with two uniformed officers. It didn't take long for Nina to explain what had happened. Ernie told her that they would deal with it and her colleagues looked as if they were handling an unexploded bomb as they led the Dean away. Soon she and Nige were alone in the house.

'What made you think she was in the garden?' Nina asked.

'The fig tree,' he said mysteriously.

Ernie could smell the woman's perfume as he helped her into the back of the car and slid in beside her. He was aware of her closeness and searched unsuccessfully for the words to reassure her. He was concerned that his sergeant would hear whatever he said, so he waited until they were getting out of the car to tell her that she needn't worry, it was probably just a misunderstanding. The formalities took a while and Ernie supervised them. She asked to ring her solicitor and spoke for some time. Finally it was confirmed that she would be along in an hour or so. Meanwhile Ernie waited with her in the interview room, sending for tea and biscuits. The comparison between this and her office was not lost on him. Eventually she suggested that he was probably busy and she would be fine in the company of one of his uniformed constables.

'I want a full report from you, young lady!' he shouted as he burst into the upstairs office. Several heads turned in his direction. Nina's did not.

'It's on your desk,' she called back, then added, 'sir.'

Without comment he strode over and picked up the folder.

'I'm off for a fag,' he shouted over his shoulder as he left the room.

Nina knew that she'd done a thorough job. Every scrap of information that pointed to the Dean was catalogued. She had included the mobile phone photos of her with Vrishti, the damage to the Land Rover, the position of the driver's seat, the pathologists report on the dust from the old coffin, the mention of a fig tree, the CCTV evidence, the letter that enticed Millie to the storeroom and the undisputable fact that Millie was found in the Deanery greenhouse. She'd put it all in the report for Ernie but she had also taken the precaution of placing a copy on the Chief Superintendent's desk. It wasn't long before he came down to find her.

'Is this woman being interviewed?' he asked.

'Not yet, sir. We're waiting for her solicitor.'

'Where's your inspector?'

'Not sure, sir,' she lied.

He left, clutching her report. Shortly afterwards she heard raised voices in the corridor and then Ernie came in, crimson-faced. He ignored Nina and went directly to his sergeant, ordering him to organise a search of the Dean's office and home, including the garden. SOCO should be sent to take her car and the white Land Rover apart. He told Mitch to check CCTV footage from the university for the period when Vrishti disappeared and the day Dani died.

Nina listened, smiling, and mentally ticking off her list of suggested locations for evidence to prove that the Dean was behind all the murders. Except of course that of Colin Hammond since poor misguided Dr Perkins had admitted that he was responsible for that one before he was taken off to the psychiatric unit for assessment. He had been fooled by Angela McGrath's innuendos that Colin Hammond had killed Joanna, when she had been responsible.

Soon Mitch had roped Nina in to make the necessary phone calls but when the desk rang through to say that the solicitor was in the interview room Ernie stood, wearily, and told Nina to accompany him. As they made their way downstairs he pointed out that she was only sitting in because the Chief Super wanted her to. He made it clear that she was to keep her mouth shut or she would be out. She experienced a nervous anticipation as she followed her boss into the room.

The smart young lawyer dressed in a black suit seated beside the Dean made a conspicuous contrast. The older woman now looked drained of her usual vitality despite her composure.

'Professor McGrath,' Ernie began after the preliminary formalities with the tape recorder, 'I have to ask you some questions. Do you know why you are here?'

She nodded and he politely asked her to vocalise her assent for the benefit of the tape.

She lifted her head and spoke clearly. 'Yes, Inspector.'

'A young woman was found drugged in your garden this morning. She was a student who was in your care following an earlier attack at the university. We are trying to find out what happened to her, do you understand?'

'Yes, of course I do, I am an intelligent woman, Inspector.'

'Of course, Professor.' He smiled apologetically and Nina cringed at his unnecessary fawning. 'So, do you have any idea what may have occurred?'

She smiled graciously. 'No, Inspector. I'd been out and just got back to the Deanery when your young constable arrived with her friends. I thought Millie had gone home to her father.'

'Why did you think that?'

'Because she told me she planned to. She was very unhappy. I suppose she couldn't face it and decided to end it all.' She leaned forward in a confidential manner. 'Inspector, how is she? I was so worried when I saw the young man carrying her up the garden like that. I thought that she might be ... well ...'

Ernie across looked at Nina.

'We haven't had a report from the hospital yet,' she lied.

The Dean sipped her water very slowly and Ernie consulted his notes.

'The departmental Land Rover, do you ever drive it?' he asked.

'No.' She was beginning to look more relaxed.

Ernie's finger moved down a fraction. 'My next questions relate to the attack on Millie Sanderson at the university.'

'Oh, yes?' She was sounding confident now.

'The girl received a letter purporting to be from you, asking her to meet you in the storeroom on Wednesday morning, at midday.'

'Did she? Well I certainly didn't write it. I was expecting to be in London all day on Wednesday. I went down on Tuesday for a special reception at the Royal Academy, organised by the Society of Antiquaries and I stayed overnight. I didn't expect to be back until late on the Wednesday.'

'So why did you come back?' Ernie asked politely.

'It was hot and I decided to give my meeting a miss.'

'And there are witnesses who will corroborate the fact that you were in London on Tuesday evening?'

'Yes, plenty. I met several colleagues at the reception and we went on to dinner afterwards. At the Ritz actually, which is just across the road so rather handy.'

She had placed him firmly back at a social disadvantage once more but he actually felt more comfortable that way.

'I'm sure someone will confirm my movements,' she added, smiling broadly.

'But you told me that you had just returned from London when I met you at the university that evening,' exclaimed Nina.

Ernie glared at her.

'That was just a manner of speech, my dear. I had dropped in to the university on my way back to the Deanery. I freshened up, and then I came into the department later on to do some work. It seemed like I was just back from London.'

She sipped her water and frowned at Nina. Ernie, head down, was studying his list.

'I don't believe you,' exclaimed Nina, 'I think you went to the store and knocked Millie out, same as you did Vrishti. You put her in that coffin, just like the other girl!'

'Constable!' Ernie was half standing. 'The detective constable is leaving the room,' he addressed the tape recorder.

Nina stood outside the door, trembling, taking deep breaths, listening to her boss apologising for her behaviour. Head down she made for the stairs, almost colliding with her superintendent who was coming down.

'Interview over already?' he asked.

'Not exactly, sir.'

'On a break?' He smiled at her.

'Sort of, sir.'

'I've just been talking to your sergeant about more staff to help get the evidence together. We don't want to lose her, do we? I've told everyone that it's top priority.'

She managed a nod and continued up to the office. She looked up the mobile number for Millie's father to let him know where his daughter was. Initially he was baffled by her call. He had not been expecting his daughter to be coming home. In fact he had not even been notified about his daughter's earlier attack. The Dean had not contacted him since he visited her at the university. Nina ensured that her boss was informed.

Later that day news came through that a bottle of flunitrazepam had been found at the Deanery, proving that Angela McGrath had access to the rohipnol. A note added that there was a fig tree in the greenhouse, and a tarpaulin with long black hairs on it that were being tested for Vrishti Bhatt's DNA.

Finally, late Saturday morning, the breakthrough came. A fingerprint matching the Dean's was found on the rear view mirror of the Land Rover. Mitch was ecstatic and generous with his congratulations to the team, which included acknowledging Nina's contribution. In private he began to criticise his inspector and suggested to Nina that he should be retired to make way for younger blood, like himself. He asked her whether she would be taking her exams soon because he would need a good sergeant when he got his promotion.

Mitch joined Ernie in the interview room and began to reveal the evidence they had been accumulating during the day. At first McGrath tried to convince them someone was setting her up, that fingerprints could be lifted and deposited in places where the owner had never been.

'Professor McGrath.' Mitch was running out of patience. 'We have enough evidence to convict you of three murders and one attempted murder. There is no way that you are walking out of here a free woman. You are intelligent, more intelligent than most, and you may have a mind capable of successfully framing another person for the murders but the man on the street doesn't. Do you think that a jury is going to buy that argument? They will listen to the expert witness telling them that the victims were drugged with rohipnol and a bottle of it was found in your dressing table drawer. What will they do? They'll put two and two together and make four. Bingo!'

The room was silent. McGrath picked up her glass and drained the water. Her lawyer leant over and spoke to her quietly.

'I would like to have a consultation with my solicitor, in private,' she announced at last.

'Certainly, Professor. The interview is terminated at four thirteen.'

Mitch pressed the button with a flourish and they left the room.

'I'll let you know when they're ready,' he told his inspector.

Nina sat waiting while Ernie paced the office. Eventually the phone went and he listened without speaking, finally replacing the receiver.

'Her solicitor says that she wants to make a statement. She's admitting to Joanna Armstrong and Vrishti Bhatt at this stage.'

Ernie allowed Nina to congratulate him on his success before he rushed back to rejoin Mitch. Nina sat at her desk, feeling considerable pleasure at the part she had played in the case and was pleased the truth had been established, despite the fact that the suspect did not fit the normal profile. What had her trainer said on the diversity course? *Crime is no respecter of boundaries; it can be perpetrated by anyone, regardless of race, gender or sexual orientation.* She had certainly been right there.

Chapter 20

Millie was discharged from hospital when the consultant returned after the weekend. During her three nights on the ward she'd had flashbacks which left her confused. She went straight to the farm, where Bridget insisted she rested for at least a week before doing anything. Although the nightmares subsided she still had the odd weird dream and Bridget was with her on several occasions when she had woken herself shouting. On the whole she could remember very little of what had happened to her and relied on what she was told by Jake. He was now back at the Wesleydale site and was working everyl day, reporting progress to her. Nige had been made a temporary lecturer and was in charge, in the absence of any other staff members, and the British Museum was going to help put right the damage that Colin Hammond had done to the excavation. Some of it would be irreparable but other parts that had not yet been uncovered would be saved.

Her first proper visitors came to see Millie later in the week. She watched with amusement as Fiona picked her way across the farmyard in her white platform sandals. Her hair had been cropped and bleached since they had last met and she was dressed in a very short skirt. Millie went over to meet her father and gave him a long hug. Inside the farmhouse Bridget was preparing lunch and Robert was pouring wine. They were very hospitable. Too hospitable, Millie thought, when Fiona became a little petulant after an excess of alcohol. Bridget invited the couple to stay the night but to Millie's relief Fiona wanted to get back to York for an evening race meeting with a live band.

Millie held on to her father as they left and promised to see him soon. She walked down the track, opening the gate for them and was left standing alone after she had waved them off. When Bridget had asked the couple how long they'd been together, Millie was surprised to learn that it was already three years and she did admit that Dad appeared very happy. Perhaps it was time to grow up, as Jake had put it, and let them have a life together. She turned back to the house, where Bridget was waiting for her and, much to Toby's delight, Millie was tucked up in bed a full two hours before he was due to have his bath.

Next day, when Nina and Nige appeared, Millie was completely distracted by Nige's new appearance. Jake had been sworn to secrecy by Nina, who wanted to surprise Millie with Nige's new hairstyle and complete change of clothes. He blushed, explaining that it was all part of his new image, now that he had a proper job, albeit a temporary one. Nina had begun studying and planned to go for her sergeant exams as soon as she was ready.

She was reticent to discuss the case but Millie and Jake fired questions at her throughout lunch until she did confide that Angela McGrath had finally admitted to killing Vrishti, Joanna and Dani, as well as attempting to murder Millie, all because she was worried that someone might find out she was harassing Vrishti. As Nina explained, she was used to having the power to get what she wanted. She was already the Dean of Science and had hopes of climbing even higher. When she thought she might lose it all through the scandal of making a pass at a female student, she fought hard to keep it. Millie hadn't known but Angela McGrath had assumed that Vrishti confided in her. She ransacked the house, looking for the note that she had sent Vrishti to entice her to her death. Nina warned Millie she might have to appear at the trial but it would not be for many months, and probably in the following year.

Millie spent the next couple of weeks quietly at the farm, reading the books on forensic archaeology that Jake brought from the library. Toby insisted that she played with him and the school hamsters outside in the orchard when it was fine, and read to him indoors when it wasn't. And every afternoon at the allotted time she logged onto the internet to chat with Phoebe, who was still very excited by her recent trip to the Rath Yatra festival. She had sent more photographs of the chariots and the procession, many of which included Priti's handsome young brother. Phoebe informed her excitedly that he was a medical student in London and she was having dinner with him at the weekend. Only after giving full details of how gorgeous he was did Phoebe announce she'd passed her resits. She would be coming back for her last year at university. Millie confided that she was going to choose all the forensic archaeology options, so that she could work on the chariot burial site for her final year project.

Neither of them wanted to go back to Jubilee Street at the beginning of term and Phoebe had a plan. She'd been looking on the internet for houses to let in the town and found one overlooking the park, close to the university. The only problem was it had five bedrooms but she was sure it would be perfect if

Millie persuaded Jake, Nige and perhaps Nina to share.

Finally, after another week, Jake and his mother agreed Millie was well enough to visit the excavation. A team of archaeologists from the British Museum and several of the northern universities had been drafted in to work on the site. She watched fascinated as the illustrator made sketches of the grave, carefully noting the position of every tiny artefact. A photographer was coming and a film crew would be following the work as it progressed. Jake was thoroughly enjoying the opportunity to work with the experts who were attempting to retrieve the damage that Colin Hammond had caused. Most of the work was being done back at the laboratory, where a conservator was painstakingly cleaning off the soil and recovering the beautifully decorated ornamental terret rings and bits. Unfortunately the wheels were virtually gone except for the rust-stained soil that was used to infill the grave but, where metal fragments remained, they hoped to find evidence of the wooden tyre. Jake promised to take Millie to the laboratory to see the conservator at work next time he went.

There was always an air of excitement at the excavation with frequent visits from the press as more significant finds were uncovered. The metal artefacts were as ornamental as those found at the famous Wetwang site and soon all Nige's focus moved from Driffield up to Wensleydale as he co-ordinated the team of university academics. The scientists agreed that the woman buried in the grave was a priestess but Millie had her own views. They seemed to have forgotten that they had found a dagger at the site because it was in an evidence bag at the police station. Surely a weapon like that would have been buried with a warrior? Millie read up about Cartimandua, Queen of the Brigantes, and she learned that she had been deposed by her ex-husband and had to step down, and the Brigantes were defeated by the Romans at Stanwick, not far from Richmond. They said she fled to Chester with her new young husband Vellocatus who had been her charioteer. Perhaps she didn't, maybe she died and he gave her a warrior's burial anyway? There may have been a few followers who remained faithful. Jake simply told her not to be so fanciful.

Phoebe was invited to stay at the farm for a few days while she sorted out the student house in town and they all got together at the weekend for the Wensleydale Show. It was an important part of the Sweeting's year and every available surface in the kitchen was covered in recent baking or vegetables that had been scrubbed and graded. Jake, Millie and Phoebe arranged to met Nige and Nina at the beer tent and they spent much of the day catching up with each other's news. Phoebe had finalised the house for the new term and, since Nina had to keep her own flat on for another ten months, Ben had been persuaded to take the fifth room.

At the end of the day they moved on to West Witton where the Bartle feast was in full swing. They were standing around drinking while they waited for the procession to begin when Phoebe asked how the excavation was going and had they uncovered the woman in the cart. Nige was horrified at her ignorance and explained how important she must have been to be buried with her chariot.

'We should drink a toast to her,' declared Jake.

'To the princess,' said Millie, raising her glass and everyone echoed her words.

'To be strictly correct …' began Jake but Millie put her finger on his lips.

'No. I didn't mean just her. I was thinking of another princess,' she said and Phoebe smiled knowingly.